The world looked like a snow globe.

She'd opened the drapes and turned out the lights to give him a view of the falling snow. Then she stood beside him. Luke should have thought it through, but he didn't. He grasped her hand, and his heart thudded when she didn't pull away.

He wished he could find out if her lips were as sweet as he remembered, if her curves were as soft.

But she astonished him by saying, "I want to hate you."

"I thought you already did."

"I did. But now I don't, and I want to again."

"Why?"

She leaned over and kissed him on the mouth. Not a tentative kiss, but the kiss of a lover who knows her man.

"I shouldn't…" she whispered.

"But I want it, too."

"That's exactly what's wrong," she said. "Sex between us was always good. Everything else was the problem."

"We could talk about it, Bri."

"Why? It's o

"Not quite." w her into a deep, hungry kiss.

D1136080

SNOWSTORM CONFESSIONS

BY
RACHEL LEE

MILLS & BOON

All rights reserved including the right of reproduction in whole or in part in any form. This edition is published by arrangement with Harlequin Books S.A.

This is a work of fiction. Names, characters, places, locations and incidents are purely fictional and bear no relationship to any real life individuals, living or dead, or to any actual places, business establishments, locations, events or incidents. Any resemblance is entirely coincidental.

This book is sold subject to the condition that it shall not, by way of trade or otherwise, be lent, resold, hired out or otherwise circulated without the prior consent of the publisher in any form of binding or cover other than that in which it is published and without a similar condition including this condition being imposed on the subsequent purchaser.

® and ™ are trademarks owned and used by the trademark owner and/or its licensee. Trademarks marked with ® are registered with the United Kingdom Patent Office and/or the Office for Harmonisation in the Internal Market and in other countries.

Published in Great Britain 2014
by Mills & Boon, an imprint of Harlequin (UK) Limited,
Eton House, 18-24 Paradise Road, Richmond, Surrey, TW9 1SR

© 2014 Susan Civil Brown

ISBN: 978-0-263-91426-9

18-1014

Harlequin (UK) Limited's policy is to use papers that are natural, renewable and recyclable products and made from wood grown in sustainable forests. The logging and manufacturing processes conform to the legal environmental regulations of the country of origin.

Printed and bound in Spain
by Blackprint CPI, Barcelona

LANCASHIRE COUNTY LIBRARY	
3011812998134 0	
Askews & Holts	15-Sep-2014
AF ROM	£3.99
Z	

Rachel Lee was hooked on writing by the age of twelve and practiced her craft as she moved from place to place all over the United States. This *New York Times* bestselling author now resides in Florida and has the joy of writing full-time.

To Allison Carroll,
for her infinite patience and kindness

Chapter 1

"Luke!"

Brianna Cole stared, stunned, at the last man on earth she expected to see standing at her front door. Icy winter air, defying the spring season, swirled around her, but she hardly noticed. Luke Masters, her ex-husband, stood there with smiling gray eyes she remembered all too well. His thick parka hung open despite the cold, showing her he still pretty much dressed like a lumberjack: plaid wool shirt, jeans and work boots. Why wasn't he back at their old place in Chicago? What was he doing in Conard County?

"Hi, Bri," he said pleasantly enough.

"What are you doing here?" Shock rapidly gave way to a sick feeling, an urge to deny what she was seeing and a swamp of memories she never wanted to think about again. How dare he?

"Well, I'm on a project. I'll be around for a few weeks, and I thought it would be better for you to find out this way. Besides, I thought we might catch up."

Catch up? The idea astonished her. They had parted three years ago for a lot of very good reasons. Well, they'd started parting ways before that, but the divorce had been finalized three years ago. Unfortunately, finalizing a divorce didn't end the pain. "Why?"

"Because there was a time we used to be best friends."

What kind of excuse was that? she wondered. Suddenly becoming aware of the frigid air, she realized she had to close the door. Either invite him in or send him on his way, but as she heard her heat kick on, she considered more practical matters. Thinking of the heat at least interrupted the emotional tsunami the sight of him had caused. "Come in," she said irritably. "But don't get comfortable."

He didn't comment on her ungracious invitation, merely stamped his feet a couple times to shake off any remaining snow, then stepped inside.

She closed the door behind him. The chill from outside seemed to reach her and she hugged herself, rubbing her arms. The forced-air heat blasted away but didn't seem to warm her.

He looked good, from what she could see. Time hadn't changed him one bit, not even adding threads of gray to his dark hair. Bitterness filled her mouth. She'd always suspected that their divorce hadn't troubled him as much as it had her. He looked fit, healthy and as self-assured as ever. On the other hand, upset had cost her ten pounds she hadn't been able to put back on, and sleepless nights had made her look like a raccoon for over a year. "This is wrong," she said. "On so many levels."

"Why? We used to be married. I'm in town. I just wanted a few minutes to see how you're doing."

"Right." She pointed to her shabby living room and told him to sit wherever. Then, because she was cold, she went to get some coffee. Then, because she wasn't naturally rude, she poured a mug for him.

Ten minutes, she thought. *I can handle this for ten minutes.* That didn't make her feel any better. All of a sudden she was staring into a yawning abyss of old pain and desire she didn't want to freshen.

Squaring her shoulders, she walked back to the man who had twisted her heart into knots and then torn it apart.

She hoped she wasn't being stupid.

The night outside began to sprinkle big white flakes of snow, just a dusting, but the flakes glittered like jewels under the streetlights. Spring was late this year.

Jack Milkin stood three doors down from Brianna's house. He liked Brianna. She was one of the few people who seemed to go out of her way to notice him and be nice to him. Mostly he felt invisible, but not when she was around. He'd been interested in her for a long time, but was always reluctant to ask her out. He knew she didn't date much. There'd been a few guys she had gone out with but it never lasted.

Jack figured he could make it last if she would just let him try.

So he'd been trying to learn everything he could about her so he could please her. Soon, he had promised himself, he would ask her out for a movie or dinner. Some safe little date. If she said yes, then he'd set about proving just how good he could be for her. If she didn't say yes, well, he'd find another way.

But now a strange man had just been invited into her house. A wrinkle. Competition? A possible threat? He thought he knew nearly everything about her, but she had seemed to know this guy, a guy who wasn't on his list of things he knew about Bri.

He approached her house at last, and when he was sure no one could see, he climbed the big old tree and then pushed through her attic vent. From up here, he could see what he needed to see and hear what he needed to hear.

The attic was empty, but it was not too cold. Heat from the house seeped up here. She needed more insulation on the floor, and he'd been meaning to offer to put it in.

Being quiet as a mouse, he eased toward the voices that drifted up to him. A minute later he was facedown on the attic flooring, looking through a tiny hole he had put there. One for each room. Stretched out, he could watch Bri. He could hear Bri.

He could find out everything about her life and all the ways he could please her.

Bri faced Luke in the living room. Naturally he'd settled on the sofa. That was his expansive style. She took the Boston rocker, safely across from him. The silence that ensued would have been funny if it hadn't been so tense. He'd wanted to talk, and now had nothing to say. She couldn't think of anything, either. She'd never expected to see him again, and she didn't like the way old hurts were rising in her.

Even less did she like realizing that she still found him attractive. Three years and a lot of pain hadn't changed that at all. Her hands curled until her nails bit into her palms. This was insane.

"I was asked," he said finally, "to evaluate the land that was purchased for a ski resort. Take a look at what problems we might face."

"That's going to be hard under all this snow."

"Some of it will be." He'd been sitting with his arms outflung, one on the arm of the couch, the other along its back. Now he rubbed his chin, sweeping her with his gray eyes.

"You're a little thinner," he remarked.

She battled an urge to tell him he had no right to comment on her appearance. None at all. Instead she chose to change the topic. Letting him get under her skin would be a mistake. "There's been talk of a ski resort forever. It hasn't happened yet. The land just keeps getting resold. Any reason to think it's going to be different this time?"

At that he smiled faintly. "Well, I'm on the job."

It was an old joke he'd always made, but now bitterness made her wonder if it was a joke at all. Maybe his ego really was that big. "Oh?"

He gave a slight shrug. "I'm checking it out, is all."

"It'll die like it always does. The county doesn't have the money to expand the airport to handle more than a few executive jets."

"The company I'm working for is planning on doing the airport as well."

The county could use the jobs and the tourist income. It would change things around here, although whether for the good remained to be seen. But she was

in no mood to be thinking about the entire county.
All she could think about was that if this project went
ahead, Luke would be around for months, if not a year
or more.

Longer than he'd been around at any point in their
marriage. Wow. Didn't that say everything?

"How are you doing?" he asked after a moment.

"Fine." Short and unrevealing. What was he expecting? A heart-to-heart?

"Still in nursing?"

"Of course."

He nodded. "You always loved working with patients."

Nothing to say to that, either. She was definitely not
enjoying the tension.

A sound from the attic above caught her attention
and she looked up. "Another raccoon?" she said more
to herself than him.

"Want me to look?"

"No. I have someone who takes care of that for me."
She couldn't climb ladders because she had a bad knee.
Wrapping it properly allowed her to work, but climbing? Not since she'd been knocked off her bicycle by
a careless motorist.

"Is it a common problem? Raccoons in the attic?"

"It happened last fall. Jack, the guy who takes care
of it for me, put up some chicken wire to keep them
out, but it might have worked loose."

"Raccoons are pretty smart. They could figure it
out."

"Probably." This conversation was pointless. He
must have come for some reason other than to warn

her that he'd be around. "Luke, what's the real purpose of this visit? Not to talk about raccoons."

He rose from the couch, and she recognized that they were about to get to the meat of the matter. He could never hold still while discussing something important. Funny that she remembered him so well when she had spent so long trying to forget him.

"As much as it hurt when you left me, I can live with it. What I can't live with, even after all this time, is you thinking I'm a liar and a cheat." He faced her, and his gray eyes seemed to flame. "I never lied to you and I never cheated on you."

He'd said that before. "You think I want to beat this horse all over again?" she demanded, rising to her feet. "It's dead. It's in the past. We went our separate ways."

"Because you believed I lied to you. That I cheated. And that matters to me."

God. How was she supposed to handle this? Old hurts were returning, opening wounds she had thought healed. All because…because why? "What difference does it make whether I believe you now?"

"It does."

Bald, uncompromising, no excuses or wiggle room.

"Okay. Whatever. You didn't lie and you didn't cheat. Feel better?"

"Why don't *you* try telling me the truth? You don't believe that."

Her hands had begun to ache from being clenched for so long. She tried putting them on her hips to ease them. Man, she could barely stand to look at him right now, as refreshed emotional agony tore into her. "Just leave, Luke. There's no point rehashing this. You said you didn't do it back then. You say now that you didn't do it. You can't prove it. And I'm the one who got the phone call telling me otherwise."

"And you believed a woman you barely knew over me. Damn that Barbara."

"How did you know it was Barbara?" She leaped on the name as if it were evidence. "I didn't tell you who called."

"She did. Eventually. When she realized I wasn't going to rebound into her arms after all. You could say the only pleasure she got out of her little escapade was knowing that she'd killed our marriage."

Something else burst out of her then, maybe the most important thing of all. She didn't know, but it rose to the surface and exploded. "You were never home. We didn't have a marriage, we had an occasional affair!"

He froze. Despite herself she looked at him and saw his face shutter as if it had turned to steel.

"I see," he said quietly. "I won't bother you again."

She listened to him leave, standing frozen herself. Where had that come from? Was it as true as it had felt when it burst out of her? Had she been harboring that kind of resentment without knowing it?

She realized she was trembling and forced herself to move stiffly to the kitchen. She hadn't had supper yet, and the tension and anger had drained her. She had to eat. She had to carry on. Her life was here now, among family and friends, not in some big city where she'd felt so lonely sometimes when Luke was away. She never really felt lonely anymore.

But looking back, she remembered how badly she had ached every time he left on another trip. She'd never gotten used to it. So maybe she'd been a fool to marry him in the first place. His absences had been built in, but she'd faced them with so much confidence, sure she could handle them.

Time had proved her wrong. Whether he had cheated or not, they had probably been doomed anyway.

She managed to make a chicken sandwich on melba rye bread, then poured herself fresh coffee before sitting at the kitchen table. As she lifted the sandwich, she realized she was still shaking.

She needed someone. Someone to talk to and let her vent. Twisting on her seat, she reached for the wall phone and called Diane. Her best buddy. The one who shared both good times and bad.

Diane said she'd be right over. Help was on the way.

Jack crawled out of the attic, content. The man was an ex who had cheated on her. No threat there. And tomorrow or the next day, Bri would call him to get rid of the raccoon. How long it took him to catch the animal would depend on whether he could afford to stay away for a few days or a week. Once he "caught" the animal, he couldn't risk making noise up here for a while. Time would tell.

In the meantime, he was sure he could let her talk to her best friend without listening in. Diane would be on his side, after all, wanting only what was best for Bri.

Jack closed up the attic, checked to make sure it was safe, then shinnied down the tree. Amazing what you could learn just by listening. He hoped that soon he'd have a chance to comfort Bri.

But first, maybe, it would be best to ensure that her ex didn't hang around for long. Better safe than sorry.

* * *

Luke climbed into his truck and nearly skidded on the snow and ice as he pulled away. Had he been out of his ever-loving mind? What had made him think she would listen to him? She certainly hadn't listened to him when he'd denied her accusations the first time.

Damn, she still had those witchy green eyes, that heart-shaped face, although it had lost some of its softness to the years. Chiseled cheekbones showed now. But her brown hair still looked as silky as ever. In short, except for the chaos between them, he'd still think she was the most beautiful woman on the planet.

But he'd seen inside that woman, and what he'd found there hadn't been all that beautiful. Not toward the end. Not when she'd refused to trust him or his honesty.

And what was that crap about him being gone all the time? She'd known that before they married. She'd refused his every attempt to get her to travel with him because she wanted to keep nursing. Her job had mattered more to her than being with him. *That* was a two-way street.

So how dare she throw that up at him? Especially at this late date?

He'd almost convinced himself yet again that the marriage had been a huge mistake by the time he got back to the crusty motel on the edge of town. He'd spent time in worse accommodations over the years, and with fewer amenities, as construction manager for DEL Inc. He barely noticed his surroundings as he entered the room, paused to wash his face, then set out again for the truck stop across the highway.

He needed to eat. He hadn't eaten during his entire

trip to this godforsaken town in the middle of nowhere. Nerves about seeing Bri again? Maybe.

The part of him that never stopped working had already scanned the town. Turning this place into a tourist resort was going to take some big bucks. The basics of the charm were there, but they needed a whole lot of touching up to make this the kind of place people with money would want to spend a few weeks skiing and hiking. Yeah, they would put a lot of good stuff out at the resort, but people often wanted to wander into town.

Conard City spoke of older times. That would help. Some sprucing up would seal its charm, make people feel they'd come to a place out of time. But boy, it was going to take some sprucing.

But first he had to get the lay of the land up in the mountains, figure out if they'd run into a few surprises about how much it would cost to build the place and put in the kinds of slopes that would appeal to everyone from the beginner to the pro. The designers had given him a rudimentary plan, but now he had to look over the actual site and see how much could actually become reality. And if it would be worth it.

He half hoped it wouldn't be. Then he could leave and be sure he'd never see Bri again.

Just what the hell had he expected, anyway? The woman had always been stubborn, she clearly hadn't trusted him and she'd divorced him. A sane man wouldn't have returned for a second round.

But he knew what he had wanted. Their marriage was dust, but it still chapped him that she had believed those lies about him. It wasn't enough to know in his own mind that he'd never cheated, he wanted—no, needed—Bri to know it, too. Somehow that mattered and had never stopped mattering.

Somehow it all still mattered, he thought grimly as he settled into a booth in the overbright truck stop diner. Three years since the divorce. Even longer if he counted back to when he'd first realized the relationship was crumbling. Shouldn't he be over it all by now?

But maybe when you'd invested that many hopes and dreams into a person and a relationship, cutting loose wasn't easy. God knew, he'd never wanted the divorce. He just hadn't had the heart to fight her anymore.

Setting her free hadn't been easy. It had been necessary.

Chapter 2

A week later, Bri was in the locker room, ditching her scrubs for street clothes. She was feeling good, all things considered. Apart from an uneasy awareness that Luke was probably still around somewhere, she hadn't seen him. A mercy. She felt she had stuffed all the painful genies back into the bottle, and that life had pretty much returned to normal.

That normalcy had been hard-won, and she welcomed its return. Even though her marriage had been running into trouble before the never-to-be-forgotten phone call from Barbara, that hadn't made it any easier to break the ties. Anyone who thought divorce was easy had clearly never been through one.

She sighed, pushing the memories away once again. She was here now, reasonably content with her life and enjoying her job. No need to hash over the dead things in her life. Looking forward had always been her salvation.

After she had dumped all over Diane, however, her best friend had left her with a question that she was trying to ignore: Why do you still care so much?

Ah, heck, she thought, closing her locker. Why indeed? There seemed to be no answer to that.

Forcing her thoughts back to the mundane, she realized she hadn't heard any more sounds from the attic. Maybe it hadn't been raccoons after all, but simply the wood expanding or shrinking. Certainly the temperatures had been unpredictable this spring. It ought to be greening out there right now, but the trees were showing more intelligence than the calendar. They hadn't even tried to bud yet, as if they knew darn well there was still snow on the ground and more in the forecast. Weird.

She was just emerging from the locker room when one of the nurses passing by stopped her. "Do you know Luke Masters?"

A week of good resolutions seemed to evaporate. "Unfortunately."

"Well, he's in the E.R. asking for you. Dr. Trent sent me to find you."

"I'm on my way." Why would he be asking for her? And what was he doing in the E.R? Her heart sped up, and she figured no amount of resolve was going to cure that until she found out what was going on.

Part of her just wanted to head for the door and pretend she hadn't gotten the message. The cowardly part. The part of herself she sometimes believed might have been the cause of a lot of problems in her life.

Sighing, she headed for the E.R, but she couldn't

imagine any reason Luke would be asking for her. She thought they'd pretty well ended any hope of talking that night last week. On the other hand, as a nurse she'd seen plenty of the worst that could happen to people, and knew how often they wanted to see a familiar face. *Any* familiar face.

Then it hit her like a ton of bricks. Luke was in the emergency room? Visions of catastrophe, drawing on graphic memory, suddenly crashed home. She increased her pace to the fast walk hospital staff used because they weren't supposed to run. It was damn near as fast.

She reached the nurse's station in front of the emergency pod. Ira Mason stood there, sorting some files. "Hi, Ira. I hear you have a patient asking for me."

He nodded. "Luke Masters? You know him?"

She caught herself just in time, holding back the statement that he was her husband. Not anymore. Man, was she going to slip into old habits that easily? A little flame of annoyance lit. "From way back."

"Bay three."

"Is it bad?"

"Well, he's not in danger of dying. Pretty messed up, though."

That was about all she was going to get from Ira. It wasn't her case, she wasn't a relative and the hospital was pretty strict about patient privacy. As it should be, she thought as she walked down the hall to the cubicles.

Sheila Gardner was hurrying toward the front with a clipboard. "Ah, you must be here to see that guy who's asking for you. Bay three."

Bri didn't fail to notice the curiosity on Sheila's face, but this was no time for a heart-to-heart about past heartbreaks. The silly phrase floated through her head, but provided no distraction. Luke was hurt, and the intervening years were slipping away as fast as a speed skater headed for the finish line. Nor did all her training as a nurse prevent her heart from climbing into her throat as she approached the bay. How bad was it? She had plenty of experience to raise horrifying images in her mind's eye.

She pulled the curtain aside and stepped in. The sight of Luke's naked leg raised and surrounded by metal framework didn't shake her. They'd probably had to stretch his leg a bit to reset bones. There was no evidence that the fracture had broken the skin—a good sign.

What got to her was the face above the blanket that covered him from chin to hips. He had a huge bruise around his eye, red and angry-looking, and his left cheekbone appeared swollen. Then she noticed that the arm lying along his side already sported a cast.

Damn, he'd done a number on himself.

She heard a rubber-soled step behind her and turned to see Dr. Trent. "He's going to be okay," he said. "They're checking the X-rays of his leg right now to see if the reset looks good or if they'll need to pin it."

She nodded quickly, wondering why her mouth was so dry. "His head?"

"So far the concussion actually appears mild. We did a CT on him and saw only some insignificant bleeding. He also cracked his cheekbone. No displacement, no movement of the bone, so we're going to leave it. His arm was a simple fracture, but his hand is a mess of lacerations and contusions. He's not going to be happy when he wakes up from the morphine."

Then Dr. Trent touched her arm. "He was pretty angry when he came in here. Aggressive. We need to keep an eye on that concussion, at least overnight. It might be worse than we think. Just watch it. There's no telling how he might react when he wakes."

She knew all of this already, but she didn't mind having Dr. Trent repeat it. Somehow it was more calming hearing it in his measured, steady voice than from inside her own head.

Then came the question she had half expected and had been dreading.

"Bri? Does he have anyone around here? Because he's going to need help, but mostly he's going to need some pretty close observation. Of course, we can keep him hospitalized…."

The idea of Luke putting up with being stuck in a hospital would have been funny under other circumstances. Heck, he was going to be upset enough about the limitations his injuries were going to cause. He was not good patient material.

"There's just me," she said quietly. "We're divorced."

Trent grimaced. "Not good. Although I guess that's why he kept demanding we get you. I don't think he knows what decade it is right now. Well, I can sure understand if you don't want the responsibility. Just let me know so I can make arrangements after we find out how that leg is."

Maybe, she thought bitterly, as she stood staring at Luke, she should call Barbara to come watch him.

Bitterness aside, though, something stronger tugged at her. At last she gave in with a sigh and sat on the one chair beside the bed. She tried to focus on the steady drip of the IV into his uninjured arm, but her eyes kept straying back to his face. God, he was a mess! That cheek alone was going to cause him some huge pain.

Sheila came in, nodded to her and checked his vitals. Then she pulled out an ice pack, flexed it to activate it, and rested it gently on his cheek. "Twenty minutes," she said.

"I'll take care of it."

"You haven't eaten, have you?"

"I just got off shift."

"Then let me bring you a tray from the cafeteria. They have a passable turkey breast tonight. Potatoes or rice?"

"Potatoes, please. And coffee. Looks like I'm going to need it."

"You should have heard him when they brought him in. Cussing a blue streak. He said somebody pushed him, but the other guy who was up there with him said no one else was around. Then he kept demanding to see you. He said he had to warn you. I mean, man, he was out of it."

Bri listened, her heart growing heavy. She knew even mild concussions could cause all sorts of disorientation. It wasn't unusual for a concussed patient who was conscious to ask every thirty seconds where they were and what had happened. But claims of being pushed? A need to warn her of what? That seemed to go beyond the ordinary confusion.

Rubbing her forehead, trying to ease the beginnings of a tension headache, she felt the first real fear. Earlier she had been concerned, but not afraid. Looking at him, however, she thought of all the deficits that could arise from even a so-called mild concussion. Sheila's description of his state when he arrived hadn't reassured her at all.

She wished his eyes would open, that he'd look at her, recognize her and be all right. Bad as things had gotten between them, she wished him no ill. None at all. But she had never expected to ever again fear for him.

Unsettled, she wanted to get up and walk outside, at least for a few minutes, to gather her increasingly scattered thoughts and emotions. Much as she tried to tell herself that she cared about him the way she would have cared about anyone she had known, the response inside her told her she was lying.

There were threads left tying her to him and the past. She had thought them cut, but they remained. She felt as if she were on a pinnacle, suddenly surrounded by the abyss of all that she had thrown out of her life. The pain remained, but something else did, too.

This was not good.

Sheila popped in with a dinner tray and Bri thanked her. She glanced at the clock above the bed and saw that the ice pack needed to remain another five minutes. She wondered what was taking X-ray so long. She wondered if she would be able to eat.

She grabbed the coffee first. Sheila had brought her two covered cups full. She downed them both, then took a stab at the turkey, potatoes and broccoli. The broccoli was a little soggy from being in the steam tray, but otherwise Sheila was right about it being a passable meal.

She paused to remove the ice pack from Luke's cheek and stood for a minute, just looking down at him. The bruise was still spreading, distorting his face even more. It looked as if he was going to be eating through a straw, she thought.

That little flicker of anger that had started earlier returned, but it was not anger at him. All of it arose from seeing him laid low like this. In the years she had known Luke, he'd always been a powerhouse, always on top of things, always independent. Maybe that had been part of what had bothered her, that he had never seemed to need her in any way. It wasn't as if she wanted him to be dependent on her, but it would still have been nice to feel needed in some way. Essential.

Wow, that was a heavy thought. She pulled back from the bed and picked up the tray again. She'd wanted to feel essential? Wasn't that a crock. She liked her own independence and had respected his. Right?

Staring down at the tray, she wondered what was going on inside her. Last week she had yelled at him for always being gone during their marriage. Now tonight she was thinking he hadn't made her feel important enough?

Whoa. Being around him again wasn't going to be good for her unless she could find a way to avoid thoughts like these. At this late date, it struck her as just more rationalization, anyway. Since the relationship was over, it was pointless to invent new reasons for its failure.

Her appetite gone, she took the tray out and put it on the meal cart rack in an empty slot. Catching sight of Sheila, she asked, "Who brought Luke in? There was someone working with him?"

"Yeah. I didn't recognize the guy."

"Where is he now?"

"He said he had to go back and pick up tools he left because he was in such a rush to get Luke down here."

Made sense, Bri thought. Just as she reentered the cubicle, Dr. Trent appeared. "Good news. We can wrap the leg—the break won't need any pins. You want to wait outside? With any luck, we'll have the cast on him before he starts to wake up."

And then what? Bri wondered as she went to the small waiting area. He'd stay overnight here, but then what?

Gloom filled her. Her mind scrambled around, trying to find other ways to manage this, but in her heart of hearts she knew she was going to wind up taking care of him, at least until he was ready to travel.

Luke Masters was going to move back into her life.

Luke was starting to wake when they wheeled him out of the bay. Bri followed, watching him stir and groan.

"You're sure the concussion isn't bad?" she asked Trent again as she passed him.

"Do a neuro on him if you want. Pupils are normal and reactive. All other reflexes are fine. He's just a little addled at the moment, but like I said, we'll keep him under observation tonight. The more you can get him to talk or at least acknowledge you, the better."

As if he were going to talk much with that cheekbone all swollen. He must feel as though he'd been hit by a baseball bat in the head. Never mind the pain he'd start feeling in his arm and leg.

Luke was placed in a room by himself, maybe because he'd been aggressive when he arrived and they feared he might disturb another patient. The ward nurse, Karen Bloom, told her she didn't have to stay all night.

"You know we'll watch him."

"I know, Karen, but he was asking for me. It might be better if I'm here." Exhaustion was beginning to break through her worry, though. She'd just worked a twelve-hour shift, which had now stretched to more than fifteen if she counted the time in the E.R.

"Your ex, huh?" Karen said. "Not fun."

Bri didn't even blink. By this time tomorrow the whole town would probably know that Luke and she were once married. This was not the place to live if you wanted to keep secrets.

"It's hard to see him this way," she said quietly, admitting a truth she was reluctant to face.

"I'm sure it is." Karen patted her arm. "Time for more ice?"

Bri looked at the clock over the door. "Yeah. Thanks. I'll get it."

She retrieved several of the instant ice packs and returned to the room. She cracked one and placed it against his cheek, feeling an unwanted ache for him. Apart from his injuries and the pain he would endure, she knew he was going to hate being cooped up. Especially inside his own body. As he'd often joked, he was a man who said "go" and his body went. This was not going to be easy.

As she leaned over him, adjusting the ice pack, his eyes snapped open. She found herself looking into those familiar gray pools.

"Bri?"

"It's me."

"I see that. Where did you go? I lost you." His voice

sounded thick, his words slurred by the bruising of his cheek.

She didn't take him seriously. Concussion often caused this kind of thing. "I'm right here now."

"What happened? Where am I?"

She'd probably answer that question a hundred times tonight. "In the hospital. You fell and got pretty banged up. You're going to be fine."

His unbroken arm lifted; his hand seemed to reach for her. She hesitated, and finally slid her hand into his. She nearly winced as he squeezed. "Don't go."

Before she could reply, he was out of it again, but he didn't let go of her. She tried to ease her hand away so she could sit, maybe stretch out until the next time he woke, but each time she tried, he tightened his hold.

A couple of minutes later he woke again. "Where am I? Bri?"

"I'm right here."

"Did someone beat me up?"

"You fell. You were out on the mountain, and you fell."

"Okay."

His eyes closed again, and this time his grip on her hand relaxed. Sagging onto the chair, she wondered if it would even be worth folding it back into a narrow bed. It would be nice to stretch out and doze, but he was coming out of the morphine now and would wake frequently. Unless the concussion was getting worse. The thought made her shudder.

She scooted the chair closer to the bed, kept her eye on the clock for the ice pack and rested her hand on his shoulder. Maybe that contact would help him.

Karen popped in and was glad to hear he'd been

talking. She noted the times, checked his pupils and told Bri everything looked good.

"Who was that?" Luke awoke again. "Who was here?"

"A nurse." She rose and bent so he could see her without moving too much.

"You're a nurse."

"Right. But I'm not your nurse. Karen is." Although it was beginning to look as if she'd be his nurse soon enough, unless he chose an ambulance ride to somewhere else. Her heart sank again.

"What happened? Where am I?"

If she hadn't been through this so many times, Bri would have been seriously worried. His confusion was normal, but she found a penlight in the drawer and checked his pupils again anyway. She needed to see for herself.

"What are you doing?"

"Making sure you're okay."

"I don't feel okay. Where did you go?"

She ignored the last question. "You fell. You hit your head and broke your arm and leg. Just relax. Everything's fine."

Everything except her.

"I lost you," he muttered. "I couldn't find you."

Oh, boy, this was going to be fun. When she could, she sat again and waited for the next round. Hearing repeatedly that he'd lost her was *not* making this any easier to take. For three years or more, she had pretty much decided he had thrown her away. Now he was saying he'd lost her?

Deliver me, she thought as she sagged on the chair. It didn't help any to remind herself that he was concussed and making little sense. She didn't want to peek into these thoughts, however addled, from a man who should have remained in her past. And she hoped like hell he didn't remember saying any of this when he improved.

They weren't words that would make either of them happy.

By dawn, Luke no longer asked where he was and what had happened. He now remembered it from one moment to the next—an excellent sign. He was even aware enough to tell Bri to go home and get some sleep. She didn't hesitate. He wouldn't be released before noon, unless he made other arrangements, and frankly she didn't want to be around for the pain he was going to experience the first time he sipped broth through a straw.

"Get him a milkshake," Sheila suggested. "He doesn't look like someone who will make it for long on broth."

"Probably not. Call me if anything develops. Has anybody seen the guy who brought him in?" That was beginning to trouble her. Shouldn't a coworker have been here to check on him?

"Not yet. I'll let you know. Girl, you look dead."

"I feel halfway there."

"At least you have the next four days off."

She'd forgotten that. She could catch up on her sleep. Maybe. Unless she needed to watch over Luke at her place, in which case she'd rather be working. It would be a great excuse to make him call someone else.

Her eyes felt gritty and burned. The bright sunlight almost hurt, and for a moment she had a wild idea that maybe the night had turned her into a vampire. Nope, her skin didn't smoke.

The silliness indicated that she desperately needed sleep. Next thing, she'd be hallucinating. Aware that she wasn't at her best, she drove with extra care and finally pulled into her driveway with a huge sense of relief. Home. Bed. Sleep.

She might have left Luke at the hospital, but she realized as she climbed out of her car that he had come home with her anyway. She couldn't erase the anguished tone of voice in which he'd said he lost her.

Concussion craziness, she told herself sternly. Icy snow still covered the ground, and she walked carefully, wishing spring would just get on with it. She needed some warmth. She needed to be able to stride freely again without fear of slipping.

Dissatisfaction followed her and she tried to blame it on a rough night. She was happy with her life, she loved living in a place with seasons, including winter, and so what if one of them lasted too long?

Dang. Her own thoughts were getting as addled as Luke's.

"Bri?"

She looked around, startled, and saw Jack standing a few feet away. A man of about thirty, he was thin enough to look like he was still a kid. His dark hair was shaggy, his dark eyes strangely penetrating. "Jack? Is something wrong?"

He shoved his hands in his pockets. "I don't know. One of the cops was here a little while ago looking for you."

"Thanks." Somebody at the hospital had probably reported that Luke had said he'd been pushed. And that she was his ex-wife. Lovely. What was she supposed to know about anything? "I'm sure they'll come back if it's important. Are you on your way to work?"

"Yeah." He nodded and started to shuffle away.

She stared after him for a moment. Somewhere in the fog that wrapped her brain, it struck her as odd that he would have known the cops were here. Then she shrugged the thought away. Jack was a pretty lonely guy, she figured. Always nice and polite, but he'd probably been walking past here when the cops came and had just waited to tell her. Made him feel important.

Inside, she barely paused. She pulled off her clothes, letting them lie where they fell as she stumbled down the hallway. Her bed was the only thing she wanted. She took just enough time to pull on a long flannel nightshirt, then crawl under the covers. She fell asleep as soon as her head hit the pillow.

Luke and all the problems he might raise could wait.

They only waited a few hours, however. The phone started ringing off the wall around noon. Like a well-trained nurse, she came instantly awake. A headache had settled in while she slept but she ignored it, reaching for the phone beside her bed.

"Bri? It's Jan. Dr. David asked me to call you. We've got a lion who wants out of the cage, but he can't be released until we know he'll have care. So…"

"On my way. What about the guy who was working with him?"

"He showed up, too. That's part of what's going on here. Plus a deputy. Sorry."

"What am I supposed to do about that?"

Jan laughed quietly. "Soothe the raging beast? I don't know. It's kind of funny, actually."

Bri sat up and realized her head was pounding. A migraine. Lovely. Funny? What in the world was Jan talking about?

Groaning once or twice, Bri struggled into her clothes, popped some ibuprofen for the migraine and grabbed a roll for breakfast. On the way to the hospital she stopped to get a large milkshake at the diner, wondering why she even bothered. Sometimes she was too nice for her own good, she thought irritably. This was not going to be a good day.

It started getting interesting, though. As she walked down the corridor in the ward where Luke was being kept, she could hear him.

"Don't you tell me I can't leave! I can leave anytime I want. You can't keep me."

Apparently he was not fully over the concussion. Luke might not like being trapped in a hospital bed, but he'd always been sensible. This didn't sound sensible.

She entered his room to find Dr. David, Jan, Police Chief Jake Madison and a strange man clad in heavy work clothes. Firmly stuck in the bed by his elevated leg and broken arm, Luke was holding forth, his words slurred by the swelling in his face.

She rounded the bed, took his good arm, put the milkshake in his hand and said, "Shut up and drink."

Luke paused midsentence, blinked and said, "Bri?"

"Who else? Shut up and drink. Let me find out what's going on."

"They're keeping me prisoner."

"You don't look ready to walk out of here. Now put the straw in your mouth and drink."

To her surprise, he obeyed. He took one pull on

the straw and looked at her. "Do you know how much that hurts?"

"Not as much as you're going to hurt if you try to stand on that leg right now. Drink."

She turned to everyone else. "How about you all tell me what's happening?"

Dr. David—all the docs here preferred to be called by their first names—answered first. "He can't leave here unless we're certain he's going to get proper care. The concussion can have effects for weeks, as you know. Then there's his lack of mobility. Dr. Trent doesn't want him walking on that leg for a week."

"A week?" It must have been a pretty bad break. She nodded. "Okay, I get that part, and from what I see he's still not quite in his right mind."

Luke stopped drinking. "I'm perfectly sane!"

"And perfectly concussed. Hush and drink. Let's figure out things so we know what to do."

She was beginning to understand why Jan could see some humor in this. She was beginning to see it herself.

"Bri…"

"If you don't behave, I'm going to tape you with my cell phone so I can show you later just how impossible you're being."

He glared at her, but resumed trying to drink his milkshake.

"Now what about everyone else here?" she asked.

The stranger stepped forward, offering his hand. "I'm Mike Hanson. I work with Luke sometimes. We were out checking out the building site when Luke fell. I brought him in. The thing is, he was insisting he was pushed, so I reported it to the chief here."

Jake Madison nodded. "We were hoping Mr. Masters might remember, but he doesn't seem to."

"That's not unusual," Dr. David said. "He might never remember what happened right before his fall."

Jake nodded again. "I'm asking Mr. Hanson here to take a deputy out to the site to see if there's any evidence that someone else was out there, but he didn't see anyone at the time."

"Not a soul," Hanson agreed. "It was awfully slippery out there, but Luke isn't a careless man. That's the thing. If he says he was pushed, I believe him."

"We'll check it out," Jake said. A moment later he departed, reminding Mike that a deputy would be by to pick him up shortly.

Bri followed him out. "Jake? Someone told me you or another officer were at my place early this morning."

"Me. When I heard you'd spent all night watching Luke, I thought he might have told you something."

She shook her head. "He couldn't even remember for ten seconds that he was in the hospital."

"That's what I was just told. Your ex, huh?"

Bri simply sighed. Jake winked at her. "Fun times. Not. Good luck."

Back in the room, a glaring Luke was still drinking his milkshake. Bri's first question was straight to the point and directed at Mike.

"Is the company going to send transport for him? He obviously can't work like this."

Mike shook his head. "They said they aren't going to hire an ambulance just to move him somewhere else. When he's ready for a car and plane ride, he can go home. They're sending out another builder."

Luke released the straw. "Nobody else is going to do my job."

Mike shook his head. "Sorry, Luke, but you're in no condition to do it yourself. You can advise, but you ain't climbing no mountains."

"I'm sure not staying here."

Dr. David spoke. "Well, you sure as hell aren't going to stay at the La-Z-Rest. You need to be under observation. You're going to need help until we can get you up on crutches, which doesn't look like anytime soon what with that broken arm. Regardless, you might be a wheelchair commando for a few weeks, and you can't be by yourself."

The freight train was bearing down on her. Bri felt as if she were standing at the end of the tunnel and could see the light coming. At least until he could be transported, she was probably the only option. She gave up the fight, hoping she wasn't making a huge mistake.

"He can stay with me, but I need to make arrangements for a chair and a hospital bed. I'm assuming you want to continue elevation on the leg?"

David nodded. "Best to keep the swelling down."

"I don't want to stay with you," Luke said.

"Sorry, buddy, but it's your only choice. Don't worry, I'll ship you out as soon as I can."

"I'm sure," he said bitterly, then fell silent.

Bri tried pretending a brightness she didn't feel. "I need to get things ready."

"I'll help," David said. "We've got plenty of rental stuff here at the hospital. We just need to arrange to move it. Are you sure you have room?"

"I never use my living room anyway." Resignation was beginning to set in. A week, maybe two. She looked at Mike. "Can you get all his things from the motel? Eventually I'm going to need his personal care products, and maybe some clothing."

"I'll do that as soon as I'm done with the deputy."

Bri reached out and touched his arm. "Come by in a few days. Don't leave him feeling cut out of the loop."

Mike nodded. "I will. As soon as I know how the company wants to handle all this."

"They really won't transport him?"

Mike shook his head. "We're all just widgets, ma'am. Every one of us can be replaced."

She wondered if Mike knew how sour he sounded. She'd think about that later. She looked again at Luke. "I'm going to need some relief when I have to come back to work."

"I'll help," Jan said. "My break is coming up soon."

Bri would have been happier if someone else had offered, but she didn't want to examine that too closely. Luke was a closed chapter, right?

Right.

By five that afternoon, Bri's living room had been transformed. A hospital bed, complete with a frame-and-pulley system to keep Luke's leg elevated, had been installed. She'd arranged it so he could see the television, and moved unnecessary items out of the way or into other rooms. Since he was going to have to get around in a wheelchair with his leg sticking straight out, at least for a while, she cleared pathways so he could get out of the living room and down the hall to the bathroom. Any way she looked at it, that part was *not* going to be easy.

"Bonehead," she said aloud. "You should have just

stayed in the hospital. Or paid someone to fly you out of here to somewhere else."

Except she didn't know where else he could go. The two of them had been orphans, their parents gone, no other family to speak of. It was either her living room or some rehab facility—and he was likely to need rehab eventually regardless. In the meantime, until the worst of the concussion passed, he couldn't be trusted on his own or without continual observation. Nor was it as if there were some convalescent facility nearby he could transfer to. One of the downsides of truly being in the boonies.

She felt ticked at DEL for treating him this way, too. He'd been injured on the job. They should have been all over themselves trying to help instead of saying he could just stay put until he could travel by conventional means. It was as if he had become useless to them.

Then another thought struck her. Could he lose his job over this? She wouldn't put it past them. A lot of these large companies looked at employees as inter-changeable parts, as Mike had said. Lose one, find another.

Pulling on her jacket, she went outside to salt her porch, steps and sidewalk yet again. Not much longer now. She put the salt away in the plastic bin she kept on one corner of her porch and stood waiting. The past, she thought, was about to descend with a vengeance.

The ambulance appeared around the corner and pulled up in front of her house. She knew both the EMTs, of course. Tim and Ted. They joked that they were the "Tim and Ted Show," and sometimes they lived up to that appellation with their zany humor and jokes. Today they were just looking busy and rushed.

She went down to them as they opened the back door of the vehicle, and saw Luke strapped into a wheelchair with his leg extended in front of him.

"Everything is *not* okay," Ted muttered to her. "Loony tunes."

"Concussion."

He sighed. "I know that. I was just warning you. Sometimes he makes sense. Sometimes not so much." He hopped up inside and passed down a couple of heavy plastic bags. "Supplies, meds and instructions, and his personal belongings," he said by way of explanation. "Open the front door for us, will you?"

Except for a couple of groans when he was inadvertently jostled, Luke remained surprisingly quiet. Ted and Tim were sweethearts and helped Luke to the bathroom before lifting him onto the bed and helping to raise his leg.

Throughout, Luke groaned sometimes but didn't complain. She gave him credit for that because he certainly had enough to complain about.

"Doc David said to tell you he had IV painkillers before he left the hospital. None of that stuff in the bag until around nine p.m."

Then Ted paused. "You can't do this alone." He pulled out a card and scribbled on the back. "Our home phone numbers. You need anything at all, call. Did you get some stuff he can eat? Because we can run to the store or something."

"I stocked up on broths and there are four milkshakes in the fridge."

Ted nodded approval. "We'll bring some more tomorrow."

Then they zipped out with cheery goodbyes.

After she closed the door, Bri thought the house felt at once strangely full and strangely silent. As if something dark had entered.

Only her own past. Hooking her jacket onto the hall tree, she went into the living room to check on her patient. To her surprise, he was wide-awake and more like himself. His gaze was sharper, as if the world had once again come into focus for him.

"I'm sorry, Bri. I'm messing up your life."

"That depends. If you behave yourself, no mess. How are you feeling?"

"Like I took a bad fall and broke too many things. I don't know what they gave me for pain, but it almost feels like it's a long way away."

"Well, that's good, anyway." She pulled over the desk chair she had brought out here because it would be easy to roll around and sat beside him. "Do you remember anything about what happened?"

"No." He didn't even try to shake his head. It probably felt as big as a pumpkin, she thought. "I know we were climbing around checking out sight lines and terrain. To build up there we're going to have to do some blasting. The last thing I remember was walking along what looked like a level path. The snow wasn't very deep. I guess it must have been slippery, though." Lifting his good arm, he waved at himself, then winced slightly. "Damn, how long am I going to be like this?"

"It's going to take a while," she said honestly. "If you behave, you might get a walking cast in a week or two, but I don't know. I'm not the doctor."

"Hell." He sighed and closed his eyes. The next thing she heard was a quiet snore.

She pulled the blanket up to protect him against

drafts. Even with the heat on it was still cold enough at night that occasionally the chill wafted through the house like frigid fingers.

His being asleep gave her time, though, to go eat her own dinner. When she'd stopped for the milkshakes, she had bought herself one of Maude's steak sandwiches and a salad, enough to keep her going for two days. She ate quickly, concerned about Luke in the next room, but she didn't want him to wake and see her chowing down on real food. He had enough misery to contend with.

After she cleaned up, she went back to check on him. His eyes were open, and despite the red and rapidly purpling swelling that covered one whole side of his face, he managed a crooked smile. "Thanks, Bri."

"Somebody had to do it. DEL apparently doesn't think you're worth bringing back."

"Probably thinks I should have stayed in the hospital."

"Maybe you should have."

"Doesn't suit me."

"No kidding." Once again she could almost see the humor in this, except there was absolutely nothing humorous about the injuries he had suffered. "Getting hungry?"

"A little."

"Broth or milkshake?"

"Milk. Please." At least that was what it had sounded like. So she brought him a milkshake and when she was sure he had a good grip on it, she sat again. "You want the TV?"

"Not really. Maybe later. I'm…having a little trouble following things."

She could well believe it. The improvement since last night was huge, but he was going to take a while to come back fully. It was a good sign, however, that he recognized he was having a problem.

"Pretty, up there on the mountain," he mumbled.

"It certainly is. I'm not sure I want to see it turned into a resort."

"You and shum—somebody else."

Her heart slammed. Had he remembered? "You think you were pushed?"

"Mike said."

So he had heard what Mike said. Not exactly evidence of anything except that he now remembered something from this morning. Impulsively, she reached out and laid her hand on his shoulder. Almost at once she snatched it back, shocked by the zing of attraction she felt for him. She knew his body intimately, and at this most inappropriate time, those memories seemed to want to come back. She had to force herself to remain professional when she had the worst urge to lean over him, kiss him and tell him everything would be okay. "Don't worry about it. The important thing is to heal. Everything else can wait."

"Never been a good waiter." Then he dozed off again. She caught the milkshake as it began to tip from his hand and set it beside him on the adjustable table that had been brought with the bed.

Sitting back, she watched him, thinking about how fast her life had been turned on end, and what it might mean if he had been right about someone pushing him.

There were certainly people hereabouts who didn't want to see anything change. They'd resisted the semiconductor plant and had celebrated when it shut down and the jobs went overseas. They barely tolerated the community college. Why would they ever want a big resort that would bring all kinds of strangers to the area?

But there were a lot more people who wanted jobs. Wanted some kind of economic infusion into this county. Ranching was no longer the big moneymaker it had once been, not since the commodities markets and ethanol had raised the cost of feed through the roof. A lot of them stuck it out, though, refusing to give up their way of life and land that their families had owned for generations. She watched them make all kinds of hard adjustments to survive.

But people in town were making the same adjustments. Church rummage sales were so well picked-over these days that there hardly seemed to be anything left for them. Nearly everyone dressed in secondhand clothes, pregnant women traded outfits, young mothers traded baby clothes, and even goods from China weren't moving fast off the racks at Freitag's Mercantile.

The place was fading, she thought sadly. Probably like a million other small rural communities. A ski resort could turn that around. It might not mean great jobs for the locals, but it would mean jobs. Business for the stores in town, as long as the resort didn't supply everything. She needed to ask Luke about that.

But the entire character of the community would change, and she really couldn't blame the folks who wanted to resist.

"Face-lift."

The word startled her back to the present and she

realized Luke was awake again. She put the milkshake back in his hand and he sipped on the straw.

"Good," he said.

"I'm glad. Who needs a face-lift?"

For a moment he looked confused, then said, "The town."

"Oh. I don't know if people will like that. What kind of face-lift?"

"Paint. Brick sidewalks. Streetlights…"

Well, none of that sounded exactly awful, she thought. If that's all that was involved. She waited, but his thoughts seemed to have drifted elsewhere.

"Great mountain," he said, then resumed sipping. It appeared to be getting a little easier.

"I love those mountains. I don't know if I want to see them shredded by ski runs."

"Not visible."

"What's not visible?"

He sighed. "Not from down here."

"Oh." All of a sudden she wished it were easier for him to talk. She wanted to ask him all kinds of questions about what DEL intended to do up there.

"Hurts," he said, this time sounding angry.

"Where?"

He just looked at her like, *Isn't it obvious?*

She glanced at the clock. "It's too soon for more pain meds, Luke. Another half hour. I guess you feel like you're being hammered."

"No joke."

"Soon," she assured him. "Very soon."

He sighed, and his eyes closed as he drifted away, a result of the concussion most likely. Or maybe the remaining morphine in his system.

"I lost you," he said, then passed out again.

"You threw me away," she answered quietly. The real pain in her heart that had never gone away, the certainty that he had thrown her away. She was glad he didn't hear her.

Chapter 3

Bri spent the night on the couch in the living room in case Luke needed something. He was able to tend to his most personal needs, so she didn't have to manhandle him down the hall to the bathroom, a relief. She had no doubt she could have done it, but it wouldn't have been fun for either of them.

By morning, though, a thought had occurred to her. She needed to look after the man for at least a week, maybe longer, depending on how soon he could travel. His cast went from his ankle to above his knee, which meant that wasn't likely to be soon.

With a sigh, she picked up the phone and called Jack. "I need a safety bar in my bathroom," she told him. "Can you do that?"

"Sure," came the prompt response. "When do you want it?"

"As soon as possible. Thanks, Jack. You're a good guy."

"Always glad to help," he responded cheerfully.

And he was a cheerful person. He worked at the hardware store, but picked up side jobs as a handyman. She'd lost count of the times he'd helped her out with something.

She tried making some very soft scrambled eggs for Luke. The man needed something for subsistence besides broth and milkshakes.

He was wide awake when she carried the bowl and spoon into the living room. "Good morning," she said.

"Morning." He looked at the bowl.

"Scrambled eggs," she explained. "No chewing. How's that jaw feel?"

"Better."

She supposed that was debatable. It didn't look any less swollen, but maybe it was on the inside. "Time for your pain pill, too. Water?"

"Please."

"You want to try to feed yourself?"

"Yeah."

So she raised the head of his bed, pulled the table over, adjusting its height, and left him to it while she went to get him a glass of water with a straw.

When she came back, he'd already put away half the eggs. "Good," he said, with what appeared to be an attempt at a smile.

"More where those came from. Just let me know."

He managed to get the pill down, too. "Coffee?" he asked hopefully.

She hesitated. "I'll have to cool it down. I don't

know how lacerated the inside of your cheek is, either. It might really sting."

"Coffee," he repeated. "Please."

Puppy-dog eyes, she thought. When had Luke learned to make puppy-dog eyes? Damn, he was tugging her heart strings.

At least she had plastic straws. "Iced coffee," she suggested. "You have to drink through a straw right now." She wondered if he had any idea of how much egg he had on his face right now. Probably not. She grabbed a napkin and wiped it gently away.

"Won't always be like this," he said.

She wondered if that was a promise or a threat. "No, you're getting better. I'll get that coffee."

She made the iced coffee in a plastic cup, then froze. He must need a sponge bath by now. Oh, wasn't that going to be fun. But it needed to be done before she changed his sheets.

She didn't want to do it. She could do it for any patient without a second thought, but this was different. This was a body she had once loved and made love with. Awkward. Awful. She closed her eyes a moment, resisting the idea but knowing it was important for his comfort, if not for his health. He was beginning to get a little ripe.

Oh, hell. She carried the coffee back to him and found he'd nearly finished the eggs. She had to wipe his face again.

He enjoyed the coffee, though, and it didn't seem to cause him too much discomfort. Of course the pill was probably starting to kick in. Maybe it would make him safely woozy for a sponge bath.

"More eggs?" she asked.

"Not now. Later. Thanks."

She sat sipping her own mug of coffee, waiting for him to start looking a bit drowsy. Unfortunately, that didn't seem to be happening.

"How are you feeling?"

"Been through a cement mixer."

"I imagine it feels that way. Listen, I need to change your bedding, and your gown. I want to do it when the pain pill is working its strongest."

"'Kay."

"But..." She bit her lower lip. "I need to give you a sponge bath, too. Will you cooperate?"

Damn him, she thought she saw a wicked twinkle in those gray eyes. "Never thought you'd ask."

"Damn you, Luke, don't be a pain. I've got to move you around. Clean sheets. Clean body, clean gown. No bedsores on my watch. That's the beginning and end of it."

"Yes, Nurse." But that twinkle seemed to remain. If the rest of his face had been more mobile, the expression probably would have been all over it.

"Luke..."

"I'll...be good."

As if he could do much else, she thought irritably. Why was she even bothered by this? Right now he was a helpless slab of meat with a devilish look in his eyes. She'd seen that from eighty-year-olds...although they tried to have the male nurses take care of these things.

"I could call a man to do it."

"Said I'd be good." He set the coffee on the table. "What am I gonna do?"

Exactly, she thought. He was utterly helpless, which gave her a momentary flash of pleasure. Luke had never been helpless. Never. Her mind suddenly served up a smorgasbord of the ways she could tease him with a sponge bath, drive him out of his mind the way he had so often driven her. Turn him into a help-less sex slave. The image amused her so much that she was able to laugh at herself, even as heat blossomed between her legs.

The knock on the door surprised her. She wasn't ex-pecting anyone at this hour, but there was Jack, safety bar and tool kit in hand.

"That was quick," she said.

He shrugged and gave her a shy smile. "I heard about the guy. Didn't figure it could wait long."

"I really appreciate this," she assured him as she let him in.

"Why do you have to take care of him?" Jack asked as he headed down the hallway to the bathroom. She wasn't surprised he knew where it was since he'd re-placed the tile for her last year.

"Do you see a convalescent home within a few hun-dred miles? He can't be moved yet."

"So how'd you get to be it?"

Good question, she thought. "Because I'm a sucker?"

He astonished her by turning sharply, looking angry. "Don't say things like that about yourself. You're a nice lady."

His vehemence surprised her so much that she nearly stepped back. Jack usually seemed so calm and pleasant. But then his face smoothed and he shifted the bar so he could enter the bathroom.

"I used to know Luke," she said finally. "It seemed like the right thing to do for a friend."

"Like I said, you're a nice lady. Where you want this bar? By the commode or in the shower?"

"He won't be taking showers while he's here. Just by the commode. To help him move in and out of the wheelchair."

"He's pretty messed up?"

"Seriously messed up."

"Too bad. This won't take long."

She was glad, actually glad, to head back to Luke. Something about Jack disturbed her this morning. He didn't seem quite like himself. But then everything in her life felt strange right now, so why should Jack be any different?

Luke had finished the iced coffee and asked for more when she got back. At the moment she was glad just to be busy. Everything was off-kilter, and ordinary tasks suddenly felt like a lifeline to sanity.

Luke was back in her life, however temporarily; Jack seemed weird; and God knew she didn't feel at all like herself.

Jack finished up in about twenty minutes. He had her test the bar to her own satisfaction, leaning her full weight on it.

"Great job," she told him.

He smiled shyly. "It's easy."

"Maybe for you."

That made him beam. "You got a vacuum? I'll get up the dust."

"I can take care of it. The store must need you back." And she needed him out of here, though she wasn't sure why. Ordinarily she didn't mind having Jack around when he was doing a job for her, but today…today something was different.

He looked surprised but finished packing his tools and headed out. She'd get a bill from the store at the end of the month, so he didn't have to even pause for payment. She was relieved to close the door behind him.

"What was that?" Luke asked.

"My handyman, Jack. I had him put a safety bar in the bathroom for you."

"Sorry. Sorry for imposing. Causing trouble."

"It's not your fault." She could say that much with truth. And at least he seemed to be growing steadily more coherent. Maybe there wouldn't be any long-term effects from the concussion. God, she hoped not. Mild concussions had been known to mess people up for years or longer.

Then a thought occurred to her. "Luke? Have you worked with Mike Hanson for long?"

"Five, six years. Why?"

"I just wondered." Because he'd been the only other person out there when Luke fell, and Luke had initially claimed he'd been pushed. "Do you remember any more about what happened?"

"No."

"Well, that's common enough, to forget what happened right before."

"I hear. I guess I stirred up a mess of trouble, saying I was pushed. Wonder where that came from."

"The concussion," she said with more surety than she felt. "People can say and do a lot of crazy things."

"How do you know what's real?"

She managed a smile for him. "By what doesn't change."

"Not true," he said, his face drooping. "Life changes. All the time."

"You're right. It does." And sometimes that was its saddest part.

Changing the sheets and sponging him down didn't prove that difficult physically, but for her it was sheer hell psychologically. She lowered his leg so she could roll him onto his side and sponge his back. She didn't care if the sheets got damp, but beneath them was a foam pad, what they sometimes called an egg crate, to help prevent pressure sores. That definitely couldn't get wet.

So she pulled out a rubber sheet, and once she had carefully rolled him to the side, she tucked it beneath him to catch any water. It was then she saw all the bruises that covered his back. She couldn't withhold a sound of distress.

"What's wrong?" He was starting to sound pretty groggy from the pain pill.

"Your back is a mess. You must have rolled when you tumbled. Just bruises. Let me know if I hurt you."

"You already did that," he muttered.

She had to resist an urge to snap at him, especially since she was sure he wouldn't have said it at all if he weren't full of drugs and concussed. Luke had never been a man to show weakness of any kind. Initially she had admired that in him. Now she wondered.

Wringing out a cloth, she began to wash him from his neck down, baring only small parts of his body to prevent him from growing chilled.

"Feels good," he mumbled.

"As long as the water stays warm," she answered. Maybe she should have gotten a heating pad to put beneath the bowl. Or she could just hurry.

She had to be gentle, not wanting to hurt him, but she hoped the rubbing of the terry cloth would stimulate circulation. And instead of going fast, she lingered. It had been years since she had run her hands over this muscled back, but time hadn't diminished the impact anyway. He was a beautifully built man, sculpted by years of physical labor, without a spare ounce of flesh on him. She knew she wasn't maintaining proper clinical detachment, but she figured that was a lost cause under the circumstances.

"Feels good," he mumbled again, drowsily.

To her, too. She worked her way down slowly, relearning every line of him, lingering more than she should have. Her breath quickened, and she felt stupid for it. This man hadn't wanted her, and anyway, even if he had he was out of action.

When she reached his buttocks, she felt him quiver, and a similar quiver ran through her. It did not help to realize that *that* hadn't died with their marriage. Biting her lip, she forced herself to a quicker pace, then covered him with a blanket so he wouldn't get chilled.

"You feeling all right?" she asked as she rounded the bed.

"Great."

"I need to get more warm water, then I'm going to turn you again."

He didn't answer and she hoped he had dozed off again. This was getting too intimate when it should have been purely clinical. Damn him.

When she returned, she rolled him gently onto his back. One groan escaped him, but only one. "It's okay," he mumbled.

She started at his shoulders and began to work her way down bit by bit. When she reached his hips and was about to move the blanket, his good hand reached out with a speed that surprised her.

"No. Not there."

"I'm a nurse," she said, hoping she didn't sound as weak as she suddenly felt.

"No," he repeated.

She couldn't help feeling relieved. Honestly, she didn't know if she could manage to handle his privates with anything approaching proper detachment. But she remembered them, remembered all too well. He was perfectly built in every respect, at least as far as she was concerned. And for a few seconds as she stood there, she realized she wanted nothing more than to touch him intimately again, to caress him and draw groans from his lips. She needed to get a grip. Quickly.

Apparently even in his present state, memory was bedeviling him as much as it was her. He'd never been shy about his body, and if it had been anyone else proposing to wash him, he probably wouldn't have objected.

Maybe more than one thing wasn't completely dead yet.

After that, though, things went faster. She made up one side of the bed with a fresh sheet, rolled him over and finished the job while he lay on the freshly made side. Man, it had been a while since she had needed to do this. Usually the LPNs handled it.

But at last he was clean and in a fresh gown. "Bathroom?" she asked.

"Nah, just give me that bottle thing."

"Call if you need help." She practically fled. Time to regroup, she told herself as she waited in the kitchen. Time to build up the time and distance he'd erased so effectively. Time to remind herself of all her good reasons for not reacting to him. Time to figure out how she was going to handle this until he could be transported.

Because somehow she had to. Sometimes the hardest part of life was just dealing. The curveballs seemed to keep coming.

Trent stopped by every evening for a quick look at Luke and three days later pronounced himself very satisfied. "The recovery is really going well," he said. "I don't see any new swelling since you left the hospital, Luke, and there's no sign of infection. At this rate we'll take you back for X-rays in a few days, and maybe we can get you into a walking cast."

"That would be great," Luke said. "I hate being stuck in bed."

"Well, the good news is, I'm going to allow you to spend some time in the wheelchair now with your leg up. It'll give you some mobility."

"Maybe even the front porch," Bri said. "We're starting to get warmer at last."

"I'd continue elevating his leg overnight, but unless you detect some new swelling, he can sit up as much as he wants." He turned to Luke. "Just don't tire yourself too much. You've still got a lot of mending to do, including inside your head. So don't push it."

Bri listened to this, wondering if Luke would follow instructions or just push himself to the brink over and over. She was surprised he hadn't grown so frustrated with his confinement that he swamped her in it. In fact, when all was said and done, he'd been amazingly cooperative so far.

"What about bending my leg again?" Luke asked.

"The break above your knee was minor. Depending on how the X-rays look we may be able to give you back the use of your knee. No promises, but if we can, we will."

"God," Luke said after Trent left, "that would be a relief."

"What?"

"Bending my leg again. Right now it just juts out there and even getting to the bathroom is a major hassle. Nothing moves right."

She turned to look at him at last and found him making a funny face. Despite her best intention to remain distant, she had to laugh.

"That's better," he said, surprising her. "The freeze around here has been amazing. It's a wonder I don't have frostbite."

She couldn't protest that he was wrong. She had been pretty much hiding out in the kitchen, appearing only when she had to act the role of nurse. Maybe it wasn't exactly friendly of her, but she didn't need to be friendly. Those days were gone and she didn't want to risk letting them back in. She'd already discovered that three years hadn't banished old yearnings and old pains, at least not entirely. Spending a lot of time with him would be folly.

So she pretended she was at work, looking in on

him as often as necessary, seeing to his essential needs, but definitely not sitting around and entertaining him.

Now his pain meds had been reduced, and she doubted he was going to continue to be such a compliant patient. In fact, she was sure his boredom would start becoming a problem. Maybe having Jan take over for her would be salvation, much as she didn't want Jan to have free run of her house. She liked the woman well enough, but at some level had never entirely trusted her. Among other things, she was an unkind gossip. Not the sort of person you wanted to share anything intimate with.

On the other hand... Well, on the other hand it turned out she didn't have to worry about Jan. She needed to worry about herself. The nursing supervisor called to say that she was putting Bri on family leave for the next week.

"But why, Mary?"

"Think about it," Mary said frankly. "I hear he's your ex. Do you really want some of the nurses here running over there to cover for you and hunting for juicy details?"

Bri knew exactly who Mary meant. Much as she wanted to escape Luke for a few hours and get back on her normal routine, she couldn't deny Mary's point.

"I know this must be hard on you," Mary said. "But it could be harder, if you think about it. So tough it out, Bri. Maybe once the guy's brain is less addled he'll figure out a way to get himself to a convalescent facility."

After she hung up the phone, she sat at the table wondering how everything had just spun her life out of control and what she was going to do about it. Transport was expensive, and even though Luke was well paid, hiring an ambulance to drive him a couple hundred miles… Well, nobody short of a billionaire would want to do that. The cost of getting a facility to come pick him up would probably be nearly as much.

Nothing like being in the boonies, she thought for the umpteenth time since the accident. Most people had family around here who could do this part, but Luke had no one but her.

Which left her the reluctant nurse. Dang.

In that instant a whole lot seemed to crash down on her. Feelings she'd been deliberately avoiding since Luke had come back into her life. Feelings about him being right there and spending most of her time trying to ignore him. Feelings out of the distant past.

And again and again the memory of how many times he'd said he'd lost her. Did he really feel that way?

She wanted to pack a bag and just run. A tsunami seemed to be headed right at her, and she wondered if she would survive it. Old wounds reopening. Old arguments rebuilding. New problems. Changes.

How long could she keep a lid on it before something snapped?

"Bri?"

The sound of him calling her name pierced her heart. She didn't want that. She didn't want that ever again.

Jack hadn't seen much of Bri since the accident, except when she ran out for a short time to get more milkshakes or things from the grocery. It made him uneasy. He needed to know what was going on.

He'd thought giving the Luke guy that shove would

have settled the matter one way or another. Either he'd die or be transported to a hospital far away.

Instead he'd landed right in Bri's house. Did she care that much for him still?

He had to know, so he'd crawled into the attic again to listen. So far he hadn't seen or heard a thing to make him nervous. Bri spent an awful lot of time in her kitchen or bedroom. She hardly talked to Luke.

That was good.

But hearing Luke call for her as though she was some kind of servant really ticked him off. He supposed he should be nice about it, considering the guy was stuck in bed, but he wasn't feeling very nice about it.

Every minute that Luke spent in her house struck him as a ticking time bomb. What if they made up?

He wouldn't be able to stand it.

Chapter 4

Now that Luke was spending more time in the chair, the hospital gown had to go. With his permission, she cut the leg off a pair of his sweatpants and soon got them on him. Then she cut the arm off a matching sweatshirt to just above the elbow and helped him into that.

"I feel almost human," he announced when she was done.

She saw he was trying to smile, an expression that was coming easier as the swelling in his cheek receded some. He was still not in great shape, but the improvement was fast and noticeable.

"Potato soup for dinner tonight," she told him.

"Homemade?"

"Yes."

"I love your homemade potato soup."

He always had. "With ground turkey," she added, knowing how much he liked that. "It's still chilly out, but do you want to try sitting on the porch for a bit?"

"Please."

He was being incredibly polite, she noticed. Almost as if they were strangers. Either he was still addled, or he was trying to pretend they didn't have a past. Either way was fine by her. Or so she told herself.

She lowered the bed to the level of the wheelchair, then locked the chair in place. He was becoming quite the expert at levering himself in and out of it with one arm.

She had a moment of concern, though, when he slipped onto the chair then lowered his head. "Luke? What's wrong?"

"Dizzy."

That was expected post-concussion, but she needed to know more. "How dizzy? Worse?"

"Not worse. Just a little." After a moment he lifted his head. "Better now."

He was still limited to short sentences because of his cheek, and the way he was talking she wondered just how cut up the inside of his mouth had been.

She looked straight into his eyes, but saw the pupils were even. Okay, then, nothing worse. Yet. Grabbing a blanket, she covered his legs, then wrapped another around his upper body as best she could. "You tell me if you start to feel chilled."

"'Kay."

"Promise?"

He just glared at her, and she had a crazy urge to laugh. Dizzy or not, that was Luke. Even when they were married he hadn't liked being fussed over.

Out on the porch she locked the chair so it wouldn't roll, then ran back inside to get her jacket. She pulled up a plastic chair beside him.

"The snow is finally almost gone," she remarked. "And I think I see some buds on the trees. It's been a late spring."

"I noticed."

"So you said the ski slopes won't be visible from town?"

"That's the plan."

"Good, because those mountains are too pretty to be scarred."

"Agree." He shifted his weight in the wheelchair. "Should all be pretty. For everyone."

"Will you have all the shops up there, or will people come to town?"

"Both."

She looked at him and realized it was getting easier to see him nearby. She was growing accustomed to his face again, to quote an old song. "How so?"

"Some people don't want to leave the resort. Others want to see more. Around here, that's this town. Build up the Old West flavor and your shops will be busy."

"If they carry the right merchandise."

"Yeah. Not my issue."

No, she supposed it wasn't. "Has your company even thought about the fact that this town serves working ranchers and local people? They can't be priced out of the place. Not like Aspen and Vail."

"Part of the charm," he said.

"What is?"

"Working town, not plastic town. They don't want to ruin that, I hear."

"They better not. I imagine a whole lot of people are already getting upset about this. They didn't like the semiconductor plant, for example, and that created a bunch of good jobs for a while. It also brought a whole lot of new people who didn't understand our way of life. You're going to face some opposition."

"Always do."

If she allowed her memory to wander to her past with him, she had no difficulty remembering occasional references to local opposition. He never made much of it, but for the first time she wondered if he had been trying to protect her from some very real dangers in his work. Look at him. She couldn't forget that he claimed to have been pushed, even though he didn't remember that now.

Ice touched the base of her neck.

"Nice to be outside again," he said. His speech was definitely becoming clearer.

"I imagine so." He'd always preferred being outdoors, but he'd also always preferred being active. "Feel like a prisoner?"

"Not much I can do about it."

"Not right now." She hesitated. "Have you thought about transport to a convalescent facility?"

His gray eyes pinned her. "Wanna get rid of me?"

Sheesh. Looking into those eyes, something inside her whispered that that was the last thing she wanted. How stupid could she be? "I'm thinking of your recovery. You'll probably get a walking cast soon. You'll also probably need some rehab." She hung back from telling him the community hospital had a decent physiotherapy department. She feared it would sound like an invitation, one she didn't want to offer.

"Sorry I messed up your life," he said. "But I'm not leaving."

"Why?"

"My job." He fixed her with his stare again. "I may not be able to climb the mountain, but I've seen enough to finish my report. This is *my* project."

"They won't take it away from you? Mike seemed pretty sure they were going to send someone else."

"Not soon. Everyone's tied up. I'll call them Monday and tell them I have a handle on it. As soon as I can walk again, I'll get out of your hair."

And go back to the motel. She had to admit she really didn't like the idea of him living there, but she also figured he'd endured worse conditions. Was he in her hair? Yes. Had he made a mess of her life? Only a little. He'd be gone soon.

"I'm not trying to throw you out," she said finally.

"But you're uncomfortable. I get it. I just wanted to say hi and defend myself, and instead I wind up in your living room. You must be thrilled."

She wasn't exactly tap-dancing for joy, but she didn't want to say that. Having him around made her fearful. Fearful that the past could be resurrected. Fearful that she could get hurt again. Fearful that she might start caring again.

But that was no reason to treat him like a junkyard dog. Hell, she'd give at least this much care to a stray. "It's okay," she said finally. "That past is past."

"Is it?"

Now it was her turn to give him a look, an icy one. "Yes. So I suggest we just go on as if we have no past. I don't want to rake that up, and neither should you."

"Fair enough." He closed his eyes a moment, then swore quietly. "I hate this."

"What?"

"Being dependent. I'm cold. I don't want to go in but I'm starting to shiver. I'm hurting. I don't want one, but I think I need another pain pill. I can't tough it out any longer."

"What are you feeling?"

"Like someone's hammering my leg, my arm and my head. It's making me crabby. I don't want to fight with you."

"Maybe if we get you warmed up, you won't need a pill. Want to try that first?"

"Yeah." Curt but to the point.

Just then, Jack came walking up the street. Bri was bending to unlock Luke's wheelchair when he called out.

"Bri?"

She straightened, seeking him with her gaze. "Hi, Jack. We were just about to go in."

"You maybe need a ramp on those steps? I mean, if your friend is going to be here a while."

Luke started to say no, but Bri forestalled him. "That might be a good idea. Let me think about it. I'll know more when Luke gets his leg X-rayed next week."

"All right. You need any help, just holler."

"I will. Thanks, Jack."

Luke remained silent until they were back inside. Then the withheld words burst out of him. "I don't want you spending that kind of money on me."

"But wouldn't it be nice to get around the block in the chair? Trent said you might need it for a while, and I'm not sure you can get very far on a walking cast at first. Sheesh, Luke, crutches are going to be hard with your broken arm."

He remained silent for a smoldering moment. "Did you hear that guy?"

"Jack? What?"

"He can't wait for me to be gone. Just like you."

Oh, boy, she thought. The concussion? Or had she really missed something? "Jack is always trying to be helpful."

"He might as well wear a sign. He's sweet on you."

"And that's none of your business."

"Nope." He shook off as much of her help as he could getting back into bed.

Without a word, she elevated his leg again, hoping it would help. "How's the pain? Head? Leg?"

"What do you care?" he grumbled.

"Luke!" She put her hands on her hips and glared at him.

"Sorry. The pain got to me, I guess. Or maybe my head did."

So she went to get him half a pain pill. He took it sullenly, like a sick kid. *Lovely.*

But, she reminded herself, he'd been through hell, he was indeed in a lot of pain and he still had a long way to go. She could hardly blame him for getting cranky, especially with the concussion. Those effects might well last a long time.

A tiny fear gnawed at the corner of her mind. What if the concussion had a permanent effect on his personality? The thought made her feel ill.

He slept for a while, which gave Bri a little time to read. Diane called and they chatted for a few minutes.

She offered to come over and keep an eye on Luke if Bri wanted to get out. The offer was tempting, but she refused it.

"He's not in the best mood right now. Maybe another time, Di."

"Sure, but I can handle cranky. Remember, I've got a husband and two sons. When they get sick they turn into real pains. Men. They can't handle even a tummy ache."

Bri laughed, because she'd seen it often enough. At the hospital men tended to be sweet as pie to the nurses, but then she'd hear all the crankiness and complaining when their wives came to visit.

Even though she tried to read an engaging novel, her mind insisted on wandering. Could Luke be right about Jack? She dismissed the idea almost immediately. Jack had been her handyman for a couple of years, and he'd never done or said anything that indicated interest. Just helpful and pleasant and nothing more. After two years, if he really was sweet on her, he surely would have indicated it in some way. She was glad he hadn't, though, because she wasn't at all interested in Jack that way.

Luke was just concussed and in pain, and probably hypersensitive about the idea that Jack might have to build him a ramp, a chore that were he well he would have knocked out himself in no time. The male ego was probably taking a real ding. That was all. Luke had never been one to like others doing for him what he should be able to do for himself.

Such as the way he had insisted on refusing almost all her help with getting back into bed. Ego again. Independence. Maybe a measure of stupidity. Certainly he had been determined to prove that he wasn't completely helpless.

She sighed and closed the book. For some reason her knee was aching. The weather must be changing. Rising, she went to the kitchen and got herself an ice pack, then grabbed an elastic bandage from the cupboard.

She was sitting in her office chair wrapping the ice pack onto her knee when Luke startled her by speaking.

"When are you going to get that knee fixed?" he asked.

She looked up as soon as she pinned the wrap into place. "When it gets bad enough."

"But it hampers you now."

"Sometimes. There's a lot of arthritis there now. But it's not to the point where I want to undergo a knee replacement. No biggie."

He grunted, which could have meant anything.

"How are you feeling?" she asked.

"Like a freaking jerk. Apologies available."

"Also not necessary."

He gave her a crooked smile. "I probably still owe you a million apologies."

"Let's not go there, okay?"

He shrugged one shoulder. "Have it your way. Watch out for that Jack guy, though. Unless you want to date him."

"I don't want to date him, and he's a perfectly nice person."

"You would know."

She straightened the leg with the ice pack on it. "I don't get you," she said. "Jack has been my handyman for two years now. He's never stepped out of line."

"He sure doesn't like me being here."

"How can you possibly know that? Did he say something? Because if so, I sure didn't hear it."

"It wasn't something to hear. But I can tell."

"Oh, you have amazing psychic powers?"

He lifted his good hand, as if to wave the discussion away, then paused. "If you were paying attention, you would have heard it. He was trying to find out if I was going to be here for long."

"By asking if I needed a ramp? Really? That couldn't have just come from seeing you in a wheelchair?"

"Maybe."

"Thank you." Sarcasm filled her tone.

"But think about it, Bri. If you wanted a ramp, you'd have called him and hired him. Asking was like pumping you for work…or information. Does he do that often?"

Bri fell silent, partly because she was steaming, and partly because he'd raised a question in her mind. But just because Jack had never asked her about work before, but had always waited for her to ask him, didn't mean he wouldn't ask such an obvious question under the circumstances.

"Cut it out," she said finally.

"What?"

"Poisoning things. Jack's a nice, helpful guy and I don't want to be suspicious of him."

"Okay," he said. "What are you reading?"

The change of topic was too abrupt and very unlike Luke, who didn't quit easily. Now she had to worry about his head again. She didn't want to worry about him, especially when he lay there in a bed looking like a dented Christmas package waiting to be opened. Everything about him awoke her sexuality, even when she was annoyed.

She stood, wincing a little as her knee complained. "I need to stir the soup. Are you hungry?"

"Getting there."

She left the living room, and now it was her turn to feel as if she'd been thrown in a cement mixer. Mentally and emotionally, anyway. Was Luke right? Was his concussion affecting him? Was there really some reason to be suspicious of Jack?

No, of course not. She answered the last question for herself. She knew Jack. All he'd done was offer to build her a ramp for her front steps. A kind and generous offer. Thoughtful. Jack was always thoughtful.

So Luke was still a bit addled, seeing things that weren't there. She supposed there'd be more where that came from.

Dang, it was easier to deal with someone she didn't know as well, a regular patient. Dealing with her ex was making every bit of this harder. Things he said struck her more deeply. He had her questioning herself in ways she didn't like.

And she wanted to get back to him with a bowl of soup. Maybe that was the scariest thing of all.

Luke lay in the bed feeling pretty crummy. It wasn't just the pounding pain, or the loopiness of even the smaller dose of painkillers. It was wondering how much the concussion had affected him.

His suspicion that Jack was sweet on Bri struck him as perfectly reasonable. The thing was, it wasn't his business. Bri was his ex. A free agent. Someone who was entitled to make her own decisions about everything. The only thing he knew for sure was that there was something he didn't like about Jack.

Well, maybe that was just an old jealousy rising up. He ought to be able to deal with that by now.

He'd said more than he should have, in a way that wasn't good, and that bothered him. How much damage had he suffered to his head, anyway? It was hard to know, being stuck like this, locked up in his own body. He couldn't get out there to learn if he could still cope with everything in his life. Hell, at this point he wasn't sure if he could still walk. All his parts seemed to be there, he could wiggle the toes on his broken leg, but the thing he worried about was the dizziness.

He hadn't mentioned it to Bri except briefly because he could tell it instantly worried her. The doc had told him he might experience it for a while, but Bri clearly feared it. She had asked, after all, if it was getting worse.

It wasn't, but if it kept grabbing him at odd times, he might not be able to get around on crutches. God, the thought of being stuck indefinitely in a wheelchair made him want to crawl out of his skin.

He couldn't stand being helpless, but he kept reminding himself to shut up and take his medicine like a man. Easier said than done. He wondered if it would have been easier if he went to that convalescent facility Bri had mentioned. Maybe his self-image would take less of a ding being cared for by strangers than by Bri.

Not that she was doing anything wrong. Considering the way their meeting before his accident had gone, he was amazed that she'd been willing to take him in. And not only take him in, but sometimes care for him like a baby.

She was a nurse, yes, but she was also his ex. They had a history. This had to be hard on her.

It was sure hard on him being around her all the time. He had plenty of good reasons not to care about her anymore, but those reasons weren't helping him much.

He'd come here the first time, all determined to defend himself. After three years. He might be concussed and not quite in his right mind, but he wondered if he'd been in his right mind when he walked in on her.

In theory, it should be enough that *he* knew he hadn't cheated on her. You couldn't make people believe what they didn't want to believe, and the only opinion that should matter was his own, anyway.

But somehow, despite all the anger, all the pain, all the fury of their breakup, her opinion still mattered. It was like having a piece of glass in his foot that he couldn't extract, a constant irritant that she had such a low opinion of him.

But changing her opinion, even if he could, wouldn't change anything else. They had split, it had been hurtful and ugly, and you couldn't take that back. No way. It would ever be there, a scar on the landscape of the past as if a huge bomb had blasted a hole into what had once been a beautiful world.

Maybe she had other gripes, too. How would he know? She hadn't said much until the end when she was so angry with him, and that had all been about Barbara. That comment she'd made about how their marriage had been more like an affair bothered him, though.

Had separation been the real death knell?

All he was sure of at that moment was that he still

craved her with every cell in his body. Medicated and
in pain though he was, addled though he probably was,
the intimacy of her care for him kept arousing him. He
hoped she never guessed how often he quickly bunched
blankets over his erection so she wouldn't see it. How
quickly he responded to the lightest of her touches.
God, he wanted that woman as much as he had ever
wanted anything. Still.

He tried to think about that, about what it might
mean considering all that had happened between them,
but he was drifting away again. He gave up.

None of it mattered anymore. He just had to heal
and get the hell out of here. His eyes closed, he let go.
He still had a lifetime to examine his screwups.

Bri let him sleep for a couple of hours, then brought
him a big bowl of potato soup. He was waking, and
gave her a half smile as she set it on the table beside
him. "That smells really good."

"Do you want me to raise the head of the bed, or do
you want to get into the chair?"

He looked down his length, at his leg once again
elevated, and thought of all the work he would make
for her by asking to sit in the chair. So he reached for
the bed control and raised himself up. "This is fine,
thanks."

"Let me know if you want more. There's plenty."
She pushed the table in front of him.

"I don't see a bowl for you," he said. "Can't even
eat with me?"

She hadn't been, but this was the first time he had
mentioned it. "Oh, for heaven's sake, Luke!"

"What? You're stuck with me for at least a few more

days. I'm tired of the ice-queen routine. Surely you can manage a casual conversation with me."

She studied him dubiously. He liked the look in her witchy eyes, liked knowing he'd put her off balance. She deserved to be a little off balance. Vengeful? Maybe. But she should have believed him rather than Barbara.

After a long pause she said, "I'll get a bowl."

"Good." Not that he was likely to have much to say. The swelling and lacerations in his cheek still made speech painful, and he figured he'd used up most of his endurance just asking her to eat with him.

His thoughts drew up short. Endurance? Was he really feeling that way, as though he was out of strength even to talk?

She returned a couple of minutes later, put her bowl on the table beside his, then brought out a TV tray that she set up in front of the office chair she'd been using.

"You're still limping," he remarked.

"Change of weather, I guess. I'm going to be one of those people who can predict rain by my knee."

She settled with her own table and soup so that she faced him. "So what's on your mind?" she asked.

Before answering, he tasted the soup. Hot and rich, the way she always made it. "This is really, really good, Bri. Better than I remember it even."

A faint smile lifted the corners of her mouth, a mouth he realized that he still wanted to kiss. Oh, cut it out. That would only cause trouble.

"What's on your mind?" she asked again.

"I realized it's wearing on me even to talk. That won't last, will it?"

"You've been through a lot, Luke. It's not like you

just had a minor injury. It'll take time to get your strength back. And the more time you spend in bed, the more strength you lose." She shook her head a little, and he wished she'd let her hair down so he could watch it swing the way it once had. "I'm hoping they can start some rehab on you when they replace the casts. That's so important. Bed rest is a bad thing."

"It feels like it, but not much I can do."

"Not yet. That'll change soon. You'll see."

For a while they ate in silence. He tried to figure out some way to draw her out, maybe about her job. He knew how dedicated she was to nursing. Hell, it had been the reason she hadn't wanted to travel with him. Getting her to talk about it should be safe ground.

But he felt like an idiot when it came to that. He knew next to nothing about what she did, even after being married to her. When they were together, neither of them had spent much time on shoptalk. They'd been too busy making up for lost time, in bed and out of it.

Maybe she was right. Maybe it had never become a real marriage, never had the chance to grow that way. Maybe it had been just an extended affair. That might work for some people, but it apparently hadn't worked for them. Not in the end. Even as she had accused him of cheating on her, he'd had his own dissatisfactions with the ways things were.

Neither of them had been willing to change. But before he brought up that bit of the past—if he decided to—he'd better be clear on how much change he'd be willing to make. They'd already burned enough bridges.

But why was he thinking this way? It was over. She had made that clear. She'd sent him packing until he wound up helpless. Nor could he say that she seemed to be enjoying having him at her mercy. In fact, she seemed utterly unhappy about it.

As unhappy as he was.

So put away those thoughts about how much he'd like to make love to her again, be grateful it was completely impossible now and focus on anything else.

It was hard, though, with her sitting so close. The itch to reach for her never went away. Even harder to face the fact that she was now a stranger to him. Maybe she'd always been a stranger.

"Crap," he said.

She looked up from her soup. "What?"

"I know I had a concussion. What I'm wondering is if my brain is working right. How can I know?"

"Well, the usual questions are about what day it is and who is president, and what's the last news story you read."

A half laugh slipped out of him. "That won't tell me if all the gears are meshing properly."

She surprised him with a rare smile. "No, I guess it won't. Is there something you can think of to do from that bed that would test it?"

"Actually, yes," he said. "I just had a stroke of brilliance."

She pursed her lips but the amusement remained in her eyes. "Yeah?"

"Yeah. After I've had another bowl of this soup, could you bring me my laptop? I could start writing my report. You can tell me if I'm making sense."

"How would I know?"

"You know the English language. That's a good start. And most of it would be common sense."

She tilted her head. "Never once when we were married did you ask me to look at your work."

"I know. I thought it would bore you."

She frowned faintly. "Really? I thought you just didn't like to talk about it."

"It's my hobbyhorse. I can talk endlessly about it. You can probably do the same about nursing."

"But I never did."

It was an admission, he realized. They were both facing what might have been a major failing between them. They hadn't cemented the bonds between them with day-to-day stuff.

Before he could say something he probably shouldn't, he returned to eating. He really didn't trust his brain right now. He just hoped he'd feel better about it after he started working again.

In the meantime, analyzing his dead marriage might only lead him down a rabbit hole. How could he be sure about anything?

After dinner, Bri brought him his laptop. The battery was low, so she plugged it in for him. "Typing is going to be a pain," she remarked.

"Typos I can live with. Not knowing if my reasoning still works, I can't."

She astonished him then, laying her hand on his shoulder and squeezing gently. "You're going to be fine, Luke. Really. Mild concussions aren't good, but from what Trent said, you should be okay."

"I wish I believed that. Maybe my whole problem is spending too much time vegging. I've been doped up on pain meds with too much time to think, and not enough to focus on."

He saw her bite her lip.

"I'm not blaming you," he said swiftly. "But I am running out of steam for talking. Sorry."

"It's all right." She patted his shoulder and retreated to her chair and book. "Let me know when you want me to look. Or if you need help."

The way the inside of his mouth felt right now, he could have chosen not to speak again forever, but he knew it would pass. It was getting better, too, just like the rest of him.

He called up the notes he'd been keeping on the local site and began an outline of his proposed recommendations. At least he could remember those with reasonable clarity, especially after reviewing his notes.

He looked up. "Well, at least I can understand my notes."

She smiled almost wryly. "Is that unusual?"

"It could have been, after that head knock." Then he went to work, feeling his spirits lift for the first time since the accident.

His ability to work hadn't been stolen.

Bri, who could still remember the sounds of him working in his home office, thought his typing sounded painfully laborious compared to what it had been, but that could easily be blamed on the cast on his arm, and maybe the aftereffects of his pain pill. She glanced at her watch, surprised that he hadn't asked for another one. He was well past due.

But as she looked his way, she recognized the expression of determination on his face. Everything else had faded from his awareness as he focused on his work. This was an important, good step. She bit back a warning not to wear himself out, realizing it was pointless because he wasn't apt to listen to her. He would do as much as he could, and that was that.

She returned her attention to the novel she'd spent all week trying to finish, until she heard his typing stop. Raising her head, she saw him frowning.

"Luke?"

"I think I'm going to need something for pain again. Using my fingers..."

She didn't need him to finish. All those tendons in his arm had been working hard, and there was probably still a lot of internal swelling. "I'll get you one."

"I don't want it."

"I'm sure, but there's no point in suffering if you don't have to."

"Read first," he said, waving at his computer.

She crossed to him and pulled the table close so she could read. Beneath the company's name and a bunch of boxes all filled out with numbers and names that were meaningless to her, she looked at the paragraph below.

"Does it make sense?" he asked.

"Actually, yes. You're asking them to move a couple of slopes because of the geologic conditions."

"Ah..." He sighed audibly, closed his eyes and let his head fall back on the pillow. "My brain still works."

"Clearly. Want that pill now?"

"Let me wait and see." His gray eyes snapped open.

"Okay." She retreated to the safe distance of her chair, because looking into those eyes at too close a distance filled her with yearnings that should have died a long time ago. "Why do you want them to move the slopes? What's wrong with the geology?"

"The designers were working from maps and apparently they weren't very good ones. While it looks pretty on paper, I want to minimize the amount of blasting we'd have to do."

"I think everyone would appreciate that."

"I'm sure. We'll inevitably have to do some to prepare parts of the slope, but less is better."

"Why do they send you out with a plan if they don't know it will work? And aren't you a builder?" She knew he had a degree in geology, but mostly when he spoke of his work, he spoke of the construction.

"They're designers, but it's my job to flesh it out in a way that works for minimal expense. I'm also a site inspector because of my geology training. Usually it encompasses minor matters, but this time, working with these mountains…" He shrugged and fell silent.

She wondered if his mouth was hurting too much. She hesitated, then asked one last question. "Will they like what you want to do?"

"Always a question. But I think the plan I intend to lay out will make for more interesting slopes."

"Ah."

"Plus, these mountains are geologically active. Don't want to destabilize them."

"Could blasting do that?"

"Who knows how many surface faults might be disturbed? Less is best."

Her curiosity had grown to a high pitch, and she wondered why they had never talked about things like this before. Had she appeared uninterested? It was possible, she supposed. She hadn't thought him interested in her nursing. Then, of course, their time together had been dominated by other things, like actually being together, like the desire that had burned so brightly every single minute. They'd probably spent more time making love than chatting.

She almost mentioned how little they had talked about their jobs, then decided to let sleeping dogs lie. Bringing up the past wouldn't change a thing, but it might lead to anger or hurt, or even an argument about whether he had cheated on her.

It surprised her, though, that three years after their divorce he still wanted her to believe he hadn't had an affair with Barbara. Why should he care at this point, unless it was a matter of honor with him?

If it was a matter of honor, though, that might mean... She yanked her thoughts back from that precipice. Thinking about whether he was simply too honorable to have cheated on her would leave her a mess all over again. The anguish of their split was not a feeling she wanted to relive. Ever.

It was odd, though, to look at him in that bed, mostly immobilized, utterly at her mercy. In her mind's eye, when she thought of him, she always pictured him in motion. He had rarely been still for long, and he'd always made her life exciting when he was at home. Quiet evenings in front of the fire or TV had been rare. He'd always wanted to go somewhere, do something, whether it was a museum, a play or a hike in the woods. So full of vitality and energy.

Which, she supposed, made his current condition sad, although oddly not one less bit sexy. He must be waging a constant internal struggle to endure his current incapacity, and he was doing a pretty good job of it. She wouldn't have blamed him if he'd become cranky.

A few minutes later he lifted his arms and began

typing slowly again. Working must feel good. She understood. She was already getting out of sync because they'd given her family-leave time. Luke didn't demand that much attention. He couldn't be left on his own yet, but she was far from being as busy as she was used to.

She almost sighed, but she knew from experience he never ignored her sighs. This was certainly one she didn't want to have to explain.

"I'm going to fix dinner," she announced, rising.

"I'd offer to help, but…" His expression was at once rueful and humorous.

"I think this might be easier on my own. You need anything?"

"A cup of coffee, if that wouldn't be too much trouble."

"You willing to try it hot?"

She could see him poking around the inside of his mouth with his tongue. "That sounds really good."

"No problem. And tonight we might try a little chewing."

"Now, that sounds even better." He gave her a lopsided smile. "Thanks."

She smiled back, perhaps too brightly, and went to make a chicken stew. She figured the chicken would soften up enough in the process that it wouldn't give him too much trouble. Plus, at this point, she wanted to see him put away some vegetables.

When she brought him his coffee fifteen minutes later, he asked for his cell phone. She had to root around in the bag of personal belongings the hospital had gathered up, but at last she was able to hand it to him.

He punched one button and a moment later she heard him say, "Hey, Greg, it's Luke. I'm working on the new proposal for the resort. I'm fine. I finished the survey before I got hurt, so I have my notes to work from. Listen, we have a bit of a problem with the geology...."

She slipped away and went back to dicing chicken breasts. Even with his appetite she figured she'd have enough stew for a couple of days at least. No point, she'd always thought, in making a stew for one, or for one meal. When she did it for herself, she froze up a lot of single-serving portions. She doubted she'd have to freeze any of this. It would probably get eaten along with the leftover potato soup in next to no time.

She was standing at the sink washing her chef's knife when she saw a shadow pass. The afternoon had grown dark with clouds, making it hard to see past the reflections from the kitchen. Curious, she grabbed her jacket and stepped out back to discover who was there. Probably a neighborhood kid.

It proved to be Jack, however. She found him around the corner headed for the street.

"Jack?"

He froze. Then, slowly, he turned. "Hi," he said.

"Did you need something? Why didn't you just knock."

He hesitated, looking down at the ground. "Sorry. I didn't want to bother you. You're kinda busy and all."

"It wouldn't have been a bother. Is there a problem?"

"I was just checking to make sure the screening I put over the attic vent was okay. I might need to fix it so you don't get more raccoons. Or squirrels."

"Oh. I thought I heard something up there nearly two weeks ago, but I haven't heard it since."

He nodded and slowly raised his head. "The screen's

peeled back a bit. I'll come tomorrow and fix it. They can do a lot of damage."

"I don't want them up there defecating, that's for sure. The disease potential is terrible." She smiled. "Thanks for taking such good care of me."

"You're a nice lady." Then he turned and hurried away, leaving her wondering why he made her feel as if she had interrupted something.

She was walking back to the kitchen when she remembered Luke's suspicions. She paused, thought about it, then dismissed it. Jack had worked for her on and off for the last two years. There was no reason to think ill of him.

Other than that he'd roused Luke's suspicions. Other than that he'd been prowling her yard without knocking to tell her he was there.

Chapter 5

On Saturday afternoon, the "Tim and Ted Show" appeared on her front porch. Tim was quite blunt.

"You haven't called for help. By now you must need a break. Go out shopping, get a coffee, meet a friend. We'll take care of the big guy."

Luke appeared a bit startled, but the two EMTs had him laughing by the time they'd loaded him into his wheelchair and pushed him toward the bathroom, promising they were going to make him squeaky-clean.

"Even the hair, man," Tim said. "That dry shampoo stinks."

"Actually it sticks," Ted chimed in. "Ve haf our vays."

Bri took the opportunity to change out the bed the easy way, and throw sheets and blankets and Luke's clothing into the washer. Laughter still came from the bathroom, so she grabbed her jacket and headed out, determined to bring back a feast to thank Tim and Ted.

It felt so good to be out and to know that Tim and Ted wouldn't leave before she got back. She could dawdle if she felt like it, spend some time doing whatever she felt like. She drew deep breaths of chilly air as she walked, then realized she smelled coming snow.

Really? Again? Was spring ever going to arrive? Sighing, she turned back and got her car. First to the grocery. She needed to restock her pantry and fridge, and most definitely get more coffee. Luke was putting it away as though there was no tomorrow, probably to fight the grogginess from the pain meds. Her knee twinged a few times, letting her know that whether she was right about snow, a change was coming.

She had a sudden, absurd image of herself hobbling on a cane at ninety telling young whippersnappers that her knee was a more reliable predictor than the weather service. Hah!

At the store she browsed the deli section. Nothing like the cities had, but it gave her some good choices. Three men to feed, so she picked up two rotisserie chickens. She added cold cuts, figuring that Luke could probably handle them, especially if she served them on thin, soft bread. By the time she finished, her cart was groaning with food and even ice cream. Luke gave her an excuse to indulge, a thought that brought another smile to her face.

The bakery was next, and Melinda topped her off with cinnamon rolls and fresh but soft bread, and she even caved and bought a baguette with Melinda's famous crust. Luke could dip it, but she wanted some crunchy garlic bread.

When she stepped out of the bakery, it became obvious her knee had been right. The temperature had dropped noticeably, the sky had turned leaden gray and snowflakes were flying. So much for stopping for coffee. If she wanted a latte, she'd have to make her own.

Back at the house, Tim and Ted came racing to help her with the groceries. Inside she found Luke sitting up in his wheelchair.

"Squeaky-clean," he announced.

"I can see that." Unable to resist for some reason, she reached out and ruffled his still-damp hair. "Looking good."

"Smelling better," he retorted. "Except for the cast. That thing is beginning to reek."

"They'll probably put a better one on on Monday," Tim said. "The new ones are great. They can even put holes in it so your leg can breathe."

"That would be nice. I hope they can wash it first. I didn't realize how bad I was getting."

"Hey," Bri said with mock indignation, "I've been bathing you. Where you would let me, anyway."

That sent Tim and Ted off into more laughter. Then they proved they weren't useless in a kitchen. They helped put everything away, then assisted her in her "feast."

They were also duly appreciative. Soon TV tables were set up, Luke's table had been adjusted so he could use it in the wheelchair, and they filled her living room to the brim. Chicken, steamed broccoli, bread and some gravy from a packet seemed to please everyone.

Luke, as always, especially enjoyed the bread and gravy. He needed some help cutting the chicken and broccoli into small pieces, but mostly he managed well enough by himself.

"You're making quite some progress," she told Luke as he used his broken arm efficiently.

"Typing seems to be building it up," he agreed.

But not everything was joking. Tim and Ted had questions about the ski resort. Luke answered amicably but Bri wondered how much of it was pure sales pitch. Bringing a business this big to the mountains west of town would also bring changes, changes most of them probably couldn't imagine right now.

"There'll be jobs of all kinds," Luke answered Tim's question. "We'll need everything from ski instructors to ski patrols, to people to deal with avalanche threats. Then there are the jobs within the resorts themselves."

"Maids," Bri commented. "Janitors. Bartenders. Waiters. Not exactly top-of-the-line in income."

"Better than they'd make in town," Luke retorted. "We have standards we want our staff to meet. They'll be taking care of a lot of high-maintenance customers. We'll bring in some experienced people, and for a month we'll have a full training staff, but then mostly local people will take over. And we don't pay minimum wage. Ever."

"Not even for waiters," she said skeptically.

"Not even. We're talking about a four- or five-star type of service and so on."

"It sounds too good to be true."

"Check out some of our other projects. I promise, people who work at the resort will make more than people holding similar jobs in town."

"That could create problems for local shopkeepers."

"It could, but most of our employment will be seasonal. We'll hire a lot of local students."

"I'm more worried about our mountains," Ted said. "How much are you going to mess them up? I hate the scars where the power lines run."

Luke nodded. "We're working to disturb as little as possible, and I've already promised it won't be visible from town."

"And what are you going to do for the town?"

So Luke was off and running with the same spiel he'd already given Bri. The face-lift and so on. He seemed to be winning them over.

"Anyway, before we move ahead, we'll have a town meeting so everyone knows what we intend to do. It'll give everyone a chance to ask questions and make suggestions."

"But will you guys listen?"

Luke put down his fork. "We try to, within reason. We'd like a friendly relationship locally."

Before they left, Tim and Ted helped with the cleanup and helped get Luke back in bed. "Don't wait so long to call," Tim told her as they were on their way out. "We don't get dinners like that very often."

She laughed and told them to drive safely. The snow was falling heavily now and the wind whipped it around.

"Some spring," she remarked as she returned to Luke. "I'm going to make a latte. Want one?"

"Can I be a wuss and ask for a half pain pill?"

She went immediately to his side and touched his shoulder. "Too much up?"

"And jostling. They were good, I needed to get clean and I'm really grateful. I think I might have been growing bacterial colonies like a petri dish. My scalp sure feels better."

"But it wasn't comfortable. I'm sorry."

"You're more gentle," he admitted.

"But they got the job done," she tried to tease.

"Yeah." He managed a smile. "But coffee and a pain pill sound really good."

"Coming up."

"Thanks, Bri. You're an angel."

He hadn't called her an angel in years. Her heart leaped and she had to tamp it down. No, no, no. She refused to risk her heart that way again. He'd leave soon, either because he no longer needed her care, or because his job here would be done. That was the way it had always been, Luke home for a month then packing his bags again, off to some exotic location or other. They'd already discovered there was no future in it. She just wished the sexual attraction would lie down and die.

Luke could handle the throbbing in his arm and leg. In fact, it slowly seemed to be lessening, although that jostling he'd taken while Tim and Ted had ruthlessly bathed him had made him pretty achy.

He worried about his head, though. The dizziness still came in spells, and it needed to go away quickly. There was only so long he could keep his job if he lost his ability to mountain-goat his way over construction sites. The thought gnawed at him.

But gnawing even harder at him was his desire for Bri. That hadn't eased at all, despite the separation, despite the painful memories, despite the fact that she still believed he had cheated on her. He'd wanted her the instant he first set eyes on her, and nothing had changed that. He'd been first snared by the curve of her hip when he glimpsed her. She'd been coming to his building to visit a friend who had just moved in, and when he saw her from the back, his interest arose. But his captivation had become complete when she turned and gave him a smile with those witchy green eyes and soft lips, when he'd seen the shape of her breasts beneath jersey. From that instant he'd become like a bloodhound that had caught a scent.

But wanting wasn't enough, a lesson he should have learned. He couldn't trust her. There was a certain irony in that, he supposed. She *didn't* trust him, and because of that he couldn't trust her.

That was one mountain he'd never be able to blast away, apparently.

With a latte on the tray table in front of him and a pain pill starting to course through his system, he felt tension easing away. Bri had resumed her seat on the other side of the room, a book open in her lap, but he noticed she hadn't turned a page in a while.

Maybe she was messed up, too, by all this. It couldn't be easy to have to be his caretaker after all the bitterness between them. In fact, considering some of the things she had said to him during their last huge fight, it was remarkable that she would do this for him.

"So it's snowing again," he said, feeling a need to hear her voice.

"Yes." She looked up. "This may be the spring that never happened. I mean, yeah, sometimes we get snow late in the season, but this weather really hasn't let up. It's May, for crying out loud. If we lived farther north, I could see it."

"This can't be good for your ranchers."

"I'm sure it isn't. Feed costs will skyrocket without grazing. I don't know how they'll manage."

"That's why this town needs the resort."

"We needed the semiconductor plant, too, but that didn't keep them from shutting down and sending the jobs elsewhere."

"Well, you can't pick up a ski resort and move it."

"True. But you need lots of people with money to burn to keep it going. You won't find many around here."

"But there are loads of them out there in the world. A long winter like this would be a boon to business, too." He paused. "Maybe DEL could do something for the ranchers. A goodwill gesture."

"Why in the world would they do that? Why should they care?"

"Image. One of the things I like about this company is that they don't come into a place and act like an eight-hundred-pound gorilla."

"Really."

"Yes, really." He fell silent, regarding her thoughtfully, wondering how much of her resistance to the resort came from liking the town the way it was, and how much came from disliking him. Maybe he had come to represent everything evil to her. Working for a big development company was rarely a recommendation to the people who were facing the development.

"We could make things better in a lot of ways," he finally said.

"Maybe. Just don't break all the eggs."

"We don't operate that way. We hire locally as much as possible. Part of that is going to be hiring for all the construction jobs. I don't know if you've got enough people in this town to provide all that we need, but you've got teachers who'll need summer work, right? And others who don't have jobs. We'll employ every able-bodied person we can. We always do that. We prefer to hire locally. It creates a more stable workforce."

"Okay." She didn't look convinced, but she also looked as if she didn't know where else to take this. She'd expressed her concerns.

"I don't suppose I could get to a window and see the snow."

"I could open the drapes and turn out the lights in here. It should give you a pretty good view."

"Thanks."

She pulled the drapes open, then turned on her porch light. The world looked like a snow globe just then. "You weren't kidding about it coming down."

She came to stand beside his bed, facing the window. Maybe he should have thought it through, but he didn't. He reached out and grasped her hand, taking care not to squeeze tightly, giving her the opportunity to pull away. His heart thudded when she didn't.

"It's beautiful," he said.

"Yeah. I'm glad I stocked up. If it keeps coming down like this, I'll be relieved I don't have to go to the store."

Practical thoughts. His weren't running to the practical at all. He was wishing he could pull her closer, draw her down and find out if her lips were as sweet as he remembered, if her curves were as soft and enticing.

There was, however, the matter of a broken arm and leg.

Then she astonished him, turning to look at him. "I want to hate you," she announced.

"I thought you already did."

"I did. But now I don't, and I want to hate you again."

"Why?"

Taking his breath away, she leaned over and kissed him on the mouth. It was not a tentative first kiss, but the kiss of a lover who knew her man.

"I shouldn't," she whispered when she lifted her lips briefly. "I shouldn't."

"I want it, too."

"That's exactly what's wrong here," she murmured, pulling back. "The sex between us was always good. It was everything else that was the problem."

"We could talk about it."

"To what end? It's over."

"Not quite." Then, without compunction, he lifted his good arm and drew her into a deep, hungry kiss. He felt an instant of resistance before she gave herself up to him.

God, she tasted good, just as he remembered. Her lips were mobile against his, her kiss heartfelt with yearning. He almost felt as if a victory song was breaking out in his head.

Then she pulled away, whirled and returned to her chair. "It's not enough," she said tautly.

"It's a starting point."

"For what? Another sexy affair when you're almost never around? I'm not doing that again. I felt like a way station on your travels. Like a mistress!"

"Really?" She'd told him during one of their fights that she sometimes felt more like an affair than a marriage, but being put in these harsh terms brought it home to him like a punch in the gut. She'd felt like his mistress?

He'd never meant to make her feel that way. Never. But suddenly the argument that she'd known what she was getting into sounded awfully thin even to him. Knowing was one thing, experiencing was another entirely.

"And here I thought I was being such a modern man, respecting your career," he said. His voice was thick again, thick with yearning, and thick with the pain pill and remaining swelling. "What was I supposed to do? Carry you off over my shoulder like some kind of caveman? Demand that you follow me all over the planet?"

She didn't reply, but she wasn't looking at him, either. In the dark, he looked at the whirling snow outside and tried to deal with the fact that maybe Barbara hadn't ended his marriage with her lies. Maybe she had just been the last straw.

So what the hell did he think he was doing here? Maybe he ought to sort that out before he made Bri any more miserable than he already had. Sure, he'd been full of a desire to convince her he hadn't cheated, but maybe he'd cheated on her in more important ways.

He loved his job, loved the travel, loved the challenges. Unless he was willing to change that, maybe he shouldn't try to reach Bri as anything but a friend. It wouldn't be fair to her. He was still the same man who had left her feeling like a convenient mistress, a port of call, as it were. God, what a sucky way to feel about herself.

It seemed he had another bunch of things to kick himself in the butt over. The question was: Was it worth it? She clearly didn't really want him back; she'd made a life here among friends and family, as far as she could get from Chicago where they lived during their marriage. Well, where *she'd* lived during their marriage. Evidently he had been a drop-in visitor.

It hadn't looked to him that way at the time. Military families dealt with this kind of thing, after all. And she'd seemed to understand at the outset that that was how it would be.

But apparently it hadn't been enough for her, and taking a good hard look at himself, he wasn't sure he could ever offer more.

So cut it out, he told himself. *Just cut it out.* He was older now, and he hoped a little wiser, and maybe some women needed a helluva lot more from a relationship than he seemed able to give.

Maybe he was just plain selfish. Maybe he wasn't willing to give enough. Inviting her to travel with him hadn't been an answer. It would have deprived her of what she loved, leaving her at loose ends for months while he worked a new resort.

Maybe it just couldn't work at all, not with Bri.

He closed his eyes so he didn't have to see her, and tried to decide if it was a failure of circumstances or a failure on his part not to recognize her needs.

Sadly, no ready answer came to him.

By ten that night, two fresh feet of snow drifted across streets and yards. Bri pulled on her jacket and stepped out onto the porch. Lifting some, she found it was heavy and wet, but the wind remained strong enough anyway to keep blowing the surface stuff around.

"I got a problem," she said as she stepped back inside.

Luke roused from what had seemed like slumber. "What?"

"The snow is heavy. Really heavy. Around here it's usually dry. I've never faced this before."

"And?"

"I don't know if the roof can bear the weight. I don't know if I should let it go until morning."

He raised the head of his bed. "I need to get into the wheelchair."

"What good will that do?"

"I won't feel quite so helpless, even if I am."

She almost laughed, but went to lower the bed and bring the chair close enough for him to slide into it. "You're getting to be quite the expert."

"Plenty of practice." Once in the chair, with a blanket over his lap, he looked up. Of course, there was nothing to see but a ceiling. "How old is this house? Have you ever seen the trusses up there?"

"I've never been able to climb up there. And the house is about eighty years old."

"Not good. No way to know how well constructed or whether there's been water damage over the years."

"I know."

"Did you have the place inspected when you bought it?"

"Yeah, but it seemed cursory. A lot of allowances for age."

"Great."

"I'm going out to see what's on the roof." She didn't wait for an argument. It's not as if she intended to climb anything. She just wondered how much snow was accumulating above their heads.

She took great care descending her front steps,

which had become little more than vaguely defined mounds of white. Snow stung her cheeks, and what had been pretty earlier now seemed threatening. When she plowed through the snow to the sidewalk and looked back, she didn't like what she saw. In places, the snow was piling really high, like around the vents and the chimney.

Swearing, she stomped her way back through the snow and entered the house. To her surprise, she heard Luke cussing a blue streak.

She raced into the living room. "What's wrong?"

"I am so damn sick of being laid up. I ought to be able to help you with this. I ought to be able to check out your attic, clear the worst of the snow from your roof. Instead I'm stuck in this damn chair."

"Can't be helped, Luke. Get a grip. It's not like you did this to yourself."

"That's a real help." Then, abruptly, he cocked his head to one side. "I was pushed."

Her heart nearly stopped. "Is your memory coming back?"

"I can remember the feel of hands on my back, shoving. I remember it as clearly as I can see you."

She found her chair and sank onto it, feeling sick. "Somebody tried to kill you?" It was hard to process, hard to accept. Cold chills began to run through her.

"Or at least put me out of commission."

She arched a brow at him. "Right. You're lucky you're not dead. Try viewing it from that perspective. Does this happen to you often?"

"Well, I was shot at once, been punched a few times, but no, this isn't par for the course."

"We need to call the sheriff."

"What's the point? He already headed up there looking for evidence. This snow will have buried anything that was overlooked."

"But now that you remember…"

He just shook his head. "Not the most trustworthy memory, I gather. No, whoever it was, they got what they wanted. I'm out of commission. It won't stop the project. Killing me wouldn't have stopped it."

Which raised an interesting question for Bri. If removing Luke wouldn't stop the resort, what was the point in attacking him? Something personal? But he hadn't been in town long enough to draw that kind of attention.

"This doesn't make sense," she protested.

"Except in the mind of whoever did it. It might have been an impulse. Regardless, this isn't getting the snow off your roof."

She looked out the window again. "If it would just stop, I'd feel better about waiting for morning." At the rate it was falling, however, she wondered if there'd be another two feet before dawn. Reaching for the remote, she flipped on the weather and waited until they got to her part of the country.

"Accumulations of three to four feet are expected," said the cheerful woman who seemed to think this was the best news ever. Bri would have bet that the only thing that would have made her happier was a tornado outbreak. She flipped it off.

"I can't wait for morning."

"You can't do this alone! You could slip and break your neck."

"Some of my neighbors must be worrying about the

same thing. Maybe we'll get a work party together. Or I'll call Jack."

"Jack." The word emerged with distaste, but she gave him credit for not adding anything to it. She couldn't understand his antipathy for Jack, but some things just couldn't be explained. Bundling up, she went back outside to see if her neighbors wanted to do something about the snow.

Luke would just have to stew in his own juices. Might do him some good.

For her part, she was glad to have a problem to solve that didn't involve Luke. The man was growing on her again, and she didn't want that. What was that old saying? Insanity was doing the same thing again and again hoping for a different outcome.

Of one thing she was sure—she was not insane.

Jack had watched the snowfall from the cozy security of his little apartment at the edge of town. He had a game going on his computer, but the snow seemed to mesmerize him more. It was a beautiful thing, all those sparkling, swirling diamonds.

He'd begun the evening planning to show up at Bri's first thing in the morning and take care of her sidewalk and steps. That was something he could do for her that her ex couldn't do. He took pleasure in that, knowing he'd made the guy dependent and useless. He *was* sorry that it had made more work for Bri, and sorry that the guy had wound up staying with her, but he was certain that Luke couldn't possibly appeal to Bri in his current condition. Helpless jerk. Too bad he hadn't died. That would have solved a whole lot of problems.

On the other hand, Bri would be making a comparison between Jack and Luke now, and it wouldn't be very flattering to Luke. Jack liked that idea.

Bri belonged to him, and nobody else was going to get her.

He smiled, watching the snow fall, eventually noticing how deep it was getting. He decided to check it out. If it was heavy, clearing roofs could make him a whole lot of money overnight, starting with Bri's place, of course.

It wasn't long before he realized he could make a few hundred bucks tonight, and more in the morning. Whistling, he got his gear together, then climbed into his battered pickup with the small plow on the front and headed straight for Bri. Feeling quite the hero, he grinned into the teeth of the storm.

Chapter 6

Bri bundled up in her snow pants and winter jacket, and found some heavy but warm work gloves. She figured she'd need some rope to tether herself in some way across the peak of the roof so she couldn't slide off.

Rope was a bigger problem than anything else. She was going to need help.

Luke was in a mood. "Get me my jacket," he demanded. "At least I can be on the front porch to call for help if anything happens. God, Bri, risking your neck like this…"

"If the roof caves, we're both going to be in a world of hurts. I'm sure my neighbors are out and about."

He looked dubious. She went and got his parka anyway, and eased him into it. At least the sleeves were loose enough to go over the cast on his arm. "Gloves?"

"In my side pockets."

Somehow leaning over him and rummaging through his pockets felt even more intimate than all the intimacies his condition had forced on them over the past days. She felt the warmth of his breath on her cheek and a shiver ran through her. If she turned her head just a little, she could kiss him. Feel again the sexy stubble on his chin.

Good heavens, she had to stop this! Sex wasn't enough. They'd proved that beyond any shadow of a doubt. It couldn't make up for absence, and it sure as hell couldn't make up for lost trust.

She bit her lip, resisting old urges and new ones all at once, and pulled his gloves out. He needed help getting them on, especially on his casted arm, but finally it was done. Reluctantly she pushed him out onto the front porch.

There was a small area by the door where the snow hadn't deepened, and she parked him there.

Late though it was getting, she was glad to see some of her other neighbors out. Apparently she wasn't the only one concerned about the strength of her roof.

She squeezed Luke's shoulder. "I'm not alone out here. So if you start to get cold, for heaven's sake tell me. I don't think you'd make a very good icicle."

"I wouldn't be nearly as fun." He astonished her with a grin and a wink of his good eye.

She wanted to slap his shoulder playfully. *Playfully?* No play between them anymore. She hoped the urge didn't show on her face as she straightened.

The roar of an engine came down the street and she looked out through the blinding snow to see headlights. The truck pulled right up in front of her house.

A dark figure jumped out, and by his shuffling walk she recognized Jack.

"Figured you'd be worrying about the roof," he said.

Luke muttered, "And the superhero arrives."

"Hush." Bri raised her voice. "I am. There's at least another foot predicted."

"I know." Jack waded slowly through the snow. "Looks like you're not the only one. Guess I get rich tonight. Not off you, though. You I'll do for free."

"Jack, no!"

He stood at the foot of the steps and looked up at her. "You're always nice to me, Bri. Not everyone is."

That startled her. "Really?"

"Really. Shouldn't your friend be inside where it's warm?"

"No," Luke said. A single uncompromising word.

Bri hastened to smooth over Luke's obvious dislike of Jack. "Not if the roof caves," she said.

Jack nodded slowly. "Well, let's get to it. I got rope, I got shovels, we'll get it down to a safer level. Then I'll clean your walks."

"The neighbors…"

"They can maybe wait. Not gonna take that long."

Jack might shuffle, he might look too thin, but Bri had long since realized he was a fairly strong young man.

He looked around. "I'm gonna climb the tree to the side of your house. I need you to catch the end of the rope when I throw it down and tie it to something sturdy, like that oak over there. I'll clean the far side first, then we'll change, okay?"

"Okay, I can do that. Just don't slip."

"If I slip I'm going to land on a pillow. But I don't

plan to. You know, you really need me to put some insulation in your attic. Bet you've got a good ice dam going. Well, I'll find out when I get up there."

Bri didn't even dare look at Luke. It must be killing him to watch Jack do something he would have been willing to do himself but for being laid up. Being the take-charge sort could become a real problem when you were helpless.

She felt bad for Luke, but really, this problem had to be dealt with.

She watched Jack climb the tree beside her house with amazing ease. It surprised her that he nearly scampered up it like a squirrel, as if he'd done it a million times. In less than a minute he was on the gable, holding on to her chimney. She watched him tie the rope around his middle.

Then he called down, "First I'm going to throw the rope down. Tie my shovel to it so I can pull it up. Next the tree."

"Be careful," she called again, then did as he asked with a shovel from the back of his truck. It was a heavy shovel, not the light ones usually used for snow.

She watched him pull it up, wincing a little as it banged on the porch stanchions, but finally he had a hold on it.

"Here we go, Bri," he said, tossing the rope down again. She grabbed it from where it lay on top of the snow and dragged the end over to the oak tree. Man, she hoped she remembered how to tie a good knot.

All of a sudden one of her neighbors was there helping her. Jim Tuttle. "Navy," he said. "I can tie any knot on the planet. Let me. Think Jack'll do my roof, too? I wasn't paying much attention until I heard the rafters groan a bit. Have you ever seen the like?"

"Not around here."

Jim called out, "Secure here, Jack. My place next?"

"You got it, Mr. Tuttle. Keep the rope fairly taut, will you?"

"Absolutely." Jim turned to Bri. "Get back up on the porch and take care of your patient."

"Everyone knows that I have a patient, huh?"

Jim laughed. "We also know who he is. Wanna see the article in the newspaper?"

"You're kidding!"

"Of course I am. Word travels fast, you know that."

Yeah, she knew that. She waded through the snow and back onto the porch. "Getting cold, Luke?"

"Wild horses couldn't drag me back inside. Nice neighbor."

"He's not the only one. It's one of the things we don't want changed around here."

"I can see why." Then, "Jack is sweet on you."

"Cut it out."

"Open your eyes, Bri. He just came racing to your rescue like a white knight. And he's not even going to charge you."

"I'll pay him anyway. He knows that."

"Maybe." Frowning, Luke fell silent. "If you're not interested, do the kid a favor. Nip it in the bud."

"This from the expert on relationships?"

He glared up at her. "I wasn't the only screwup. And maybe I've learned something."

"You know, I think I'm going to take you back inside."

"Wild horses." He folded his arms. "Being in a wheelchair doesn't make me completely helpless."

"What are you going to do? Scream and hang on to the door frame?"

"Don't put anything past me right now."

Her anger had been reaching a good simmer, but suddenly something else penetrated. An awareness she couldn't quite define. A concern that turned down the temperature on her annoyance. She squatted.

"Luke? What's going on?"

"I hate being laid up. I should be clearing that roof. But hey, maybe nothing real is going on. I had a concussion, after all. Maybe I'm just—what did the doc call it?—addled."

For the first time it struck her how hard it must be for him to be wondering about the state of his own mind. Maybe he was being annoying. Maybe he was overreacting to Jack. But to be wondering if his thoughts were real or the artifact of the concussion? She couldn't imagine how many times a day he must be questioning himself.

"God, that's hard," she murmured. The wind nearly snatched her words away.

"What?" he demanded.

"Wondering if you're thinking properly."

"It's no picnic."

An ache filled her heart, one she didn't want to feel for this man, but it came anyway. "You're doing a whole lot better."

"But how am I supposed to know if I'm slipping?"

"It'll become less of a worry with time."

"Time. Yeah. Damn, I need to get back on my feet!"

There was little she could say to that. He must be

feeling like a caged lion, but until they changed out his casts, and even then, he was going to be restricted.

"Try putting it in perspective," she said finally.

"Really?" His expression was dark as he looked at her. "How?"

"These things usually heal in about six weeks. A little rehab to get your strength back and you'll be right as rain."

"Maybe."

She didn't dare ask him what he meant, and as it turned out, she didn't have to.

Jack called down from the roof. Jim answered him and began to untie the rope. "Going for the front side now," Jim said. "I need to make my way around back."

"Thanks," Bri called. She was going to have to make a pie for Jim, she decided. He was being really helpful, and as an older bachelor, he seemed very appreciative when someone brought him a casserole or some baked goods.

Now the view changed. As Jack shoveled snow off the front of her roof, it fell in a huge shower of heavy clumps. Before long her front yard looked as if a river ice dam had broken in it.

"He was quick about it," Luke said almost grudgingly.

"Jack is good at a lot of things." As soon as the words slipped out, Bri wished she could snatch them back. Knowing how Luke must be feeling that he couldn't help with this problem and she'd said something like that? She peeped at him, and saw his expression had grown stony.

Then another question struck her. How many times had things slipped out of her during her marriage?

She'd never had the best guard on her mouth, and apparently while she knew her limits at work, she'd never learned them in her personal relationships.

Memories started floating back, unwanted but coming anyway, of times she'd blurted things and Luke had gone utterly quiet. He'd always gotten over it quickly, but now she wondered how many times she inadvertently hurt him without even knowing it. Without even intending it.

"Luke…" But she didn't know what to say. She hadn't meant to imply anything at all about Luke. Not one thing. Only after she spoke did she realize how he might hear it.

God, this was awful.

Jack and Jim finally came around to the front of the house. "All done," Jack said. "I'll get your steps and sidewalk now. You do have some ice damming along your eaves, though. It'll make it hard for snow to slip off. Gotta do something about that."

"Not right now."

"Of course not." He turned to Jim. "I'll be right over to your place, Mr. Tuttle. Just want to clear the path in case Bri's friend has an emergency."

Bri could almost feel Luke seething beside her. She wanted to say Luke wouldn't have an emergency, but she couldn't guarantee that. She spoke quickly. "Let me pay you, Jack."

"No, ma'am. You can pay me when you let me put in that insulation."

Luke spoke quietly. "I'm cold."

So Bri opened the doors and pushed him inside, wondering what was coming next.

* * *

Luke had had enough of watching that skinny kid act like the hero. He knew he was being unfair, but he didn't care. That kid—in Luke's eyes he looked like a kid—had been helpful. He was helping the other neighbors, too. But it galled Luke to be stuck in a chair when he should be helping Bri himself.

He shouldn't have needed the kid. Bri shouldn't have needed him. Luke should have been able…

He drew himself up short and told himself to stop being an ass. Bri needed the kid's help because there was no one else. She didn't have a husband, and only now was Luke beginning to accept that he deserved some of the blame for that.

Double damn, he thought bitterly as Bri helped him out of his jacket.

"Something hot to drink?" she asked cheerfully.

What he wanted, what he'd been trying to ignore, was that the only heat he wanted was Bri's body in bed with him. Over him, under him, he didn't care. Coming back here had been a major mistake because all he'd managed to do was remind himself how he craved this woman. Despite everything, despite her accusations, despite her refusal to trust his word, despite it all, he still craved her.

His groin throbbed whenever she came near. It was the main reason he'd never let her go below his hips when she bathed him. He wouldn't put either of them through that, although he supposed she might suspect what was going on. Since they'd been married, she could hardly think it was modesty on his part.

Or maybe she didn't think about it at all. She seemed

to be handling their enforced closeness a lot better than he was.

The damn wheelchair was uncomfortable, too, with his one leg stuck straight out in an unnatural position. Like it or not, he wanted to climb back into the bed, but she'd gone off so fast to make them hot drinks that he was still wearing his parka and gloves. He managed to ditch the gloves on the floor, but pulling off a parka from a seated position didn't work, no matter how he tried to twist.

"What are you doing?"

Bri had entered the room, mugs in hand.

"Getting my parka off," he grumbled.

She frowned and put the cups down on an end table. "You need help for that. Like it or not."

He didn't like it, but he bit back complaints about it as she assisted him.

"God, you're grumpy tonight," she remarked as she pulled the last sleeve of the jacket off him. "What got into you?"

"All of it." Nothing and everything. He considered apologizing, then thought, to hell with it. It didn't matter anymore what she thought of him. That had been settled years ago. When he got out of her care, he swore he was never going to look back again.

The resolution lasted until he was back in bed with his cocoa on the tray in front of him. "Sorry," he said.

"I get you're miserable. You've been handling it very well."

"Don't patronize me."

Her head jerked back a few inches, then she went to sit on the chair she had been using. She stared down into her mug and remained mute.

A wave of self-disgust washed through him. He had no right to snap at her or take this mess out on her. After all, she'd taken him in when she would have been well within her rights to demand he find a way to get to a convalescent facility no matter how much it cost him.

"Bri?"

She didn't look up.

"I'm sorry. I'm really cranky. And it's not just about being cooped up. You know I hate being cooped."

"I gathered." The words were sarcastic.

"Oh, let's not go there," he said. "If you want to talk about the past, let's just lay it all out for once. In the middle of all the yelling and accusations, I figure we never got to the root of the real problems we had."

At that her head raised. "So sure?"

"Actually, yes. If our relationship had been firmer, if I hadn't been gone so much, you probably would never have believed Barbara's lies."

She lowered her head again, and frustration surged in him because he couldn't read her face. "Maybe," she said finally.

"No, it's true," he argued. "We both thought we could make a go of it, the way things were. And we couldn't, could we? I heard what you said about it feeling more like an affair than a marriage. You're right about that. My fault."

Now she looked straight at him. "You asked me to travel with you."

"Yes, but that would have messed up your own career. Fact is, we weren't fair to each other. I get it. We were so crazy in love we thought we could handle it all. Instead we made a royal mess. I certainly did. How were you supposed to trust me when I was almost never there? And when we were together, we were too busy making love and romancing to get to the real nitty-gritty of relationship building."

She cocked a brow at him. "Have you been getting therapy of some kind?"

"No, I've been lying trapped in this bed and doing some serious thinking for the first time in my life. Thinking I should have done a long time ago."

"It doesn't matter now," she said finally. "It's over."

Something inside him sank like a stone. "I know," he admitted quietly.

"So why rake it all up again, Luke? Answer me that. Hashing over our marriage isn't going to change a thing. It didn't work, it got ugly and we split. End of story."

"Is it?"

"Of course it is." She stood up. "Nothing's going to change. You'll finish this job and move on to the next one, and I'll still be here doing what I love. What could possibly change?"

Then she left the room with her cocoa, making it clear as she put the bell on his tray table that she would not come back.

He stared at the ceiling, thinking about what she had said. The devil of it was that she was right. Absolutely right. They had an insurmountable obstacle, and unless one of them was willing to make a radical change, there was no point even trying to figure out what had gone wrong the first time.

Because it was obvious as the ceiling overhead that there was no future.

* * *

Bri took her cocoa into her bedroom. Unless Luke rang for help during the night, he was on his own. Somehow, someway, he had made her want to weep.

Weep for what? Lost dreams? A dead marriage? Great sex? Because when she came right down to it, great sex might have been the sum and substance of their entire marriage.

Postcards from exotic places hadn't made up for his absences. Brief letters from her, with little to say because she didn't write him about her work and there was little enough when he was away. Coffee with her girlfriends. A movie. She'd read a lot of books and watched too much TV, and you didn't write about those things.

Then, finally he'd come home, practically a stranger again, and they hadn't talked nearly enough. Except about immediacies. Except about what they were doing at the moment.

Hell, they hadn't even built any dreams. There hadn't been talk of a later, because later had only looked like the present.

What had they been thinking? What had they thought they were doing? She had begun to feel like a way station on his trip through life, and she wouldn't have been surprised to find that he had felt pretty much the same at some level.

How did military families handle this? she wondered. Well, they had kids, for one thing. She and Luke hadn't even gotten around to discussing that. If it had been mentioned at all, it had been reserved for some vague day in the future.

A day when things would be different. But they were

never going to be different. They hadn't shared enough of the really important things, maybe because they were too busy panting for each other. Or maybe because they couldn't figure out how to fit those things in.

To this day, she couldn't have said which of them had been more reluctant to talk about years down the road. Changes. Family. Future. It was as if they had been caught in a soap bubble, in their own little universe.

God. Sitting on the edge of her bed, looking backward in time, she saw it all so differently than she had then. Maybe the entire marriage had been a mistake from the start. Phone calls had always devolved into sexy talk. So had their occasional Skype conversations when they could get together at the same time. They had spent an awful lot of time communicating on one single level.

They had, she realized, never built a truly sturdy framework. Whether because they'd been so randy for each other, or because time had always seemed to have such a short horizon, or because they'd been blind to really essential things, they'd built a house of cards and a wind had blown it down.

But what good would it do to talk about it now? Nothing would change. Nothing *could* change, and there was too much old pain between them now.

She sat for a while, turning things around in her head, seeing them differently. She'd been too young. Maybe he had been, too. Too late now, though.

Then she remembered his certainty that he had been pushed on that mountain. Someone had tried to kill him. He seemed sure of it.

Her heart squeezed with a fear she couldn't ignore and she got up, returning to the living room.

He was still awake and merely looked at her as she entered.

"You're sure you were pushed?" she asked bluntly.

"Like I said, I can still feel the hands on my back. I don't think I'm imagining that."

She shook her head and perched carefully on the edge of the bed. "You can't be alone," she announced.

He glanced down at himself. "Obviously."

"That's not what I meant. If someone wants you out of the picture, what makes you think that was their only attempt?"

"But I told you, getting rid of me won't stop the project. It would hardly slow it down."

"Maybe. Or maybe someone had another reason."

His gray eyes widened. "Reading too many mystery novels? Bri, I hardly know a soul in this town. I haven't been upright long enough to make an enemy."

"Maybe. Maybe not. It doesn't have to be personal."

He gave a slight nod then nearly knocked the wind out of her. "I never asked. Did you want kids?"

When she caught her breath she asked, "Where did that come from?"

"Plenty of time to think about what an idiot I was. You'd think a guy would ask his wife about something like that."

"A guy would, if he had a wife."

"Oh, man." He closed his eyes and let his head fall back on the pillow.

"Yeah," she said. "I don't know what it was, Luke, but it wasn't a real marriage. That's where we went wrong. I've been thinking about it, and it's inescapable. We had a great romance, but that was it. We never got to the point of planning a future, discussing where we'd like to be someday. I'm not even sure we even thought about the future. It seemed limited to the next time you'd be home."

He nodded, but didn't speak immediately. His answer came slowly. "We'd have had to make some big changes."

"Changes neither of us wanted to make. Neither of us wanted to change jobs. I don't think you'd have been happy staying at home and working a desk. I know I wouldn't be happy without nursing. So there we were, benighted lambs, thinking that somehow, magically, it was all going to work out."

"We never did the hard work, is what you're saying."

"Mostly, no. And by the time we had to face the things that were wrong, it was blowing up. Maybe for some people it would have been enough. It wasn't for us. Or at least it wasn't for me."

"It wasn't working for me, either, toward the end. I could feel you pulling away, and I didn't know why. Color me stupid. Maybe it wasn't pulling away, maybe it was just finally seeing the reality of all that was missing."

"Maybe," she agreed quietly. "There was certainly a lot missing as I look back on it."

"So tell me, Bri. If you could paint a future, what would it look like?"

"What difference does that make now?"

"I'm just curious."

She rose from the edge of his bed. "It's none of your business."

As she walked back to her bedroom, however, she

realized one thing for certain: she still wasn't dreaming of a future. She still hadn't even thought about it. She was stuck in the same bubble, only this time alone.

Chapter 7

Monday morning brought some good news. Tim and Ted showed up to transport Luke to the hospital for his X-rays. Bri followed in her car, not because she felt she needed to be part of his treatment but because she was beginning to feel like a caged rat. She missed work; she wanted to get in touch with everyone, get her finger on the pulse of all that was happening.

While he was examined and treated, she wandered the corridors, touching base with her friends and co-workers. It seemed she hadn't missed anything except a car accident on the night of the heavy snow. Everything else was pretty much standard illness, injury, surgery and so on. She was welcomed warmly by everyone, but she had to admit to a lowering feeling that everything had gone just fine without her. Well, of course it had. She was a nurse, not a brain surgeon. Every nurse here was capable of stepping into another's shoes. They had to do it often enough.

It would have been nice, though, to hear just one person say, "We sure missed you when…" Instead they all hastened to assure her she could take as much time as she needed. They were glad to cover for her, and were sure she would do the same for them.

Well, she would. Still. She knew she was being petty, but Luke seemed to bring that out in her. She was beginning to wince at some of her recollections of their marriage. Craziness. What was this need to feel important? Why should she feel any more important than the next person?

Sighing, she eventually made her way back to Luke, who was now sporting soft casts on his arm and thigh, and a sturdier one on his calf. He could bend his knee again, and was doing so with great delight as Dr. Trent watched his range of motion.

Trent looked at her as she entered. "Great recuperative powers here. This guy is officially allowed to use crutches, but only around the house. It's still too icy out there, so chair outdoors. We're setting him up for rehab starting next week, unless he decides to go elsewhere."

Well, that sure left a question hanging, Bri thought. She took the patient instructions and started scanning them while they helped Luke back into his chair. "Can he get into my car now?"

"Push the seat back if you can. Can you? I don't want him bending that knee too far yet. It's a little less than stable after a week of immobility."

"I can push it back."

Luke spoke. "Do I get a say? I'd really rather travel in a car."

"There are the steps," she remarked. "I salted them, but…"

Trent put his foot down. "No steps. Absolutely no steps. Let me call Tim and Ted for you."

"Ah, hell," Luke said quietly.

"Hey," Bri said, "they're nice guys."

"Very nice guys. I just want…" He stopped himself.

Trent grinned. "I get it, but be a good patient. You don't want to make anything worse."

Luke nodded grimly, and argued no more.

"I'll get that ramp built," Bri said, feeling for him. "It'll give you a lot more mobility."

That didn't look as if it sat well with him, either. "If you get a ramp, I'm paying for it."

"Okay by me."

Neither of them, she thought as Tim and Ted finally appeared to take care of transport, had even mentioned the possibility of his moving out. That gave her pause, but when she thought about it, she had to admit she was in no hurry to evict him. While they really hadn't talked all that much about the past, the conversations they had shared had eased something within her, like an old grief beginning to let go. Maybe by the time he was ready to take care of himself, the past would be dealt with in a way they could both live with. That at least was hopeful.

Because sometimes she had wondered just how much their ruined marriage had affected the woman she had become and the way she was living her life. Maybe when they popped the bubble with their fights and divorce, they'd replaced it with something much harder to get rid of: amber.

So once again she followed the ambulance back to

the house and unlocked the door so Tim and Ted could get Luke inside. They even brought in the wheelchair.

She thanked them profusely, watching them leave, reluctant to go back inside. The night of the storm Luke had asked her to paint her future and she hated knowing that she still had no idea what she wanted from her life.

Frozen in amber indeed. Something had been truncated by her marriage to Luke. These days she couldn't remember if she'd had any dreams even before she met him. She must have. Didn't everyone?

As she was standing there on the porch, noticing that the heavy snow was melting at last, garbing every house in sparkling icicles like a winter wonderland, one of the sheriff's cars pulled up.

Immediately, she felt herself tense.

Gage Dalton, the sheriff, climbed out and limped toward her. A bomb explosion years before had killed his first family and left him burn-scarred and limping. He approached with his patented crooked smile. "Big guy still here?"

"He's inside."

"Okay if I talk with him?"

"Of course. You don't even need to ask. Do I look like a gatekeeper?"

Gage laughed. "You're a nurse. That makes you a gatekeeper. Besides, it's your house."

She had to laugh with him. "Come on in. Coffee?"

"I never say no."

She went to make the coffee while he went in to greet Luke in the living room. She returned while the coffee brewed in time to hear Gage say, "It's good to see you can bend your leg again."

"It feels like heaven," Luke admitted. "I can hardly wait to start crutching my way around here."

Gage chuckled. "I can imagine. Been where you are, years ago. I hated it. By the time I was mobile again, I was ready to rip out walls."

"That's about how it feels."

Bri felt the understanding pass between them. The moment stretched, so finally she said, "Coffee in just a couple of minutes."

Gage nodded, then said, "We need to talk."

Bri didn't like the sound of that at all. Gage had taken the office chair, so she sat on her battered couch that had been moved as far out of the way as possible against the wall. "What's going on?"

Gage looked at Luke, who waved his hand that it was okay.

"Well, it's probably best to tell you both since we don't have a clue what's going on here."

"Which is?" Luke asked.

"You were right. Somebody pushed you. The deputies who went up there with Mike, your coworker, found footprints in the snow. It would have been easy for someone to sneak up on you there, with the wind blowing and the trees so close. Pop out, push and disappear."

Bri's jaw dropped and her heart began sinking. She'd feared this since Luke had mentioned that he could remember the feeling of hands pushing his back, but there'd been a slender hope he was remembering wrong because of his concussion. That hope had just died. Now there was evidence.

"But why?" she whispered. She felt almost light-headed from the shock of knowing for certain.

"Exactly." Gage turned to Luke. "Any enemies who might have followed you here?"

Luke shook his head. "None that I know of. A big part of my job is trying not to make people angry."

"Well, I'm having a lot of trouble trying to figure out why anyone around here would do such a thing. Nobody really believes we're going to get a ski resort this time. Countless others have tried, as they say. That land has changed hands six or seven times while I've lived here. It never pans out. So while some folks would really like to see it, most are sure this is going to fall apart like every other attempt. We've hardly reached a point where anyone should want you gone that way. It just doesn't add up."

"No, it doesn't," Luke agreed. "If anyone in town asked me about it, I made it clear we weren't going ahead without a big meeting with the town first. Ideally, we'd like people around here to support the idea, and to get that we need their input."

Gage nodded. He leaned back a bit in the office chair, which creaked, and winced as he did so.

"You okay?" Luke asked him.

"I'm as okay as I'll ever be. Back trouble. All right, no obvious suspects hanging out there. Dang." Then he flashed a grin. "There almost never are. Still, whoever it was chose an interesting method of dealing with you. No face-to-face, no explosive confrontation, no weapon. My guess is he wanted it to look like an accident, but again that doesn't tell us a whole lot. All right, we'll keep working it, and you be sure to let me know if anything occurs to you. I don't care how off-the-wall it may seem."

"Can do," Luke agreed.

"Now for the rest of it," Gage said. "Assuming someone wanted to kill you, not just mess you up—and from your injuries and the fall I really think this was an intended kill—we need to consider something else."

"Which is?"

"Whether you should get the hell out of town for a while."

"I can't leave my job. In fact, I won't. As soon as I'm getting around again, I need to talk to the townspeople about this."

Gage's mouth grew crooked. "You mean you won't be driven out. Well, I'd like to point out something else to you."

"What's that?"

"If someone's after you, do you want Bri getting caught in the middle?"

Luke's entire face tightened. "I'll move back to the motel."

"Don't be stupid," Bri snapped. "You can't take care of yourself there. Don't give me nightmares of you trying to cross an icy highway to get to the truck stop diner. No way."

Gage stood. "That's my exit cue. You two work it out."

Bri rose as well. "You haven't had your coffee."

"I'll have it another time. I know when to exit."

She saw him out and came back to the living room. Luke, sitting in his chair, rested his chin in his hand and looked like one very unhappy man.

"I can't leave town," he said finally. "If I do that, I can kiss off my job. You have no idea how much time I spent this week convincing Greg I could get it done."

She nodded and sank slowly onto the office chair.

"I don't want you to get fired." Although maybe a secret part of her did. She couldn't decide if that was petty or some absurd hope that they could get back together again.

"So he's right. I can't put you in the line of fire by staying here. If that guy really wants me dead, he might try again."

"There's no way to be sure of that. None. Maybe he figures you're already out of the way. It's not like anyone else knows you're still working."

"Mike is still running all over the mountain collecting information."

"But that's Mike. And I find it curious that nobody has bothered him."

That brought Luke's head up. "You're right."

"This isn't making sense. But one thing I know for sure, you're keeping your job and that means staying right here. And why isn't Mike dropping by, anyway?"

"We're talking by email. I guess he doesn't want to inconvenience you."

"Well, tell him it's no inconvenience. Maybe he has a sense of something. We ought to talk to him, too."

"Bri, I'll leave. I couldn't stand it if something happened to you because of me."

"Ditto. So you're staying. Period."

It had been a surprisingly easy decision for her to make. She wondered about it as she got coffee for Luke and peered into the refrigerator, trying to decide on dinner for later.

Why had the decision been so easy? At first she hadn't wanted to take care of Luke at all, hadn't wanted him back in her life. Now here he was, evidently with some potentially deadly trouble on his heels, and she told him to stay? It would have been the perfect excuse to move him out. But no. Had she just gotten stubborn? She had a tendency to do that.

But as she stared blindly into the fridge, another thought wiggled into her mind. Did she *want* him here? Had something in the dynamic between them changed that much?

She knew she was still fatally attracted to him, but that route had brought her nothing but pain in the past. Maybe she was a closet masochist. Muttering under her breath, she wondered what she was thinking. Somewhere in the spaghetti of her thoughts there had to be an answer. She needed to know her motivation. What she hoped for from this, if anything. Or if she was just being remarkably stupid for some reason?

At that point she would have bet on the stupidity. Nothing else made any sense. There had never been much that really mattered between them the first time around. It wasn't as if there was anything left to resurrect except the sex.

But the sex had been good. Great. Better than great. How many nights had she lain awake in her empty bed while he was away and relived every moment of their glorious lovemaking? She'd been so busy enjoying the hazy glow of their passion that for a long time she'd never realized anything was missing.

Except him. He'd be gone for six months or more at a time, then pop back in for a few weeks. It was like brand-new love all over again, every time. New relationship energy, she'd heard someone call it once. Where everything was as fresh as springtime, colors

were brighter, sensations were more vivid, and there
was a constant song in the air.

But that ended. She had enough married friends to
know that the fever pitch of new love didn't last forever. It settled down. It became real life, where other
things had to be dealt with, where friendship had to
grow, where couples had to do the hard work of making a life together.

She and Luke had never really gotten there, at least
not until the end. What wore out for most people in
six months or a year had lasted much longer for them
because of the way they were living.

But it had begun to wear off, and with its waning,
all the flaws and lacks had started to become apparent,
at least to her. Though she hadn't quite understood her
growing dissatisfaction, it had eaten at her, making her
edgier and crabbier when Luke was at home. Something was missing. She knew that much.

It had been easy to blame it on Luke's having an
affair. She didn't know if she was ready to accept that
Barbara's phone call had been a lie, but she could now
see how she had become prepared to believe it.

An affair provided a ready excuse for all that she
had begun to sense wasn't there. He was devoting himself to someone else. Of course. Snap explanation.

She closed the refrigerator door, realizing she wasn't
thinking about dinner but was running up her electric
bill. Slowly she sat at her kitchen table and tried to sort
through her tangled feelings.

It was too late to do the two of them any good. Their
life together was over, with too much bitterness under
the bridge. Yet she needed to understand or she'd never
hammer her way out of the amber that had locked her

in an unhappy time, made her distrustful of men and reluctant to risk falling in love again. She needed to sort it out for *herself.*

And it all would have been so much easier if Luke weren't in the next room. His very presence was confusing her more, even if it had begun the cascade to self-understanding.

Lovely. How was she going to deal with this?

She heard the creak and rattle of the wheelchair moving on her old wood floors. Moments later her nemesis entered the small kitchen partway. Given its size and the presence of the dinette, it would take some maneuvering to get that wheelchair in, but it could be done. "Need something?" she asked, trying not to look directly at him. It might be a risk, given the way her thoughts were running. She was beginning to feel as if she were losing her emotional control.

"More coffee, if that's okay." His voice was subdued, as if he weren't any happier than she. As if all of this had been going on too long.

She tried for forced cheer. "No problem. Still feeling good to bend your leg?"

"Like heaven. I'm working it like he told me."

"Let me know when you're ready to crutch around. I'd like to be close by the first few times. You never know. Do you want your coffee here or in the living room?" It wouldn't be easy, but she'd get him in there.

He eyed the table. "I don't think I can slide under that."

She remembered the crossbar. "Probably not. Go on back and I'll bring it to you."

But of course it wasn't that simple. He hadn't been wheeling himself around that much yet, and couldn't turn the chair on a dime. He got stuck with the chair only partly turned in the doorway. When he cussed, she laughed.

"Let me help. You'll get it before long."

"Probably about the time I'm able to walk again." But he smiled and shook his head instead of cussing.

"You could use the bell next time."

"I hate ringing for you like that. It seems…demeaning to you."

"Hardly. I'm a nurse. People ring for me all the time."

She got him to wheel himself a little farther into the kitchen so she could get behind him and begin the process of turning him and heading him in the right direction. Once he was faced the right way, he took over. She followed with two mugs of coffee.

"I need to call Jack to make that ramp," she remarked. "Then you could actually get out of here and go around the block." As soon as she suggested it, though, she remembered their discussion with Gage. Would it even be safe for Luke to go around the block alone?

She wasn't used to thinking this way, and a sour taste filled her mouth. She trusted her neighbors, but there was apparently one who couldn't be trusted at all. Maybe not on this street. Maybe not even in town, but she didn't want to start becoming suspicious of people.

She seemed, however, to have no choice.

"Well, maybe not by yourself," she hedged.

Luke was beginning to look tired, hardly surprising after a week in bed, followed by getting his casts changed that morning. His energy had to be at a relatively low ebb, but she decided not to suggest he get back into bed. He'd probably bite her head off now that he was free to bend his leg and no longer needed to spend hours with it elevated.

"I don't want you worrying about me," he said. "I'll be fine."

"Really? Don't make me laugh. You're not exactly in black-belt condition right now. It'll come back, but it's not here yet."

He arched a brow. "Are you enjoying having me at your mercy?"

"Well... No, actually. I'm not enjoying it at all. I keep thinking how rough it must be for you. Nothing ever slowed you down before."

"You did."

She caught her breath. Her mind seemed to go entirely silent and still. Her heart accelerated.

After a moment he said, "I guess I shouldn't have said that. But you know what? I'm getting tired of evasions, and things being off-limits. We have a past. I looked you up to discuss it. It's still there. It's the elephant in the room we keep dancing around."

She managed to find air but her heart continued to hammer. She didn't want to discuss this with him. Her mind shrieked that it would be dangerous. Nothing between them could work except sex. She ought to know that because she'd lived it. "Discuss what?" she said finally.

"All of it. The mess we made. How we could have done better. I don't know about you, but it haunts me. I feel like I totally screwed up, even without Barbara's lies. Do you think I didn't feel your dissatisfaction toward the end? Of course I did. I may appear to be deaf and blind sometimes, but I was aware of it. Damned if I knew what to do about it."

She spoke very carefully, quietly. "Because we didn't talk."

"Not about the right things, apparently. I wanted to fix it, Bri. But I couldn't figure out what was wrong. And I was too idiotic to just come out and ask."

She cleared her throat. In fairness to him, she needed to be truthful. "If you'd asked, I wouldn't have been able to tell you. It's just that simple. I didn't know, either."

He eyed her grimly. "Do you know now?"

"I'm not sure. But I've been thinking about it. Luke, what difference can it make now? We burned that bridge. It's gone. We can't go back. Does either of us even want to?"

"I want to understand. That's what I want."

"Me, too. I need to understand. I figure I've spent the last three years locking myself away from that whole part of life because I'm afraid of it. No boy-friends, no serious dating, no future."

He sighed and passed his hand over his face. "Same here. I can't move on without knowing how I so royally messed up something that started out so good."

They both grew silent. It felt as if there was no way into this conversation, yet it was clear they needed to have it.

"We didn't discuss anything," he said finally. "Even when we melted down. Accusations were flying, but nothing added up."

She winced inwardly since she had been the one making most of the accusations, then getting frustrated because his response had been mostly silence, except to deny he'd had an affair. But how could he have responded to her? She'd been blaming him for things that even now she could see were totally out of line. Frustration had led her to make claims that had no basis in fact.

"I got pretty wild," she admitted.

"I couldn't figure it out. It wasn't adding up to anything except you were unhappy with me. It didn't tell me what to do. Didn't give me a direction."

"That's because most of it was just ugliness pouring out of me because I was becoming miserable and I didn't know why." She paused, then lifted a hand. "There, I admitted it. I was flailing around trying to find reasons, and since I didn't know what they were, I made up things. How were you supposed to respond to that?"

"Like that time you picked me up at the airport and wouldn't even let me kiss you hello. I wondered what had happened, and I kept waiting to find out, but you didn't say. And then you seemed to get over it again and for a week or so everything was fine."

She looked down, knowing he was right. "I didn't know what the problem was. And that was the whole problem, wasn't it? No talk, then we'd fall into our usual romantic habits, and you'd be off again. The air never got cleared."

"Not really, unless you want to count those fights at the very end."

"They weren't real. I just told you."

"So what was the problem? Have you figured it out?"

She hesitated. "Luke, this is pointless."

"Not if it lets us move on."

For some reason hearing him talk about wanting to move on actually made her chest and throat tighten. Was she nuts? She'd divorced this man, had been sure she never wanted to see him again, and now the thought of him going back to his life and out of hers once more *hurt?*

She was over it. Or she should be. All these years...

"Bri, you're doing it again. Just talk, please."

For the first time she wondered if she hadn't been the biggest problem in their marriage. Not the long separations, not the lack of future planning, but her, and her unwillingness to open herself, to talk, to be vulnerable.

She took what must have seemed like a tangent to him, but a memory welled up in her, and she knew suddenly that it was extremely important. "When I was a kid, about thirteen, I was going through a painful time. Doesn't matter why—that age is just full of angst. I tried to tell my mother what I was feeling."

"And?"

"She turned from the pot she was stirring and snapped, 'Bri, quit being so dramatic.'"

"Just that once?"

Bri shook her head. "No. She was never really interested in what I felt. Almost as if the fact that I had feelings made her feel threatened."

"So you learned to be a clam."

"That's what I'm getting at."

"Anything else?"

"Actually, yes. I was taught very early, in just so many words, that my feelings didn't matter. I can still remember my father yelling at me one day when I was angry that I was too young to hate anything, too young to even know what hate was. Stuff like that."

It was as if some huge understanding was ripping open her insides. As if, finally, she was getting it. No feelings allowed. Didn't know her own feelings. Her feelings were invalid, or extreme, but whatever, they weren't real.

"So you don't even trust your own feelings?" he asked quietly.

"Guess not. Getting better at it but…" She hesitated. "I guess that's why I could never tell you what was wrong. Why I could never know what I felt, and why I kept dismissing those feelings. Like being mad that time when you came home, then sweeping it under the rug."

"I wish I'd known."

"I wish I'd figured this out years ago. Whatever, I'm glad I got that out. But when you said you couldn't figure out why I was unhappy, it suddenly got so clear, Luke. I never told you. I never trusted my feelings. I've been thinking about how we never talked much about the real stuff, and then just now I realized I was the one who wasn't talking."

"How could you, raised like that?"

Another understanding dawned. "I just figured out something else."

He leaned forward as if he wanted to be closer. "What?"

"That I was taught that if I asked for something I would never get it."

"What?" The word almost erupted from him.

She shrank back. "It's true," she said in a small

voice. "That was a rule when I was a kid. Ask and you won't get it."

He swore savagely. "So you weren't allowed to share your feelings, you were taught your feelings were suspect, and then you were taught that if you wanted something you'd better not ever ask for it."

She gave a sharp nod. She still couldn't bring herself to meet his gaze. Right then she felt like an open, exposed wound.

"They crippled you," he said harshly.

"I don't think they meant..."

"I don't care what they meant. I dealt with the results of it. They crippled you. No two ways about it."

She had begun to feel pretty small, and now shame filled her. She was broken, and she had made this man pay for her brokenness. God, she was a mess, not fit to be anyone's mate.

"Bri?"

His voice had grown quiet, gentler than she had heard it since the early days of their marriage. "What?" she asked dully.

"Don't blame yourself. It wasn't your fault."

"My fault that I ruined our marriage? Maybe it was. Like you said, I'm crippled."

"I meant that it wasn't your fault you couldn't talk about your feelings. I can't imagine what it must have been like growing up and having everything you felt devalued. Everything you wanted denied if you dared ask. I just can't imagine it, but I know it wasn't your fault. Children are impressionable and their parents are always right."

She made a sound somewhere between a laugh and a sniffle. Her entire chest ached with pent-up feelings,

feelings she couldn't give voice to. Feelings she didn't even know how to sort through or identify. She'd been skimming the surface of life, she realized, afraid of the depths beneath. "I guess I should get some therapy."

"Maybe. Or maybe you could just keep telling yourself that any feeling you have is as valid as anyone else's. You know, I'm no expert on kids but I have buddies who have children. I learned something from them."

"What's that?"

"Kids' feelings are true, whole, unsullied and real. They may blow over like a summer storm once expressed, but they're real, Bri. They aren't hemmed in by a lifetime of being told to hold things in. They let it fly. And yes, a kid does know the meaning of hate. The difference is, their emotions are strong and right up front, and usually short-lived. It's life that teaches us that expressing some feelings isn't good under most circumstances, but that's a matter of expression, not validity."

"I told my father I hated him. But I didn't. I loved him."

"I'm sure. But when you said you hated him, you meant it. With your whole being. It might have been only a few minutes, but you felt it, it was real and he should never have told you that you weren't old enough to know what it was. You knew. He just didn't want to hear it. He should have just said that it's not nice to say things like that. You'd have felt very differently, wouldn't you?"

"Maybe."

He sighed. "Okay, I'm not a shrink. I should probably shut up. But now I get what was going on, and I can't tell you how much it saddens me."

At that she stole a look at him. "Saddens you?"

"Absolutely. If I'd had any idea, I'd have driven you crazy until you started expressing yourself. I wanted to know what you were thinking and feeling, even if I wouldn't like it. How else could I do anything about it?"

She hadn't thought of it that way before, but she realized he had just identified the root problem clearly and concisely. She'd muttered on about how they never talked, but the truth was that not only had she been the one avoiding talking, but she'd closed off any opportunity of fixing things because of it. She had defined the problem without understanding all the ramifications.

"Wow," she whispered. "Oh, wow."

"What?"

"I need to think about this. I need to think about just how skewed I am. Was. How much I bottlenecked every possible path for improvement."

"I guess you were afraid."

"I guess. Afraid of being vulnerable."

"Afraid of me acting like one of your parents. I hope I'm more mature than that. But how were you to know?"

She just shook her head, unable to speak as her thoughts whirled almost crazily. Seeing herself from a totally different perspective shocked her. She'd thought she knew herself, and now she was looking at a stranger.

Luke spoke after a few minutes. "I'm tired. I think I'll stretch out."

"Want something more comfortable to wear?"

"I'm fine. What I'd like is for you to lie next to me."

"Luke!" The idea seemed fraught with serious peril.

"Just lie beside me, nothing else. I promise. I just don't want you to be alone right now. You're looking shell-shocked."

"I'll be fine."

He smiled faintly. "I'm sure you will. But not within the next five minutes, or even within a few weeks. The things you told me…" He shrugged one shoulder. "I just don't want you to be alone. You don't have to say a word."

I never said the important words, she thought. Never. But as she watched him lever himself into the bed, then scoot over to make room for her, she realized she didn't want to be alone, either. The turmoil inside her felt like an icy gale, and even silent companionship sounded far better than solitude.

So she took the risk, realizing that she trusted his word. He just didn't want her to be alone. And neither did she.

Chapter 8

Luke was exhausted. He hated to admit it, but the whole accident and the week in bed had left him feeling a bit like a noodle. Not completely, but a bit. He tired faster, too, but that might be part of the healing.

And he still didn't trust his own mind. They had told him the concussion appeared to be past the worst, but that he might still occasionally have problems, from dizziness to scattered thoughts, until fully healed. If ever you fully healed from one.

Still, he knew what he'd heard Bri say, and he knew her words had plummeted into his heart like a stone. Even the awful, horrid realization that he was failing her in their marriage, that she was going to leave him, hadn't exceeded what he felt for her now.

He tried to imagine the way she had grown up, and how that must have deprived her of the most important part of her voice: the ability to identify and express her feelings and needs.

He remembered his own frustration, the sense that things were going wrong but he didn't know why. Couldn't figure it out. Couldn't fix it. He'd have laid himself down on train tracks for her if he had thought it would help, but as it was, he had no idea what might work. None.

Now at least he knew why, and he felt sorrier for her than he did for himself. Whatever her dissatisfactions, she had been voiceless. Unable to tell him. Maybe unable to recognize them herself. And if she had figured out what she needed, she'd been trained not to ask for it.

A hell of an emotional box to put anyone in. He supposed it was a huge breakthrough for her to have identified the problem and its source. But it must have left her feeling as if she were an emotional blender, everything swirling around with no place yet to rest.

He cursed the casts that made it impossible for him to lie on his side, because he'd have dearly loved to put an arm around her. Just a light hug to let her know he was there and that he cared.

Probably just as well he couldn't, though. He hadn't missed that she had lain down with her back to him. She wasn't ready for any kind of intimacy with him. She'd exposed herself enough for one day, and he had to respect her boundaries.

But all of this was putting him in a blender, too. He had thought the past was past, except for the little matter of his honor. He'd convinced himself that the only reason he wanted to see her again was because he happened to be in town and he wanted to correct the record about Barbara. Bri's willingness to believe he'd had an affair had been rankling for years.

But now he wondered if that was the only reason he'd knocked on her door. Maybe there was a whole lot more left to deal with. Hadn't he just realized it? Just now when she was talking he'd faced how much her emotional cage had scarred him.

He was a man used to getting things done. Fixing things. Taking charge and dealing with matters until everything was right. Bri had made that impossible for him. Of all the things he had done in his life, Bri alone had stymied him. She'd been a puzzle he couldn't solve, a problem he couldn't mend. She was the one and only problem in his life that had left him feeling as if he stood on quicksand.

How many times had he asked her what was wrong? And how many times had her frown vanished to be replaced by a smile and the answer, "I'm just a bit crabby."

Crabby? Maybe that had been true on occasion, but now he was amazed how many times he had let that excuse pass. Or how many times he had watched her mood shift and smooth over without any explanation at all.

What had he been thinking?

Before he could answer that question, however, sleep crept up and carried him away.

Rest, said some corner of his mind. *You need it.* So he did.

During the afternoon, the street outside was quiet. Everyone was at work, and it was a day that didn't exactly invite people out into their yards. Snow and ice still blanketed everything, and the thaw was just making more ice.

Jack took a chance, knowing he had a lot of good excuses if someone happened to see him shinny up the tree beside Bri's house. It wasn't likely—the tree wasn't in plain sight from the street—but his excuses were ready anyway.

He needed to know if anything had changed between Bri and her ex. It was eating him alive that the guy was still with her even though his leg had improved enough that he could have gone back to the motel.

He knew that because he saw Tim and Ted carry him in. Luke's knee could bend now. With a wheelchair and crutches he ought to be able to take care of himself. He didn't need Bri's nursing anymore.

But he'd come back here anyway. Jack felt as if a whole bunch of fire ants had been unleashed in his brain. They wouldn't leave him alone. They wanted answers. He wanted answers. He needed to know if Luke was becoming a threat to him.

No one saw him climb the tree. Or if they happened to, they didn't think anything of it. That was one good thing about being known as Bri's handyman, not just the guy at the hardware store. He was a common sight working around Bri's place. No reason for anyone to wonder what he was up to.

The attic vent squeaked a little as he opened it, and he made a note to oil it next time he went up there. Then he slipped inside and closed it, becoming invisible to the world.

He crept slowly across the rafters, avoiding making noise. If Bri thought she had another raccoon, pretending to get rid of it could only be complicated by

Luke's presence. He couldn't rely on Bri's believing he'd removed the animal while she was at work. Not with that man watching.

His jacket caught on a nail and he fought with it in the dark for a few seconds before pulling free. Trying to be utterly silent frustrated him even more.

He realized he was reaching some kind of internal boiling point, and forced himself to draw some deep breaths. You had to have a plan to act. If he hadn't figured that out before, he sure got it now that Luke was still alive. That fall should have killed him. Instead he'd gotten hung up on an outcropping that had been invisible under the snow.

So no action without a thoroughly considered plan.

But he still had to know what was going on between these two. Just how much of a threat Luke posed.

Resuming his crawl along the rafters, a very slow crawl, he headed for his peephole over the living room. He couldn't see a whole lot through that hole, except Luke's bed, but he could hear, and hearing was what he was after. What did those two talk about? Must be interesting, being divorced and all that. Jack would have found it impossible to talk to someone who'd divorced him.

He paused, thinking about it, and it occurred to him that if someone tried to divorce him, he could arrange a fatal accident. Get at least some satisfaction out of it.

But he'd never been married, so he'd never been divorced, and all he wanted to do was make Bri happy, so happy she'd feel like a queen. As the nicest person in this town, with the possible exception of Reverend Laura Potter, Bri deserved it.

Thoughts of making Bri happy settled his mind a bit

and made him feel better. He finally reached the hole and put his ear to it, listening. The house was utterly silent. Had they gone out?

But no, Bri's car was still out there and Luke was too crippled to get out anyway. Bri should let him build that ramp. Not because he wanted to help Luke, but because it would help Bri. She could get some time off babysitting.

He liked that term, babysitting. Yes, she was a nurse, but right now she had to feel as if she were caring for a baby. Hardly romantic.

But the room continued to remain silent.

Finally he looked down the hole and saw the two of them lying on the bed together. They weren't hugging or anything, but that didn't matter.

Jack's brain exploded.

Luke roused a bit from sleep, with the feeling he'd heard something. He didn't open his eyes, but waited. When the sound didn't repeat, he dismissed it. It was enough that he could feel that Bri was still beside him. She never stirred, but he heard the faint sound of her breathing. It soothed him and he dozed off again.

Bri was astonished to awaken to a day that was darkening into night. When she had climbed into this bed, her brain and emotions had been running around so frantically that she had never believed she would fall asleep. She stirred, thinking she needed to close the drapes against the night's chill, then call Jack to come build a ramp. She had to at least get that started before she went back to work later this week.

Not that going back to work sounded good to her

right then. No, she was feeling too messed up to want
to deal with anything other than her own turmoil. Selfish, but true.

She stirred.

"You have a hole in your ceiling," Luke remarked.

"What?" She scooted until she was on her back.
"Where?"

"No biggie. I never would have noticed it except I've
been staring at the ceiling for the last half hour or so.
See?" He pointed. "It's really tiny."

She peered until at last she found it. "Must have
been that dang raccoon. Probably punctured it with
a claw."

"Probably."

"Jack will fix it," she said, yawning. "When I can finally pay him to put in more insulation." She stared up
at it, though. "I wonder why I never noticed it before."

"Do you spend a lot of time staring at your ceil-
ings?"

At that she had to laugh. "Actually, no. If you were
awake, you should have shaken me. You must need
something by now."

"I'm fine, although motoring to the bathroom is beginning to sound good."

She rolled out of bed and brought his wheelchair
close. "Or are you game to try the crutches?"

"Let me try crutching. Just follow close with the
chair in case this doesn't work. I've never used crutches
before."

"The important thing is to put your weight on your
hands, not on your armpits."

"Got it."

* * *

Overhead, Jack had snapped back from the hole and held his breath, as if they could even have seen him from down there. Damn it, how had that guy spied that tiny little hole?

But their voices drifting up to him reassured him. And just as soon as they got to the bathroom and started making noise in there, he had to get out of here.

He couldn't believe he had fallen asleep. What if he had snored?

He had to get his act together.

And he had to make a plan soon. It sounded to him as if those two were getting a bit too cozy.

The wait seemed endless. He had to endure more laughter as Jack made his first attempt with the crutches. Eventually their sounds faded toward another part of the house. Moving as quickly as he dared, he headed for the attic vent.

Yeah, he thought, he had to figure out something to do soon. Especially since it was beginning to feel as if Bri were in danger of cheating on him.

He wouldn't allow that. No way. He just had to decide how to prevent it.

"I can't believe how tiring that was," Luke practically exploded as he sank onto the edge of his bed again and passed Bri the crutches. "Damn, I'm as weak as a kitten."

"Cut yourself some slack," Bri told him as she tucked the crutches within reach but out of the way. "You were doing that on one broken arm and a broken leg. Which probably meant half your body was doing eighty or ninety percent of the work. I could see you were favoring your injured side. Then you had a week in bed. Amazing how fast that saps muscle strength. I thought you did pretty good considering how banged up you are."

"I need to get going on that physical therapy. How long did he say?"

She picked up his patient care papers. "You can relax. They have you scheduled for the day after tomorrow. In the meantime, I wouldn't overdo the crutching. Let them decide what's best."

He glared at the crutches. "The doc gave them to me. I ought to be able to use them."

"You just did. Short hops only. Remember that part?"

He eyed her glumly. "Sorry. I'm a lousy patient, I guess."

"I've had far worse. Now relax for a few while I try to rustle up some dinner."

Oh, this was bad, she thought as she escaped to the kitchen. First she'd made some stunning discoveries about herself, which put the blame for the failure of her marriage firmly on her shoulders, and now she was feeling a deep ache for him that he was so laid up?

She almost wished she could go back to blaming him for everything. It had been a comfortable world to live in, very black-and-white. He had cheated, therefore it was all his fault.

But it wasn't. That much had become agonizingly clear to her just a few hours ago. Barbara hardly figured into it at all anymore. If Luke *had* cheated, given what she had learned about herself this afternoon, she could hardly blame him.

She couldn't imagine what it had been like for him.

As her dissatisfaction had grown, he'd felt it. Occasionally flashes of it had shown. But then, like the good little girl she'd been trained to be, she had buried it and pretended it didn't exist. She couldn't discern her own feelings because she was so sure she must be feeling things that were invalid, and even if she had, speaking them would have been taboo.

So how was he supposed to handle that? No incoming information, just a growing perplexity on his part. He knew something was wrong but didn't know what it was, or what he could do about it.

Yup, crippled was a good word for her.

Standing at the sink, peeling some potatoes while the chicken breasts thawed in the microwave, she tried to reach back in time, to find that woman again, and parse her feelings that something wasn't right.

But that woman was gone, and would never yield her secrets now. Sure, it had felt more like an affair than a marriage, but what exactly had she meant by that? What had she been missing? She'd never faced it head-on in time to even know for certain. They hadn't talked about serious things very much, but that was her fault, not his.

She'd just kept sweeping up her emotional detritus like a good maid, but instead of actually getting rid of it, she'd put it under the rug. Eventually that rug had become lumpy enough that it could no longer be ignored.

Then had come the bursts of anger and even fury in which she still couldn't explain what was wrong. All she could do was attack him, often for imagined slights, sometimes over things so small they shouldn't have mattered at all.

Except that she had been living on her own personal

emotional volcano and when it erupted it magnified everything. He must have wondered if he was dealing with a madwoman.

She put the potatoes in a bowl of water, then checked the thawing chicken. Almost there. She let it stand, rather than risk partially cooking it in the microwave.

Right now, even with her new self-knowledge, she didn't know how to sort through this tangled mess. Then there was the undeniable fact that someone had tried to kill Luke.

The fear that pierced her every time she thought of that was enough to let her know her feelings for him weren't utterly dead. Far from it.

But his for her must be. He appeared to be a well-balanced person, unlike her, and there could be no reason on earth why he'd want to get into her emotional mess again. He'd suffered enough from it, in big ways and small ways.

"Bri?"

She whirled around and saw Luke standing in the kitchen doorway, teetering on his crutches. "Can I come in and sit?"

Even as she pulled a chair out for him, she began to scold. "I told you to rest. You shouldn't try this yet without someone to keep an eye on you."

"I know, I know. Just grab me under the shoulders...."

Without a thought, as he readied himself to sit, she slipped her arms under his and locked them behind his back. "Slowly," she cautioned. "Lean into me so I can keep my back straight." She spread her legs and tried to keep her back as straight as possible. This could be dangerous for them both. She ought to make that bit clear.

But the whole professional angle vanished quickly as their bodies met. Matters instantly became dangerous in a whole new way.

All this time, even though she had felt the awakenings of her old desire for him, she had managed to keep it at bay. But she had forgotten, she realized. She had forgotten how good it felt to have him pressed to her, to have her face nearly buried in his shoulder. How good it was to feel his arms lock around her.

In an instant, the simmering pot reached a full boil, bubbling over the top of every wall she had ever built. An almost agonizing shaft of desire speared to her core, causing her insides to clench. Breath escaped her and refused to return as if she'd been tossed into a vacuum. Only by the greatest effort could she manage to remember that she was helping him sit.

But then he folded into the chair with his legs between hers and he didn't let go. Nor, in fact, did she, although now she was bent over. Their arms remained tightly locked around each other, telegraphing something approaching desperation.

She gave in, pressing her face into his shoulder. Then to her amazement, she felt him draw her onto his lap, their hips and torsos meeting fully. The cut-up sweatpants he wore left little to her imagination. He was hard for her. He wanted her.

At last she drew a deep, gasping breath, grateful to find oxygen again. "Luke…" It came out a mere whisper of sound.

"Just relax," he murmured. "I'm hardly in any position to ravish you. But damn, I missed this. I missed *us*."

She pulled her arms out from under his and wrapped them around his neck because she was incapable of doing anything else at that point. He had suddenly become the only rock in the storm-tossed sea of passion that was rolling through her in huge waves.

It had always been like this between them. Always. It had been about the only glue that had held them together for four years. As it filled her now, it altered her memories of the past, reminding her of the good things she had tried so hard to repress.

Dangerous? Yes. But oh so good, and she wasn't in any hurry to give it up. Just being held... It seemed like forever since strong arms had held her and made her feel as if she had come home. It was a feeling she didn't want to relinquish, however ephemeral it might be.

Even as her center throbbed for him, a kind of relaxation filled her, softening her, easing tensions she hadn't been aware of bearing. She welcomed the softening, needing it as much as the passion. How could she have forgotten that he had this power, the power to make her feel soft and safe?

Because she had fought it in ways that really mattered, never fully giving him herself and her trust. Crippled.

Slowly she lifted her head, hating the space she was about to place between them. She hated the coward she had somehow become, hated the loss of the most wonderful thing in her life because self-doubt had turned her into a weakling. She had been afraid to do the very things that might have strengthened what they had had. Too confused to do them.

But as he felt her start to pull back, Luke cradled

the back of her head in his palm. "Stay," he murmured. "Just a little longer. You're safe, I promise."

Safe from what? She would never be safe from herself. But she pushed her concerns aside—all too easy for her to do, she thought sadly—then gave herself up to the moment and the magic.

Stolen moments she was sure she would have to pay for. One way or another, life exacted a price.

But she didn't care. She needed these moments as badly as she needed air to breathe.

Their hips felt almost fused together by the hunger between them. Her legs went weak, causing her to sink even more into him. His arms tightened, welcoming her, and she felt him shift, just a bit, as if trying to ease his own ache.

Heat zinged through her. She knew him all too well and was reading his body language like an open book. He wanted her, too. A flutter of panic struck her. She hadn't sorted out her own problems, and anyway, wanting wasn't enough. It could only end badly once again.

But before the panic could fully take root, he turned her head and his until their mouths met. No one had ever kissed her like Luke. No one.

His mouth was soft on hers, not demanding, but the gentleness of his lips sent more waves of soft heat through her, reminding her of how he could make the whole world go away. Whenever she had been in Luke's arms, nothing else had existed.

Nothing else existed now. This was a familiar path, but no less inflammatory for that. Maybe it was even more inflammatory because she knew so well where it could lead.

He made a quiet sound deep in his throat, not quite

a groan, but she knew what it meant. She opened her mouth and gave him entry so that their tongues could duel in an ancient dance, a mimicry of the ultimate act. The warm and damp meeting, the tangling, twisting and teasing of tongues, created needs she would never be able to ignore. He still had that much power over her.

His arm slipped down her back, circling her rump and pulling her tightly into him. In an instant, her aching need for him grew into a hard-edged hunger. She had been starving for him and had barely realized it.

At that moment, she'd have given him anything possible in order to find the satisfaction only he had ever brought her.

But then he pulled his head back. His breath rasped loudly in her ear. Reluctantly she opened her eyes.

"Sorry," he said. "I seem to remember promising not to ravish you."

She didn't want to move, but knew she had to. Everything seemed to be careering off course, and the little cocoon she had made for herself was in danger of rupturing wide-open.

She couldn't let that happen. Not with Luke. They had too much history to mend. It would only lead to more pain.

But pushing herself off his lap proved to be among the hardest things she had ever done.

When she at last stood across the kitchen from him, every cell in her body felt drained of strength, every urge within her directed at him.

He just looked at her, saying nothing, his eyes a bit heavy-lidded as if he were feeling the same way.

She forced words to pass her lips. "This can't work, Luke."

"Maybe not." He sighed and closed his eyes, and in that instant she realized just how vulnerable he had made himself to her. He'd let her know that his desire for her hadn't waned. That he still missed her. He'd exposed himself in ways she had rarely dared to.

She pivoted quickly and stared into the sink full of potato peelings. If anything, her confusion had grown. Was there any hope of rebuilding? Did he want to try? Could she change enough, open up enough, figure herself out enough?

Gripping the edge of the counter, she squeezed her eyes shut and ordered herself to calm down before she did something stupid that might hurt them both. Sex was not enough. It was never enough.

If she were to decide she wanted Luke again, she was going to have to figure herself out, and right now that didn't look too likely.

She would have to discern what she needed beyond sex from him. What kind of future she really wanted. What she needed around the corner. Picket fences? Kids? Less travel on his part?

Learning that would mean plumbing her dissatisfaction with their marriage. Honestly looking at what had made her unhappy, all the things she had felt without ascribing them to anything, all the things she had swept under the rug.

It would mean finally knowing herself and whether her feelings were valid. That scared her. It scared her almost as much as losing the most important thing in her life had: Luke.

"I'm scared," she said finally.

"That's a step in the right direction. Wanna talk about it?"

"Not yet."

"Fair enough. But thanks for telling me."

"Aren't you?" she asked.

"Scared? Hell yeah. I didn't realize until you opened the door to me the first time how much I wasn't over you. I came to defend my honor, and instead found out just how much I'd never wanted to let you go. Why wouldn't I be scared?"

"So it's not a crazy feeling?"

"I don't think any of your feelings are crazy. Just talk about them. Please. And in the meantime, rest assured I'm not expecting one thing from you. We tore something down. We shredded it. I have no great hope that we can find a way back from that. But whatever, I'd at least like to know whatever you can tell me about what happened, about what's going on now. I'm not afraid of your feelings, Bri. Just keep that in mind."

He wasn't afraid of them, but she was. From a very early age she'd learned her feelings were wrong. Almost all of them. If she wasn't happy, something was wrong with *her*. Intellectually she could know that probably wasn't true, but the lesson had been learned at a much deeper level.

Now here she was, just past thirty, and she still didn't know what was true and false.

Silence lingered for a long time. Finally Luke broke it, changing the subject entirely. "How do I get ahold of Jack to build that ramp?"

After a moment she turned. "I can call him. You don't like him."

"I don't have to like people I hire. I figured that out a long time ago. But this is a job he's going to do for *me*."

She studied his face and saw determination there.

His jaw appeared tight, and the faint creases around his eyes had deepened. Too much determination for such a small thing, but she could see no point in fighting it.

"It's on auto dial. Just grab the phone."

She went back to slicing the potatoes into a saucepan so she could make mashed potatoes to go with the broiled chicken breasts. Broccoli with cheese sauce would come next. Simple but important tasks, important in that they gave her some space and allowed her to calm down from her close encounter with Luke.

She felt amazed that the passion could still flare between them that way. It was as if the ugliness of their final fights and separation had never happened. She wouldn't have thought it possible that he could still awaken her hungers so easily.

Clearly he could, and that made him one very dangerous man.

She tensed when she realized he had reached Jack. Luke's dislike of him was so obvious that she anticipated it had to bleed into his voice as they spoke, but it didn't. Luke was both pleasant and professional.

"You mentioned building a ramp for me the other day. I'd like to hire you to do it. I don't want Bri paying for it." Silence. "That would be great. And do me another favor, please. Charge me up front for taking it down when I'm able to move out. I don't want her to have to deal with the mess when I'm gone. Thanks. I really appreciate it."

As easy as that, he'd hired Jack. She wondered how this was going to work out. Luke was a geologist, but he was also a builder. What if he critiqued Jack's work?

"I can almost feel your tension all the way over here," Luke remarked. "I was pleasant."

She turned toward him again. "You're not going to criticize him, I hope. He knows what he's doing."

"I'm sure he does." Luke paused. "And I'm equally certain I'm going to watch him do it."

"Luke!"

He shrugged and half smiled. "Nothing like two guys discussing a carpentry project. A great way to make friends."

She almost asked why he would want to do that, given that he'd made his opinion of Jack clear. But then she decided it didn't matter. As Luke had said, he'd hired plenty of people he didn't like. Maybe this was his way of getting past it.

The doorbell rang and she quickly dried her hands on a towel before going to answer it. Mike Hanson, a long, lean guy who adopted the appearance of a mountain man complete with beard, stood there, a smile on his face. "I thought it was time I dropped in on the boss man."

She had to laugh. "I wondered where you were."

"He's had me playing mountain goat for him. The guy doesn't let up, Bri. Ever."

"Come in. He's in the kitchen. I'm making dinner. Want to join us?" Doing a quick mental calculation, she decided she had time to thaw some more chicken.

"I'd love to, but you didn't plan on another mouth."

"No problem," she said as she closed the door behind him. "I'm still at the point where I can adapt."

She led the way to the kitchen and waved him to one of the dinette chairs. "You guys might be more comfortable in the living room."

"If you're not throwing us out," Luke answered, "I'd rather stay here. I need the scenery change."

She poured coffee for both of them, then went back to work, half listening to their conversation. This was, she realized, the closest to Luke's work she'd ever gotten. These conversations had always played out elsewhere.

"That snowfall the other night didn't help one bit," Mike said. "You can hardly pick out the terrain up there now. If we had open ski slopes, we'd be jammed with business."

"That's the idea."

"Yeah, but right now…" Mike trailed off, then said, "I've been using that ground-penetrating radar like you told me. We've got some fault lines up there just like you thought."

"I could see some of them when I was up there. So show me."

Bri looked over her shoulder and saw long rolls of paper being spread out. To her it looked like a bunch of lines.

"We're going to have to move some of the slopes a little more than we thought," Mike went on, clearly pointing out areas of interest. "But the important thing is to do some blast testing to see how stable these areas are."

"It's mostly the surface faults I'm worried about. I don't want rock slides falling on the slopes."

"We can manage that. I'm just saying we're going to have to do more blasting than we thought. I don't know how HQ is going to feel about that. At some point clearing the risks away is going to get expensive."

Luke continued to pore over the printouts and was nodding as he did so. Bri turned back to peeling a couple of extra potatoes and getting those chicken breasts thawed.

The things she'd never thought about. Surprise took her as she realized she was genuinely interested.

"I don't think it's impossible," Luke said. "Not yet anyway. Damn, what kinds of maps were the designers using?"

"Topographic, probably. Not every inch of these mountains has been surveyed for faults. I'm starting to wonder if that's why the plans for this place keep dying."

"Yeah." Luke sighed. "We could find more open places for the slopes. We might have to. Places where a rock slide couldn't roll far enough to reach them."

"Slides are inevitable, but I agree we need to minimize them."

"So let's start looking for wider bowls between the peaks. Safer places. I know we'll have to run one expert course through the roughest terrain we can find, but clearing the way for just one slope wouldn't be as expensive."

"Agreed."

After that the conversation grew too technical for Bri to follow. She only vaguely listened, but was glad to hear Luke sounding really involved and interested. After that concussion, she'd been so worried about long-term effects, but there didn't seem to be any, except once in a while he mentioned being a bit dizzy. As a nurse she knew that no concussion could ever be treated lightly, so he was one lucky guy in that regard.

But why would someone have pushed him? It just made no sense to her. Trying to kill him wouldn't stop the onrush of progress if the people with the money wanted it. They'd just send someone else to do Luke's job, and maybe hire a few security guards.

But she couldn't imagine anyone around here having it in for him personally. He hadn't been in town that long—little opportunity to make a serious enemy.

So that left someone who was either remarkably stupid, or crazy. Neither one felt very good to her.

She was glad Mike had come by, though. It had cut the growing sexual tension between her and Luke, switching it off as effectively as if he had turned off the power. She simply wasn't ready to deal with that again. There had to be more between her and a man than last time. Luke could get her motor humming all too easily, and when that happened everything else ceased to matter.

Until she had started to feel that something was lacking, something was wrong, something she couldn't even identify. Worse, Luke had always been good to her. Kind, gentle, loving, caring. All those greeting card sentiments wrapped up in one man. So what had there been to make her so unhappy? Hell, she'd often felt absolutely ungrateful for those times when she felt a lack, had told herself to appreciate what they had.

She'd worked her way out of every single one of those moods and back to happy Bri. Or happy Brianna as her parents had called her as a child, until she started to grow up and express another side of herself. How many times had her mother asked her, "Whatever happened to our happy Brianna? We nicknamed you Happy, you know."

Yeah, she knew. But life had been happening to happy Brianna. Growing up, fights with friends, the inevitable teenage sense of alienation, boyfriends who didn't work out. Hormonal changes. Everything seeming to change, for that matter, at lightning speeds.

So basically, she hadn't been a blissful idiot anymore. She'd had problems, and new feelings to deal with. Sometimes strange feelings. Longings she could barely contain. A future that sometimes looked exciting and sometimes terrifying. All the adolescent mess.

And no one to share it with other than her girlfriends who were shooting through the same rapids.

So she hadn't been perfectly happy, but any time she wasn't she'd been criticized or even condemned for it. She'd learned to hide and then dismiss those feelings. Clearly something was wrong with her.

But if something was wrong with her, maybe it hadn't been her feelings. Maybe it had been locking them away. Remembering what Luke had said about not knowing what he could do when he didn't know what was wrong made such sense to her.

She had cut him out of her emotional life and then signaled again and again that she wasn't happy, only to pivot around and be happy Bri again.

God, she must have been confusing to deal with. Worse, she had attributed her feelings to him. If she was unhappy, so must he be. But had she ever asked? No. If he was unhappy, why wouldn't he cheat?

What a mess!

She was beginning to think that the very least she owed him was a huge apology.

She was glad at last to put dinner on the table, grateful for Mike's presence as the conversation turned to lighter matters. They told her stories about some of the jobs they had worked on together, keeping her entertained. She noticed that Luke was beginning to look awfully tired, but she suspected that if she suggested he get back into bed he'd argue, at least while Mike was here.

She wondered if he was concerned that Mike was reporting to their bosses on how well he was doing. That maybe he could still lose his job, even though he'd gone into high gear pretty quickly, touching base back home, letting them know he could manage quite well.

Her head was beginning to hurt from all this thinking and speculation. So, nice as Mike was, she was glad when he left.

When she came back from the door, she found Luke teetering on his crutches near his bed.

Exclaiming, she hurried to steady him and ease him onto the mattress. "Overdoing it is not going to make you heal faster."

"I'm resting now, aren't I?"

"Too late," she retorted. "I'll bring you coffee after I take care of the dishes."

"No rush, Bri. That was a wonderful dinner."

"And you could chew it!"

At that he laughed wearily. "I sure did. Do you want to potty train me next?"

She laughed, too, and went to clear up from dinner while she made a fresh pot of coffee. Coffee, the staff of life. When Luke was home there was always a fresh pot except when they were in bed.

Memories of that made her cheeks color, surprisingly enough. It wasn't as if she hadn't done all those things with him. In fact, she'd entered exuberantly into whatever foreplay he'd invented. For her, limited though her experience was, he had proved to be an absolutely great lover.

Smothering a sigh, she put the last dish in the dishwasher and poured the coffee. Roaming through those memories could only lead to trouble.

She brought the coffee out to the living room. He'd raised the head of his bed and was looking at the laptop computer on his tray table. Moving carefully, she set a mug beside it. "It's hot."

"Good."

She retreated to the office chair. "Luke?"

"Hmm?"

"Are you worried about your job?"

At last he looked at her. "A bit. I'm a replaceable part."

"Really? I wouldn't have thought so from the projects you head up."

He shook his head just a little. "I'm not unique. Well, if they decided to lay me off because they figure I can't do this job, there are others out there. At least my skill set is in demand. Or maybe I could do something really harebrained and settle in some place to build houses."

She hesitated. "But I thought you loved the travel."

"I used to."

"What happened?"

"It cost me my wife."

A giant vacuum suddenly sucked all the air out of the room. His gaze never wavered, as if he was expecting a response. Her brain scrambled wildly seeking any answer to what he had just said.

But then he looked away from her and resumed staring at his computer. "It wasn't your fault, Bri. You were right. It was more like an affair than a marriage. I can understand why you were growing less happy. Who wouldn't? We never did the things married couples are supposed to do. Planning and dreaming seemed to be out in the cold."

Just then the phone rang. The worst time imaginable. She felt awful that he was blaming himself, acutely aware that she'd played a huge role in the problem.

But she couldn't resist the ring of the phone. She was still a nurse and sometimes…

"Bri," said the familiar voice of the nursing supervisor, "we need you. There's been a serious pileup on the state highway. We need all hands on deck."

"One sec." She turned to Luke. "They need me at the hospital. Emergency. Will you be all right on your own?"

"I have been for a long time."

That stung. "Just promise me you'll use the wheelchair to get around while I'm gone."

"Promise."

He never even looked at her.

"I'll be right there," she told Mary. "Fifteen minutes."

"Make it ten. ERT is flying in some really bad cases."

She hung up and raced for her jacket and boots. She'd get her scrubs at the hospital.

"Wheelchair," she called over her shoulder as she opened the door.

"I promised already."

The familiar words *I love you* almost passed her lips the way they had so often in the past when one of them had been leaving. She caught them just in time and swallowed them.

They sat in her stomach like lead.

Chapter 9

Sleep took Luke even though he wanted to keep on working. Mike's visit had filled his head with all kinds of information that would give him a sound basis for making recommendations. As soon as his brain had returned from la-la land, he had set to work proving his ability to manage the progress even though he was laid up. Defending his job.

Still, he was exhausted, and despite his best effort of will, he needed sleep. He kept dozing off in the middle of the sentences he was trying to type, and finally he slipped from a doze to a deep sleep.

His dreams were troubled, and they mostly involved Bri. When eventually he woke, it was deep in the night and by the light of the little lamp they had been using as his night-light, he stared upward at that boring ceiling and thought about it.

Today had been a mistake. She was right. No way could they recover from the mess they'd ended up making, so what was the point? Yet today for the first time he'd understood what Bri's problem really was, and it pained him.

He gathered from what she had said that it wasn't her happy feelings that had been bottled up, but the other, less pleasant ones. Anger. Frustration. Irritation. Bottled to the point that she couldn't even tell if they were justified, and from what she'd indicated, whether they were even real or what was causing them.

It wasn't right, damn it. Those feelings had reasons, however silly they might sometimes be, and expressing them was necessary to clearing the air. To solving problems. That emotional truncation had left him wondering what was going on and what, if anything, he could do about it.

It had worked for a while. He'd watched those moments in her when there was obviously something that bothered her. Then they'd blew away rapidly, leaving him to believe it had nothing to do with him.

Increasingly, though, he had realized those ephemeral moments were very much grounded in their marriage, but by then it was too late. Unspoken, unexpressed, they had become a bomb that had finally exploded, destroying everything.

How did you deal with that? He'd never dissuaded her from talking. He'd often asked what was wrong, because he really wanted to know. Then the smooth, smiling face would return and everything would get lost again in lovemaking or some other romantic pastime.

Glumly, he faced the fact that he'd never really known her. She hadn't allowed it.

Compounding his idiocy, he had drawn her onto his lap today. Had held her and kissed her and rediscovered the passion that had apparently never died. That was going to make things smoother. Not. He still ached for her, he still wanted her and, damn it, he wanted to really get to know her.

She'd always fascinated him, always seemed like a bit of a puzzle, but now he wished he could put that puzzle together. It might turn out that they had never been suited at all, but that was better than wondering, as he did all too often, where he had gone wrong and whether he could have done something to salvage their relationship.

There were questions that had never been answered, and he still wanted those answers. Even after three years. He needed to know where he had failed. That failure plagued him constantly, enough that he hadn't dated seriously since.

He refused to place the blame entirely on her shoulders. Clearly he had been doing things wrong or he wouldn't have seen those flashes of unhappiness.

He had gathered that she was reluctant to date, too, because of the first muddy mess they'd made of everything. Well, that wasn't fair to either of them. Somehow he needed to find a way for them both to sort through this so they could move on.

Because it was quite clear now that he wasn't the only one who couldn't move on. She'd said as much, and considering that he'd half expected to find her remarried when he knocked on her door, it was a little shocking to realize she still bore the same wounds he did.

Failing at marriage was no small deal, evidently.

Sighing, he sat up and reached for his chair. Nature called and he'd promised. Much as he hated it, he was going to keep that promise. He still endured the occasional bit of dizziness, and he'd deserve every bit of brimstone that would rain down on his head if Bri came home to find he'd taken another fall.

Then he wondered if she had somehow come back but hadn't wakened him. He listened intently but heard nothing at all. A truly silent night.

He made his way to the bathroom without trouble, extremely glad he no longer needed help for this chore. Then he peeked into Bri's room. A pale shaft of moonlight poked through her curtains, enough to tell him she wasn't there.

Making up his mind, he headed for the kitchen. Even a simple task like making coffee was difficult in that chair, but he managed. He remembered other nights when she had come back from something like this, all wound up and unable to sleep. A glance at the clock on the microwave announced she'd been gone for nearly five hours.

It had been bad, whatever it was. Yeah, she was going to arrive home all keyed up, pacing, maybe even needing to talk. They hadn't shared much about their jobs, but when she'd come home from a really bad night, he'd watched her try to pace it off, and sometimes she had talked, just a little.

He couldn't remember if he had ever told her how much he admired her for the work she did. He couldn't imagine the horrors she must have seen, and the sorrows that had come with them. Nor had she ever really said. All he could see was her reaction to the adrenaline that had been pumping through her for hours as she helped battle to save a life.

He clearly remembered her decision to get out of the emergency room into another branch of nursing. Apparently, out here, that didn't matter when the sky fell and they were shorthanded.

He wondered about the nightmares she must live with, nightmares she never talked about. It had to have affected her. No escaping it.

He wished he could break down her walls and get her to just spill it. But that hadn't worked before, and he doubted she had changed that much.

Hell, she'd taken her ex into her house and treated him well. Whatever animosity she must bear toward him, she had swallowed it once again.

He cussed. The coffeepot finished and he stretched to get a cup out of the cupboard.

Well, he promised himself, she wasn't going to come home to a silent house tonight. He'd be here. Whether or not she wanted to talk, she wasn't going to be alone.

He wondered if that would even help.

Black ice. A five-car pileup including a van carrying a family of six. For hours there had been no time to think about anything except treating and stabilizing.

Some were flown out as soon as they were stabilized. Others could continue their treatment right there. Bri didn't see the dead, but there were dead, one of them a small child who had been hit by flying debris, unprotected by her child safety seat.

When they let her go, she was wound tight as a drum. Fifteen peoples' lives had been changed inalterably by a slick road. It didn't make sense. It never made sense. Sometimes she wondered if *anything* made sense.

Or if it even mattered.

By the time she arrived home, she felt as if every muscle in her body had tensed. It would take time to ramp down, time for exhaustion to hit her. Then she'd fall asleep and have dreams, ugly dreams that always seemed to pursue her after something like this. Somehow she never got used to it.

Pulling into her driveway, she saw that the kitchen light was on. So Luke was up. She pressed her forehead to her steering wheel, wondering if she could handle that, too.

Part of her wished he'd never shown up. Part of her wished she'd never uncovered her own lacks to realize she had been a major problem in the marriage. Part of her wished he'd never held her and kissed her, reminding her indelibly that some things apparently never died.

But part of her was also glad she would not be walking into an empty house. Part of her was glad that it was Luke waiting for her. He'd never said much, had just been a solid, steady presence after events like these, comforting just by being there. Maybe that hadn't gone away, either.

Sighing again, she climbed out of her car and headed for the mudroom that was just off the kitchen. Because she hadn't been paying much attention to the steps and small porch, she clung tightly to the railing. Evidently Jack had cleared the worst of that heavy snowfall, but the world had been slowly thawing and she should have salted this area.

But she hadn't. She'd let a lot of things slide, she

thought. Mainly because of Luke. The fascination remained.

Shaking her head a little, she let herself in. Some snow had clung to her boots, and she stomped it off on the mat. Then she doffed boots and jacket and headed into the kitchen.

Luke was sitting there in his chair, and the smell of freshly brewed coffee filled the air.

"Welcome back," he said.

"Thanks." The coffee probably wouldn't help her unwind one bit, but she didn't care. It smelled good, and she was hungry suddenly. Searching the fridge, she found a couple slices of cheesecake. She pulled them out and slid them onto plates, one for her and one for Luke. Then she got her coffee and two forks and joined him at the table.

"Thank you," he said when she passed him a fork.

"Welcome."

"Bad?"

"As bad as it gets."

He sat silently for a few minutes, and she ate a few mouthfuls of the cheesecake. Slightly tangy, but creamy enough to settle a stomach that right now felt it might never settle again.

"I can't imagine," he said finally. "I can't imagine the things you've seen, the awful things you've dealt with, or how it must affect you."

Slowly she looked up. The grace of adrenaline numbness was beginning to wear off. "It's awful," she agreed. "But I'm not the only one. Lots of medical people have to deal with this."

"I know, but I'm talking about you. I see the aftereffects, or at least I did when I was around, but that's all I know. That you run on adrenaline and then it hits you. You think I don't see it, but I do. Some nights when I was lying beside you, you had nightmares. I never woke you from them, but you'd mumble in your sleep and I'd know where you were. Fighting death. Fighting to save shattered bodies. I got it, Bri, even though I don't actually know what it's like."

"Nobody should have to know what it's like," she said quietly. Adrenaline was turning into grim steel, not that that would help for long.

"You're amazing."

"I tried to run from it."

"No, you did it for as long as you could stand it. Not everybody is cut out for an entire lifetime of trauma medicine. That's not a failure. That's facing reality."

"Something I don't seem to be very good at."

"Bri." His tone chided her gently, but he said no more.

She went back to sipping coffee and eating. She desperately needed some fuel. "Not everybody made it," she said a minute later. "Some may still not make it."

"Traffic accident?"

"Yeah. The worst of it was, five cars piled into one another on black ice, some coming from the other direction. Bad enough except that they were there for a while before another motorist came upon them and called for help. Have you heard of the golden hour?"

"Vaguely."

"It's the hour after the trauma. The hour when we have the most hope of saving a life. You get much past that and the odds start diminishing. We're not sure how long they were out there. We were battling a time clock we couldn't see."

She wondered why she was telling him this. She'd never talked about this subject before. It was something to be locked away from those who'd never been there. At least to her way of thinking. Why share all that terrible stuff with someone who was innocent of it? Although to judge by the reality programs she had begun to see on TV, emergency rooms had become something of a spectator sport. She always switched to something else. Even the sanitized horror the TV showed was too much for her because she knew what lay behind it. The harsh reality.

Then, for some reason, she kept talking. "We lost a few, including a little girl. Some of the patients kept crashing. Hard to stabilize them at all. Those are the ones we might still lose. Some were transported to a trauma center—in time I hope. We're just a little community hospital. Yeah, we deal with almost everything sooner or later, but wherever possible we transport people who need the best expert care to have any hope. We're just not equipped…" Her voice broke. "Not equipped to deal with this much. Fifteen people were involved."

"My God."

"Yeah," she said dully. "My God. I think we emptied the supply room. All hands on deck. Some are hanging around to keep an eye on the patients. I go back at seven a.m. to help spell them. Everyone needs sleep."

"Are you going to get any?"

"I need to try. I don't want to make a mistake that could kill someone. Or doze off on the job."

She stared blindly at the remains of her cheesecake. She was coming down now, coming down hard.

"Let me just hold you," he said.

Her head lifted wearily. "How's that going to help?"

"We'll see. Come on."

He managed to turn his wheelchair and head out to the bed in the living room. To his amazement he heard her dragging steps behind him. He jacked himself into the bed, turned onto his side and scooted until he'd left plenty of room for her.

"Just lie down, Bri. Try it."

She didn't know why she did it, but she did. She climbed in beside him, still fully clothed, her head pillowed on his good arm. Then his casted arm rested across her waist, encircling her. Telling her he cared.

She needed that caring just then almost as much as she needed to breathe.

Then, quietly, helplessly, tears leaked out from behind her closed eyelids. She kept thinking of the children.

The children. That was the most awful part of all.

Luke felt the tears dampen his sweatshirt and felt a sympathetic pain for her that was so deep his chest ached with it. He'd seen the toll her job sometimes took on her, but never to the degree she showed him tonight.

He cursed his lack of imagination, cursed his unfamiliarity with the kind of trauma she faced. He'd never known how bad it was, would probably never know. He certainly hadn't known how to help her, and holding her like this seemed almost ridiculously useless.

The helpless feeling was all too familiar to him. So much time spent, especially toward the end, wondering what was wrong and how he could fix it. Now here he was again. This time he had some idea of what troubled her, but absolutely no way to fix it. He couldn't erase what she had dealt with tonight, couldn't ease the anguish and terror she had seen. There was no bandage for this one.

God, what was he thinking? Getting involved again with the one woman on earth he had loved beyond all reason only to discover there was no way possible to make her happy?

Although, she had talked to him tonight, however minimally. She'd expressed her anguish, a little bit, and told him something about how it all affected her. That was a step forward, he supposed. But still, as she had said more than once, they couldn't recover what they had once had. Together they had managed to trash it all beyond hope.

But moving forward? Even if they could, was he willing to take the risk again? No easy answers came to him. The only thing he was sure of was that a repeat of their marriage was totally off the table.

But being this close to her, smelling her familiar scents, tinged with the hospital, felt so good. Having her close always aroused him, and tonight was no different. He'd never responded sexually to a woman the way he responded to this one. That much was inescapable.

He could have turned her right then and found some awkward way to make love to her. Not even his injuries could impede him, he was sure. The world would spin away for both of them as it always had, and they'd climb to the pinnacle together, sweaty, aching, needing, until they found heaven in each other's arms.

He was so tempted. His entire body flexed as if he were about to do it. He squeezed his eyes shut and battered down the hunger. Bad time. Big risk.

It could only end wrongly. So he controlled himself and waited for the urges to pass. They seemed to want to linger, but he ignored them as best he could.

No future in it, he told himself. None whatsoever.

The realization increased the sorrow that had never departed since their breakup. She'd left a hole in his life that he sometimes thought would never be filled.

Man up, he told himself, *deal with it.*

But in the night, that seemed like an awfully tall order.

Bri's cell phone chirped at 6:15 a.m. She nearly groaned. Sleep had felt so good and she didn't want to give it up, but duty called.

As she started to slip out of the bed, she felt Luke's arm tighten around her waist.

"I have to go, Luke."

"I know. Sorry."

She knew exactly what he meant. In her drowsy state, with her barriers down, she wanted to turn to him and take advantage of the moment. To make love with him again. God, it sounded like heaven.

But instead she eased out of the bed. "Will you be okay?"

"I'm fine. I can get coffee and cereal all on my own now."

"Watch it with those crutches."

"I will."

She hurried toward her bathroom, grabbing some clothes on the way, and hit the shower, making it fast. People were depending on her to show up, and every one of them was as exhausted as she felt, some even more so.

When she emerged dressed, her hair towel-dried and clasped to the back of her head, she smelled the coffee. Luke sat at the table in his wheelchair, eating cereal. She grabbed some coffee in a travel mug.

"You need to eat," he said.

"No time. I'll grab something at the hospital."

"When will you be back?"

"Maybe four hours. I can't say for sure, but I don't have a full shift today. I doubt many do. We'll probably be part-timing it until we're all caught up."

"Take it easy."

She waved, then grabbed her parka and boots. Time to go. As she drove down the street, she wondered if that was Jack she glimpsed in the rearview mirror. Then she shrugged it off and turned toward the hospital. The load would still be heavy this morning. Patients coming out of surgery, others clinging by a thread. No time or energy to waste on anything else.

But it sure would have been nice to snuggle in with Luke.

Bad thought, she scolded herself. No good lay that way, a lesson she had learned painfully. She needed to get her head screwed on straight before she made a huge mistake.

Jack had seen. He'd known about the accident last night, and he had worried about Bri, so he'd hung around until she got home safely. Then he'd seen her lie in bed with Luke.

A furious hammering had begun in his temple and remained. He knew they hadn't done anything, but still. It was a bad sign that she was turning to him for comfort, even the small comfort of a hug.

He wanted her to turn to him. He'd been patient for so long now he sometimes thought he couldn't be patient any longer.

But Bri was special. He didn't want to do anything too soon, didn't want to make her uncomfortable. He had to find just the right moment.

But since Luke's return, that moment seemed to be slipping away. The guy was no threat, not physically, but given where he was living now, taking action against him was out of the question.

Which left Jack only one surety. If she turned back to Luke, he would not let Luke have her. She was Jack's, and he'd do whatever was necessary to keep her.

Even if it meant no one could have her at all.

That particular line of thought always disturbed him. He didn't want to hurt Bri. He didn't want to kill her. But he sure wasn't going to let anyone else have her.

There had to be another way. There *had* to be. He just had to find it. But lately, everything seemed to be getting messed up. Royally messed up.

Damn, he wished Luke had never come to town. Then his original plan to steadily get closer to Bri and gain both her interest and trust would have worked.

Instead everything was speeding up. And he was beginning to feel he was losing control of it all.

Chapter 10

Luke came home from rehab feeling pretty much like a wrung-out rag. They'd worked him hard; not just his knee, arm and feet, but all of him to counterbalance his inactivity.

It appalled him to be so easily tired, but there wasn't a thing he could do about it. It was what it was. One of the hardest things to accept in life, that you couldn't just wave a wand and make it all better.

Shortly after Tim and Ted deposited him at home, Jack appeared. Luke was beginning to loath the sight of that scrawny young man, and more, he was beginning to think the guy looked shifty. He forced down his feelings, reminding himself they might be unjustified.

The late-afternoon sun was golden, but the snow was a long way from disappearing. Luke wheeled himself to the door and managed to open it.

"Hi," Jack said. "You still want that ramp?"

Luke managed a smile. "Absolutely. I'm starting to feel like a caged tiger."

Jack's responding smile was weak. "I guess so. I brought all the stuff, so I'll just get started on it."

"Mind if I watch?"

Jack seemed to hesitate. "Why?"

"Because I'm going to sit there wishing I were helping. Self-torture."

At that, Jack actually laughed, although it sounded uncertain. "You do a lot of carpentry?"

"Usually on big projects, but I like to get my nail gun in on the action from time to time. So if you don't mind?"

Jack hesitated, then shrugged. "Why would I mind?"

"I'll be out as soon as I get my jacket."

"Okay. I'm going to unload my truck."

Luke sat watching him for a few moments before wheeling around to grab his jacket. There was something off about that guy, but he just couldn't put his finger on it.

Maybe it was just jealousy, Luke thought as he crammed his arms into the sleeves of his jacket. Maybe Luke was just jealous that Bri seemed to like Jack, even if it wasn't in *that* way. How stupid could he get?

Plenty, he decided. The last few nights Bri had slept in her own bed and he'd lain awake for hours, wishing she were beside him. Wasted time, wasted sleep, but he might as well face it. If it weren't for the job he was fighting to keep, he'd have been smart to get on the next bus or plane out of here.

Because trouble was brewing. He could feel it all the way to his soul. Whether the trouble was within

him or external he could no longer tell. All he knew
was that his instincts were gearing up, sensing impending dangers. Maybe it was a result of his concussion,
though. How would he know?

Other than the fact that someone had tried to kill
him, he was actually feeling pretty safe, physically.
Here in town was a whole different situation from
standing up on that isolated crag looking down a val-
ley toward a dot that had been Mike.

Maybe he'd just had a run-in with some crazed her-
mit who didn't want anyone on his mountain.

So why this sense of impending doom?

He wheeled out onto the porch at last, picking the
side away from the plywood and two-by-fours that Jack
was laying out on the other side.

"Good materials," he remarked.

"Only the best for Bri."

At that Luke's hackles rose, but he ignored it. Whatever it was about this guy, he seemed determined to
please Bri. That was the beginning and end of it, right?

The world still bore a heavy blanket of white, although the drifts that had looked chunky after they'd
been shoveled off of roofs had melted into softer
mounds.

"This snowstorm was unusual, I take it?" he said,
trying to make conversation with Jack.

"We should be enjoying spring about now," came
the answer. No elucidation. Not a very talkative guy.

So Luke joined the conspiracy of silence Jack evidently wanted. It was not too maddening to just sit and
watch. Better than being inside trying to amuse himself with a book or TV.

Jack was very businesslike as he measured the

length of the ramp and its angle. Equally businesslike as he measured the wood and marked it with a carpenter's pencil. The guy knew what he was doing.

Finally Luke broke the silence. "You do a lot of carpentry?"

"Here and there." Short response.

"You're good. I could use someone like you at the job site when we start construction."

Jack paused, pencil behind his ear, two-by-four under his arm. "Yeah. I do pretty good at the hardware store and picking up odd jobs. Hate to lose something steady for something temporary."

"That's a point. Thing is, we often need carpenters year-round. You'd be amazed how much damage guests can do. Not to mention the cold and other stuff. Regardless, we pay union wages. Think about it. We can talk details if you're interested."

Then Luke sat there wondering what the hell he was thinking. The guy was indeed a capable carpenter, at least at this level. But offering him a job? Was that a reaction to feeling guilty for his instant dislike for no real reason? A sop to a conscience riddled with guilt?

Well, at least it was a change of pace for his confused head. Between Bri and the concussion, he wouldn't have bet money on the soundness of his mental functioning. That woman was driving him crazy.

He itched to help Jack carry the table saw up to the porch, but the man didn't seem to have a bit of trouble with it. Thin though he appeared, there was surprising strength in that gangly body.

"You own all your own tools?" he asked as he watched Jack hunt for the electrical outlet outside.

"Nah. Shop lends them to me. I'm good for business."

"I bet you are."

Again silence fell until the saw began its keening, followed by raspier sounds, and the two-by-fours slid through the blade.

Then came the explosive sound of the nail gun as Jack began to put the frame together for the ramp. Much as Luke didn't want to think nice things about Jack, the fact remained: the guy knew what he was doing.

"Coffee?" Luke asked.

"Sure. Black."

So Luke angled his way back into the house and started another pot. That much hadn't changed. He and Bri had always had a pot of coffee at hand, like two addicts. When it finished, he called Jack to the door.

"Sorry, I can't carry the mugs myself. This chair needs a table."

Jack mounted the steps between the frame he'd finished building. "I could make you a table for that."

"I may take you up on it. Of course, inside I'm still using the hospital table, so I guess it's not really necessary unless I want to carry something like this."

He followed Jack into the kitchen and insisted on getting the coffee himself.

"You and Bri were married," Jack said.

The statement came sideways at Luke. He simply hadn't expected it. "Long ago," he said carefully.

"Must've hurt, losing her."

Luke didn't answer. He didn't care how much Bri liked this guy, it wasn't his place—or even his desire—to share personal information with Jack.

Jack carried both mugs outside, handed one to Luke, then got back to work on the ramp without another word. He finished it in quick order, even placing slats to slow the wheelchair down on descent.

"There you go," Jack said when he finished. "Wanna try it?"

"I think Bri would kill me if I tried it when she wasn't here. It looks great, though." He stuffed his hand into his pocket and pulled out his wallet so he could pay Jack. Jack took the money without counting it and shoved it into his jeans pocket.

"I'm not painting it because it won't be here for long. It'll hold long enough."

"I'm sure it will. You did a good job."

One corner of Jack's mouth lifted. "You better get back inside now."

Luke tensed. "Why?"

"Because I'm going to knock down some icicles. Wouldn't want somebody to get hurt."

Luke looked along the eaves and saw that he was right. Any number of icicles that had grown through the thaw-freeze cycle since the snowstorm looked as if they could kill a grown man.

Again the frustration overcame him. He ought to be able to do that. God, he hated this enforced helpless-ness. "Thanks," he said at last, and turned to do as he was told. Jack put both empty coffee mugs in his lap.

He put them in the kitchen by the sink, then went to the front window to watch Jack knock down the icicles. It was a dangerous job, and Jack kept his distance by using a two-by-four. Still, the sight of those icy teeth hitting the snow, or shattering against the porch rail-ing, made the danger clear.

He hated to admit that it had been good of Jack to think of that. It hadn't even crossed his own mind. Which brought him back to wondering if his head was back to 100 percent or not.

He was inclined to think not.

Spring twilight and the mountain of snow didn't seem to go together very well, Bri thought as she drove home after her shift. The light was all wrong for a world that seemed to scream winter despite the late hour of the day. Weird. Her brain seemed to be noticing the conflicting cues and trying to organize them somehow.

Or maybe she was just tired. Twelve-hour shifts had a way of doing that, and they still had a number of accident victims who, while improving, needed a lot of care.

Her knee, which rarely gave her trouble on an ordinary day, was hammering at her tonight. Her back ached, too, something she wasn't used to. She must have been walking funny because of her knee.

Pulling into the driveway, she saw that Jack had built the ramp. It looked odd, all that fresh wood in front of a house badly in need of paint, but she was glad to see it. Once the thaw quit icing over the sidewalks, Luke could get out and get around.

Then she noticed that all the icicles were gone as well. Jack must have read her mind, because she'd been thinking only that morning that they were growing to a dangerous size.

One of these days she ought to cook the man a dinner to express her gratitude for the numerous ways he looked after her. But as soon as she had the thought, a chill seemed to creep through her. Jack was her handy-man. She didn't want him to think he'd become per-sonally important to her.

Then she realized she wouldn't have given it a sec-ond thought if only Luke hadn't mentioned that he thought Jack was sweet on her.

Dang. Really? Was she going to let Luke warp her? But wasn't he already warping her? He'd shown her that she had a major hang-up. Okay, that was justified. But passing judgment on the people she knew?

Worse, she was thinking about Luke a million times a day now. He'd almost vanished from her thoughts until he had show up at her door, but now he was firmly camped in her head again.

Maybe he'd even reclaimed a small bit of her heart.

God, no! One epic disaster had been enough. She'd have to be a fool to set herself up for another.

She walked around to the back door to enter by the mudroom. She saw that Jack had been busy here, too. The icicles were gone, the steps and small porch care-fully salted.

The oddest feeling came over her. She should be thinking how nice Jack was, how kind of him to do all this, but instead she felt a chill run along her spine. He hadn't done this much before Luke's arrival. He'd been friendly and glad to take any kind of job she had, but he hadn't gone over the top like this.

This felt almost...smothering. Claiming. As if he were treating her property as his. She didn't like it, kindness or not. It felt like encroachment.

Unless Luke had paid him to do all of this?

The uncomfortable feeling remained, however, fol-lowing her inside as she ditched her outerwear. In the kitchen she grabbed the inevitable cup of coffee and an ice pack for her knee before she headed for the living room to see how Luke was doing.

He appeared to be fine, tapping busily away at his laptop from his wheelchair. His face, while still purple and black from bruising, had nearly returned to its normal dimensions. His knee bent normally now, too. "Hi," she said.

"Hi. Give me a sec."

She was willing to do that. Without giving it a second thought, she stripped off her jeans, bent over a few times as she tried to ease the stiffness in her back, then sat on the askew couch to unwrap her knee and replace the neoprene knee wrap with the ice pack. The ripping sound of opening Velcro must have caught Luke's attention.

"Bad?" he asked.

She looked up. "A bit. I didn't get a break today. My back's stiffening up, as well."

"After you get done with the icing, I'll see how much of a massage I can give you. Probably not a very good one."

She had to laugh. "Not from a wheelchair."

"I could teeter on my crutches."

"You'll be hanging on too hard to the crutches to rub."

"Objections, objections. Think positively."

"I will. And a couple of ibuprofen will help a whole lot with that positive thinking."

"Funny, I have a bottle of that right at hand. Wonder why."

She laughed again. "I'll get some in just a minute."

"Can you take it with coffee?"

"In moments of desperation, I can take it dry."

Luke pushed his table to one side, grabbing the pill bottle on it, and wheeled her way. "If you want water, I discovered today that I can manage that, too."

She smiled. "Soon you won't need me anymore."

She might as well have dropped a stink bomb in the room. He froze. She froze. The urge to say she hadn't meant it that way seemed to glue her tongue to the roof of her mouth, because she wasn't sure it was true.

"I'll be glad when I no longer need you as a nurse," he said, finally breaking the awkwardness. He passed her the bottle and rolled his chair back a few paces.

All of a sudden she grew acutely aware that she was sitting there in her panties and a fleece shirt. Too much skin lay exposed, and she knew he was tracing her legs with his eyes.

Well, she had put them on display. Desperate to change the atmosphere, which seemed to be growing heavier and even a little musky, she asked, "Did you ask Jack to take down the icicles? At least I assume it was Jack."

"His idea. He finished the ramp for me, then got right to it. Why?"

Her reaction was probably all messed up. Jack was just trying to be nice. She was imagining that he had encroached a little too far. Just being neighborly.

"Bri? You're doing that thing again. Looking disturbed but not saying why."

She realized he was right. She had this crazy, uneasy feeling and she was already dismissing it as invalid. But it sounded so nuts she didn't want to say it out loud.

"It's crazy," she said finally.

"Try it out on me," he suggested. Rolling closer, he

took her hand. "Let someone else decide if it's crazy. Just try it."

She hesitated. He'd been right about her and all the feelings she had dismissed over the years, feelings she probably should have at least expressed so they could be dealt with instead of becoming a restless graveyard of fears and resentments.

"Okay," she said at last. "I was hoping you'd asked Jack to take care of the icicles."

"I never even thought of it, which I guess makes me a fool."

She shook her head. "That's not the point. It suddenly struck me as I was coming in that he'd gone way past the point of doing a task he was hired to do. Yeah, he could just have been being neighborly. I get it."

"But you didn't feel that way?"

"No. Actually I felt as if…as if he was encroaching. Trying to make a claim, as if this house were his. That's stupid."

"Is it?"

"Probably."

"Well, has he always done things like this?"

"No. Usually he does just what I hire him to do."

She stole a look at him and was relieved to see his expression didn't seem to indicate that he thought she was nuts. Far from it. He looked soberly at her.

Finally he spoke. "Keeping in mind that I recently had a concussion, frankly I think your feeling is right. It started since I got here, right?"

"The extras? Yes."

"He was asking about our marriage."

Bri caught her breath. "That's none of his business!"

"All of this could be passed off as just being friendly."

"I know."

"But I'm with you anyway. That young man is pushing boundaries with you."

"But why?"

"Because he wants you to like him and depend on him. I'm here, I'm your ex, and maybe he's just trying to show you how useless I am. Especially now."

"You've never been useless!"

"Not until I took that fall. Regardless, I can't do any of this stuff for you, so he's making himself look good. Like not wanting to be paid for clearing your roof. I told you, he's sweet on you."

Bri looked down at her knee. Almost time to remove the ice pack. This time she couldn't dismiss what Luke was saying. Jack *had* been popping up an awful lot lately, offering to do things for free, going out of his way to take care of things that she hadn't even mentioned.

She really didn't want him to be sweet on her, as Luke put it. She liked Jack, but she didn't feel anything more for him, and after all this time, surely she should have felt some spark of attraction if that were going to happen.

"Oh, God," she said finally. Another mess confronted her and she didn't know what in the world to do about it.

"Talk to me."

She glanced at him. "I don't want that."

"Okay." He waited patiently.

She struggled to voice more, knowing that he was trying to get her to talk about things, a lesson she seriously needed to learn. She stumbled around, trying to give expression to her feelings.

"It's not like I led him on or anything," she said eventually.

"That's not always necessary. All that's necessary is for him to want you. I think he's trying to woo you, and he's pushing harder because I'm around."

"But we're divorced! The whole town seems to know that. Why would your being here cause him to do more?"

"Because you invited me in. You didn't have to do that. Ergo, you might be reconsidering."

"God," she said again, appalled and feeling bad all at once. "I don't want to hurt him. He's always been so nice. But friendship is as far as I'll go. Heck, I've never so much as baked something for him. I pay for his work. Business relationship."

"That's how *you* feel. His world is a different one."

She sat glumly, contemplating that. She valued Jack, but as a wonderful handyman who always did a good job and never let her down. Once again she started questioning herself. Had she made mistakes? Sent the wrong signals without realizing it?

Anything was possible, she supposed. He might have taken her being nice in an entirely different way than she intended. Especially considering that she had sometimes been effusive in her praise.

"Do I send out a lot of wrong signals?" she finally asked Luke. "You said you were confused when we were married."

"I think you were sending the right signals, you just didn't explain them, then you blew them off. That's different from encouraging a guy when you don't mean it. It's possible he's reading more into how you treat him than you mean by it. But that's on him, not you."

Well, there she went again, feeling as though everything inside her had been thrown in a blender. She hated to think she might be hurting Jack. She hated to think that he was seeing Luke as a threat. Although if she were to be perfectly honest with herself...

She stopped. Honest with herself? Did she even know herself well enough to be truly honest even inside her own head? Dismissing her feelings, especially unpleasant feelings, had helped ruin her marriage. Maybe it was time to spew some bile.

"Do you have another ice pack?"

"I have a ton of the instant ones from the hospital for you." She looked at him and couldn't help remarking, "Your face looks so much better."

"Just a little mottling from the bruises. It sure feels better. Bri, are you evading?"

She was, she realized. Easier to talk about his face than about the things that had once made her angry or disappointed, than to talk about the messiness inside her now.

He didn't press her, but she could feel him waiting. It was as if he wanted some dam to break inside her so he could really understand. Well, if she got to that understanding herself, she might just do it. How much of her life had she wasted and ruined by doubting her every unpleasant thought and feeling?

She looked at Luke again. He sat in his wheelchair like a wounded warrior, but his expression was one of utter patience. And maybe a little sorrow, as if he were contemplating all they had lost for lack of communication.

"It's not easy for me!" The words burst out of her.

"I know. It's not easy for most of us to be vulnerable, but for you, harder than most thanks to the way you were raised. If you say something not nice, you expect a bad reaction. You weren't allowed to have those kinds of feelings. But truthfully, Bri, I'm not afraid of those feelings. They're as important to me as they are to you."

"Well, I already blew everything up. I suppose I could hardly make it worse."

He smiled. "You might even make it better for both of us. God knows, I think confusion led to the mess more than anything. Except Barbara and her machinations. I really did *not* have an affair with her, you know."

"I think that's where we started this conversation."

"Seems like."

She hesitated. "I believe you."

The look of relief on his face made her heart feel as if it were cracking. After all this time she apparently still cared deeply about him. Maybe not the way she had before when they were married, but she still gave a damn.

"I'll get you another ice pack while you think."

She watched him wheel out of the room, then laid her head back, ignoring the ache in her knee. The past and the present seemed to somehow be melding in her mind, along with the addition of a problem named Jack.

Feelings she had thought long behind her surged and reminded her of all her dissatisfaction from their marriage, most of which were really only a few things.

Then there were the feelings he was eliciting in her now. She wanted him. That had never died, but she was also rediscovering the absolutely stellar man he had always been. Whatever she had blamed him for had come from within her, not from his failings.

That made it all the harder to think about. The admissions she needed to make would not be easy. They'd be embarrassing, and they probably weren't even fair. But here she went again, trying to dismiss them.

As for Jack… She could put that on the back burner right now. He might be trying to woo her in some crazy way, but she couldn't address it unless he said something. That would be a huge step out of line, would probably be hurtful, and she and Luke could both be wrong about his feelings.

Luke returned with another ice pack but she didn't crack it. "Ten more minutes," she said as she laid it by her side.

"Coffee? I can carry one mug at a time."

She glanced at the cup she had put on the small end table. "I still have some."

"Probably cold by now. Give me a thermal mug any day."

So he was off again, and it occurred to her that after all the care she had had to give him initially, it probably felt good for him to be able to do for her. She could understand that.

And once again her mind turned backward to the past, to the morass of feelings she had never sorted through. She had voiced one of them when she had said they'd had more of an affair than a marriage, but what did she really mean by that?

Luke ferried to the kitchen again to get himself some more coffee, but then he came back. Once again he took her hand as if to give her silent support. When he'd been around, he'd been as supportive as she would let him be. She knew that. So what the hell had been wrong with her?

He was still waiting. She could feel it. He might need the answers to what had happened even more than she did. For all she'd dismissed her own feelings, she at least had some idea what she was ignoring. He had none.

"I still want you," she blurted.

"Oh, darlin', you have no idea how much I missed you saying that."

Darlin'. How much she had missed hearing that endearment from him. His voice always changed when he said it, growing deeper, drawling slightly. He squeezed her hand.

"But it was a mess, Luke. From my point of view, it just kept getting messed up."

"How so?"

Well, that was the crux, wasn't it? "I missed you when you were gone, but you knew that. What I didn't tell you was that it was getting harder, not easier. I felt alone too much, and lonely."

He nodded, offering no commentary.

"I started to resent you going away." God, that sounded ugly. She had married him knowing how it would be. It wasn't as if he'd started traveling later. He'd been doing the same while they dated.

She was grateful that he didn't bring that up. It would have killed her to hear, "Well, you knew that at the outset."

Instead he said, "You can't really know what something is like until you've lived it for a while. It was hard. It was hard on me, too."

"Really?" She looked almost hopefully at him. "I wasn't just being unreasonable?"

"Every time I left it got harder."

"But it was your job! You couldn't just quit."

"If I'd known you were feeling the same, I might have looked for another line of work, one that didn't take me away so often or for so long. I guess I screwed up. I never told you that I'd begun to think of changing."

"And I never told you I was needing a change," she admitted.

"Was that so hard?"

"Not now. Not with nothing riding on it."

She watched his face darken, and felt the panic begin. She'd said the wrong thing again. She should just keep her mouth shut. But he surprised her.

"I get it. The real shame is that nothing I ever felt about you was riding on the fact that you wanted me around more. Nothing would have ever changed if you'd told me you were resenting my absences. God knows, I was."

"Maybe I should have traveled with you like you suggested."

He shook his head. "More resentment. You'd have given up the job you love. I'm not in love with mine. I enjoy it, but I could enjoy other things just as much. But that's not all of it, is it?"

She shook her head, reached for the ice pack and cracked it, squeezing it between her hands. She leaned forward and placed it on her knee. "I think that's enough for one night. I need a break. It's been a long day, and trying to figure out my head is taxing. Some of it I have to reach back a long time for. How do I know I'm remembering correctly?"

"Maybe we should just move forward with a new policy of honesty."

Her heart quickened. He was talking as though there might be some kind of future for them here. But that was impossible. All that hurt they'd felt at the end of their marriage couldn't just be erased, or overcome in a single leap. It would always be there, like a scar. What if they fell into old habits and wound up in the same place? She had heard that was the hardest part of a second marriage: reacting to the first one even when it was a different person. How much harder would that be when it was the same person?

Yet a little seed of hope persisted deep inside her heart. She had once loved this man, heart and soul, and the idea that they might be able to salvage something was almost irresistible.

But for that, he was right. They needed real honesty. Even if all they did was move on separately, both of them needed to deal with what had happened and why.

She sighed.

"How's the knee?" he asked.

"Better. I can probably stop icing it after this."

"Good." He pushed his chair closer and astonished her by running his hand down her bare leg. A shiver pulsed through her, and sweet passion arose in an instant.

"Aren't you cold?" he asked. "Want a blanket?"

"I'm fine." Because she was. His touch had ignited an internal fire that made any chilliness go away.

He stroked her leg again. "If I weren't laid up, and your knee weren't hurting, I'd…"

Her mouth turned dry. Her heart climbed into her throat, not with fear but with hope. "Honesty," she croaked.

"You promise it in return?"

"Absolutely."

"I'd pick you up and carry you to the nearest bed and make love to you until we were both too exhausted to move."

"And I'd let you," she said, even though it was hard to admit how utterly vulnerable she was at the moment. Then a giggle escaped her.

"What's so funny?"

"Look at us. You in three casts, me with ice on my knee. It's ridiculous."

A smile dawned slowly on his face and he gave a lazy shake of his head. "It would call for some creativity."

Her breath stuck in her throat. Her mind scrambled around trying to imagine how they could deal with their impediments.

"I think I saw a chair in the kitchen," he said huskily. "One without arms. You could sit on my lap."

"I don't want to hurt you." It was a weak but honest protest.

"I don't think you could. You're light as a feather. If your knee didn't hurt, I'd ask you for a complete bed bath. Think of the fun that would be."

A smile began to crack the astonishment she was sure must cover her face. "It would certainly be a first. You'd be at my mercy."

"So I would. You could really drive me crazy."

"You're very inventive."

"Needs must, as the saying goes. You have no idea

how hard it was to let you bathe me, then make you stop at my hips. I wanted you to go all the way."

"I thought about it," she admitted. "Briefly. It was so unprofessional of me I cut it off."

"Hey, I wasn't your usual patient. You're allowed to have lascivious thoughts with me."

She'd always had lascivious thoughts with him. That had never been the problem. Unfortunately, she was tired, and it seemed too much effort to explore anything intense right now. "I need to make us dinner."

"Another evasion." But he was smiling. "Hate to tell you, but someone named Di dropped by this afternoon with a ton of food she put in the refrigerator. We had a nice chat, but the main purpose was she felt you might need a break from cooking under the circumstances. I'm not sure which circumstances she meant."

"Di's my best friend." Bri suspected she wanted a chance to see Luke, too. "How many blanks did she try to fill in?"

"Very few. She's either a very sensitive friend or you've talked about me a lot. Not one intrusive question beyond how I was doing and why would anyone shove me off a cliff. So everyone in town must know I was pushed."

She nodded. "You came into the E.R. bellowing about it. The cops came. In this town, there's almost always someone who will talk."

"What about patient privacy?"

"I'm not sure that extends to the claim that someone tried to kill you. Besides, how many people might have heard you beyond the medical staff?"

She pulled off the icepack and reached for the neoprene wrap, which she expertly placed. "All set. I'll go see what Di brought us to eat."

And she'd also get a pair of sweatpants out, because she could still feel Luke's hand running along her leg, like a brand.

But sex wasn't enough. It simply wasn't enough, as they'd proved.

He was right. She needed to talk, however silly or ungrateful or ugly it made her sound. The air needed clearing.

But it wasn't going to be easy. Not at all.

Chapter 11

Despite a relatively active day, Luke had trouble sleeping. Dinner conversation had been desultory. Either Bri hadn't been kidding that she was too tired, or she'd gone back to hiding. He'd have given even odds for either possibility.

He stared into the dark, trying not to think about how Bri was only two rooms away. Trying not to think about how much he wanted her. Maybe he'd been a fool, but he hadn't expected the rebirth of their attraction when he'd first sought her out. Yeah, he'd been living with a lot of messed-up feelings because he never really understood how everything had fallen apart, and he'd sure been furious that she believed he had cheated on her, but he hadn't realized that nothing had died.

Not the pain, not the desire, not the caring. Maybe the love was gone, but the rest of it remained like a ghost from the past popping up at unexpected moments, grabbing him in a vise that hurt.

What was a guy to do? Leave town? He couldn't. Even if he hadn't been laid up this way, he had a job he was fighting for. Move back to the motel? He couldn't do it right now, and despite his independent streak, he had to admit it. Crossing that state highway, whether on crutches or a wheelchair, would be an exercise in suicide. He couldn't look after some of his most basic needs, either, like cleaning himself. He supposed he could hire someone, but what kind of care would he get? In that motel. With that creepy bathroom. He needed someone with Bri's expertise, and he just had to face it.

Maybe it was time to let her know how much he needed her, at least right now. Then a thought pierced him. Had he ever made her feel needed? His inclination toward independence might not have been a strength in their marriage. She had to know he wanted her, but had she ever felt that he needed her?

The night seemed to stare back at him like a living thing, full of hints of mistakes made, errors committed, and perhaps worst of all a string of omissions.

It was too easy, he supposed, to presume that when you said "I love you," all the rest was obvious. Maybe it hadn't been obvious at all. As it was, he'd been gone so much he couldn't blame her if she had wondered just how much she really mattered to him.

Nor was the excuse that they both had jobs satisfying him right now. Yeah, they had jobs. Yeah, both of them had insisted on keeping their careers. But that left a whole lot of blanks that had never been filled in.

All well and good to blame her for never telling him

what was wrong, but he should have recognized some of it all on his own. The lacks, for example. A dozen roses didn't make up for six months away, followed by another departure in two weeks. It didn't make up for never being there to deal with all the stuff that made up day-to-day living, good or bad. Or all the things they'd never discussed, like the future, or a family, or eventually settling down to a less mobile life.

Hell, he wished he could climb out of bed right now and go wake her, just to talk to her. To tell her how sorry he was. He had personified the absentee husband to perfection. Even when he'd known she was unhappy, he hadn't questioned her. He'd waited. Always waited to see what she would say. But she never spoke, and the tough moments passed like a quick summer thunderstorm.

He supposed that put him up for an award as a fool. He'd been too quick to assume that if it passed, it had nothing to do with him, or it was unimportant. The test of time had proved him wrong. Very wrong.

He opened his computer and glanced at the time. Bri had turned in at nine, but it still wasn't quite three in the morning yet, and even so he didn't want to disturb her sleep. She *had* seemed tired. He wondered how many times he'd failed to notice how much a twelve-hour shift took out of her. Or how many times he hadn't been there to see. More often than not when he was home, she took vacation time.

Now he was seeing the way it really was for her. Her dedication impressed him. Something else he'd never told her before.

He sighed, facing his own failures. There were a lot he'd never told her, he supposed. A lot he'd never seen or understood. They'd been moving in separate worlds most of the time, intersecting only briefly, filling their time together with lovemaking and romantic little stuff, as though they were still dating. Except they'd gone past dating, and at some point their relationship had needed space to grow. They'd denied it that space, for what seemed like good reasons. Hardly surprising it had died like an undernourished plant.

He heard the wind keen. Unable to stand lying in the bed any longer, he levered himself into the wheelchair and over to the front window. God, it looked like another blizzard.

He turned to the TV, which he'd only switched on a few times to watch the news, and hunted for the weather station Bri had turned on the night of the big snow.

"Holy crap," he said moments later.

"What?"

He twisted, astonished to see Bri just inside the living room. Even in the flickering light of the TV, she looked adorable in a flannel nightgown and fuzzy slippers. "More blizzard. I'm sorry, did I wake you?"

"I heard voices and I wondered if you needed help."

"I'm fine, but take a look at this."

She came to stand beside him, while a weather forecaster made this mess sound like the best and most exciting news he'd had in a while.

Bri spoke. "I'd like that guy better if he didn't sound as if this was making him happy."

"I hear you."

She dropped into her office chair and walked it over to his side. "This is awful. Tomorrow's going to be a bad day at the hospital."

"Maybe folks will get a clue and stay home."

"You'd think."

"Aren't you supposed to have tomorrow off?"

"Not if we get some real trouble."

He knew that, and wondered why he was making empty conversation. Because he didn't want her to go back to bed?

"You should get some sleep, then."

"I'm wide-awake. So are you, apparently."

"Should I make coffee or warm milk?"

She shook her head and rose. "Coffee for me. And I'm hungry. I guess I didn't eat enough dinner. How about you?"

Twenty minutes later, with warmed-up leftovers and coffee on tray tables in front of them, they watched the storm reports.

"Sleet and freezing rain," she remarked. "Worse than heavy snow, I guess."

"It's sure going to make a mess of the snow that's still there. How fast will your sand trucks get out?"

"They're probably already starting, but this is supposed to go on all day. I don't know if they'll be able to keep up."

"I seem to remember there's a temperature below which salt won't even clear the ice." He pointed to the screen. "Ten below? Some spring."

"We've all been saying that. The trees had finally just started to bud out. I hope this doesn't kill them." She shook her head. "The past couple of years, winters seem to be lasting longer. It's weird. I keep hoping it'll go back to normal." Then she looked his way. "It'll be good for your ski resort, though."

"That depends. You need powder for skiing, not sleet and ice." Then, "I hope you don't get called in."

"Me, too."

It was the only opening he was going to get, so he dove into it. "I want you to know something. I never realized before how hard you work, and how much it takes out of you. I was gone most of the time and had no idea. I'm sorry I didn't know, because I think you're admirable."

He heard her draw a quiet, sharp breath, but then an annoying beeping from the TV interrupted any response she might have made. Across the bottom of the screen the winter storm warnings began to run, an endless list of dangerous conditions, advice not to drive at all, to stay indoors…

"I hope everyone listens," she said presently, then rose to clear away their dishes. When she returned, she freshened their coffee.

The moment had been lost. He had no idea how to reopen the conversation between them. Her mind appeared to be firmly fixed on the weather, and he could almost see her pondering just what kind of catastrophes would face her today.

He wished he could take her off duty, sweep her away from such thoughts and provide her with a much-needed break, but he couldn't think of a way.

All right, maybe she hadn't been the only one with a communications problem in their marriage. Man, he ought to be able to think of something to say, something to turn her attention back to them and all the empty spaces they'd created. Spaces that they needed to fill at least somehow.

But then she astonished him. She turned to look

at him. In the flickering light from the TV screen her eyes appeared wide, almost frightened.

"I may have only a short time," she said. "If people don't heed these warnings when they get up, there's going to be trouble."

So he said the generous thing, even though his instincts wanted him to follow an entirely different direction. "Then you should try to get more sleep."

"I'm not sleepy."

He arched a brow. "What are you?"

"Horny."

The bluntness of her declaration astonished him, but he liked it. "I haven't stopped wanting you since I set eyes on you. But, Bri…"

"I know. Sex won't fix anything. It sure wasn't enough the first time around. But it's what I'm feeling. You told me to be honest."

"I'm loving it," he admitted.

"Then don't complain. We can have at least this much before all hell breaks loose."

"Maybe that won't happen."

"I don't believe that anymore. It always happens, sooner or later." She went to the window and looked out. "Nobody should go out in this. Nobody. Look, the icicles are already coming back. If you don't have livestock, you should stay inside."

"Can't argue with that."

She dropped the curtain and faced him. "But they'll still go out. They'll be afraid of losing jobs. Some folks coming down the highway won't even know this is hitting until they run into it."

He nodded, watching her closely, wondering what was going on and where she was headed with it.

The TV beeped again and he wished it to hell. She leaned over, took the controller from him and switched it off. "I'll find out soon enough."

"Has it occurred to you that you should maybe not even drive to the hospital in this?"

"Oh, yeah. And they may be hoping they don't have to call anyone in. But if they have to save lives, they will. It's the job, Luke. You understand that."

For the first time he considered which of them had the really important job, and he squirmed uncomfortably as he realized that he'd always thought what he was doing was important. Building resorts for the wealthy? It didn't rank anywhere near the importance of the work this woman did.

"I was never fair to you," he announced. "I considered both our jobs important, but I never really thought about how much more important your work is."

To his surprise, even in the nearly dark room, he could see her lips curve faintly upward.

"Bri?"

"You're right. It was one of the things I resented."

He felt punched in the gut. "Really?"

"You bet. Do you remember how you'd fly in and I'd try to take the time off, but sometimes I got called in?"

"Yeah."

"You never seemed to really understand why I had to go. You made me feel small for leaving you."

He swore, with a lot of feeling. "God, I'm sorry."

"And I wondered if I was wrong, if I wasn't caring for you well enough. If I really wasn't as important as I thought."

"No wonder you hated me."

"I never hated you. Never. Well, maybe for a while

after Barbara. But I wondered if I was overemphasizing the importance of my job."

His hands had clenched into fists. "I'm sorry," he said again. "Talk about oblivious and self-important."

"I thought I was the one being self-important."

"Saving lives versus running around the world building resorts? I don't think there's even a contest there."

"Maybe not, but I was uncertain, feeling like maybe I was being a bad wife. Then there were other times when I needed someone and you were halfway around the world. I resented that, too. I'd come home from a day like the other day and there wasn't even anyone to hug me. Or pull off my shoes. Or help me to bed where I could forget."

He drew a deep breath, facing his own failings for the first time. Really facing them.

"I thought I was being a baby about it. It wasn't fair to you, was it? You *had* to travel. But sometimes I felt as if when I needed you most you weren't there. I kept pushing the feeling aside, because it was stupid to feel that way. I'd managed *before* you, so what had changed?"

"Maybe that having a husband meant you had a right to some support from him."

"Maybe. Anyway, the list went on, it seemed to grow with time, and I got to the point where I couldn't even see a future with you because we weren't building one. How's that for a dump?"

"Keep going."

But she flatly refused. "This is meaningless right now."

"Why?"

"Because we still don't have a future. But we have a past, it's getting in the way, and right now I want to pretend it doesn't exist and just lie in your arms with you, naked. Loving. Finding the one thing we ever did right."

With that she put him squarely on the horns of a dilemma. He didn't want to hurt her again, and this had the serious potential to be hurtful. Nor did he want to resurrect the old, bad habits, like tumbling into bed and forgetting everything else in the world. But at the same time he burned for her. He wanted her so much his skin seemed to tingle with electricity, and his groin throbbed painfully.

"Bri..."

"What?" she asked quietly. "You don't want me anymore?"

"I already told you that I do. But what you're suggesting... Damn it, it could mess us up all over again. We were always good in bed. It was the other part of life we kept messing up."

"What difference will it make? You're going to be leaving again soon anyway. And this time you won't be coming back at all."

That felt like a spear to his heart. Such a hopeless vision, but probably true, which made it all the harder to hear.

"We're a mess," he said finally, utterly without other words to capture anything else.

"We always were. We just didn't know it." She sighed and flipped the TV on again, as if closing the subject. The cheery forecaster resumed predicting an icy apocalypse.

A bubble of anger burst in him then. He'd asked her

for honesty, for her feelings. She'd given them to him, however limited, and he was turning her down? Pushing her away? Rejecting her as he apparently had so often without realizing it?

Except this time he realized it. What's more, judging by the way she had turned on the television again, she had once more shut down. Because of him. Because of the way he had responded to the truth she had offered him.

Hell. Was he renewing her childhood experience? Was he protecting her in the wrong way?

He stared at the side of her head and wondered what he was supposed to do. This conundrum approached the point of the impossible. How to deal with it? He suddenly wished he were a psychologist instead of a geologist.

"Bri."

"Forget I said anything."

"No!" His voice thundered and for once he didn't care. She was twisting him into knots again, probably twisting herself into her own set of them, and he wouldn't, couldn't, allow this to continue.

"Don't yell at me."

"I'm going crazy and you're putting me there. I asked you to express yourself. Now all I seem to be doing is messing things up more because I'm trying not to do the wrong thing."

"The wrong thing for who?" She was mad now, too. "I told you what I want. Apparently you don't. So I guess I'm wrong again."

"You're not wrong," he roared. "I am!"

Her head jerked backward. "You?"

"Yes, me. I would love nothing more than to make

love to you right now. If I could, I'd stand up and sweep you off to bed. But you know what I keep seeing?"

"What?"

"All the empty spaces in our marriage. All the silences. All the unspoken words. All the buried feelings. Making love won't cure any of that. God, did it ever strike you that we had some kind of addiction?"

"Addiction?"

He wished there were more light, because right now he thought her lower lip was quivering, but he couldn't be sure. "Addiction," he repeated. "You're a nurse. What do you tell people with a drug problem? Certainly not to take the cure by repeating the mistake."

"Good God," she whispered. "You think we were addicted to sex?"

"I think we were addicted to each other in that particular way, yes. And I'm still an addict. Living with you has been like a trial by fire. That part of our relationship never faded, Bri. The craving is as strong as ever."

"But that doesn't mean it was wrong?"

"It was never wrong." God, could he get any more ham-handed with this? "It was always right. Too much of the rest of it was wrong. Like I said, empty spaces we never filled with things we should have said."

He decided it was time to shut up and listen. If she would talk, that was. She'd shared a surprising bit with him tonight, but it couldn't end there.

"You're confusing me," she said finally. "Addiction or not?"

"Considering the strength of the craving we still feel after all the hurt there was between us, maybe it's an addiction. I don't know. I just know that it's nothing to build on. There'd have to be more. And I'm not sure I want to love you unless I think there's at least a possibility of more. Of a future."

He heard her draw a sharp breath. This was it, the telling moment. He felt as if he sat on pins and needles waiting for what she might say.

Her voice was quiet when she answered. "If there's one thing I've learned, it's that there are no guarantees. If you're saying you want to take a stab at putting us back together…well, I'll consider it. But I can't promise. The old problems are still there. You traveling and me keeping too much to myself."

Silence fell between them. The wind picked up again, a banshee's keen around the house. The weather guy looked as cheerful as a kid on Christmas morning.

The phone rang. Everything inside Luke stiffened. There went the moment. There went the chance. She was being called in, and he'd sit here the rest of the night wondering if he'd handled this all wrong.

She rose and went to get the cordless set that had wound up on the bed table beside his computer. "Hello?"

Moments later, "Okay then. Call if it changes."

She hung up and he waited.

"That was the hospital. They're holding the night shift over because they don't want staff taking risks on the road."

"You weren't going in anyway."

"No, but basically they're cutting back to minimal operations unless all hell breaks loose."

"What's that mean exactly?"

"That a lot of people are going to take turns on the

cots in the break room. They're safer staying there, and the rest of us are safer at home."

She went to the window and pulled the curtain aside again. "I can't believe how fast those icicles are growing. This is bad."

"Not according to the TV guy."

She laughed. "Way too cheerful under the circumstances. More coffee?"

So she wasn't going to barrel out of here. And coffee suggested she was willing to continue talking. Okay, then. He'd better be very careful. He didn't want to leave her any more scarred than she was.

Although he already knew that he wasn't going to escape unscathed. Too late for that.

The guy on the TV thought it was really cool that this storm was breaking records. Luke sat wondering about an entirely different kind of storm.

Bri preferred a small coffeepot these days. She only brewed four to six cups at a time, partly because she often only had time for a cup or two, and partly because she preferred it fresh-brewed. At least it gave her some time to consider what was happening here.

Her cheeks heated as she thought about so blatantly telling Luke she wanted to have sex with him. That had been no secret in the past, and she was kind of surprised that she felt so exposed now for having admitted it.

But fear of exposure had kept her silent for many years, and speaking out had felt good. If only briefly. Now she was back in the cycle of wondering if she should have just kept her mouth shut after all.

She had revealed her own pettiness, as well, resenting his absences, feeling as if she lacked support when he was away. It all sounded so childish. Maybe it was. How would she know? She'd even thought she was being a bit childish at the time, yet the resentments had grown.

Half of her didn't want to go back in there and face him after all that. Another part of her felt drawn, as if it was something she needed to do regardless of consequences.

Face it, she ordered herself. *Just face it.* This kind of thinking had probably magnified all her petty resentments, rather than banishing them in the adult way: by dealing with them and talking them through.

If nothing else came out of this, perhaps she could learn a good lesson: swallowed resentments festered.

She returned to the living room with two fresh mugs of hot coffee. This time, though, after she set them down, she scooted her chair closer to Luke. She could tell he needed another bath, but his aroma was purely masculine, as if the pheromones had multiplied. He smelled so good she almost didn't want to wash it away. But she also knew that even though it hadn't been that long since his last bathing, he was probably feeling a bit uncomfortable. During their marriage she had learned he was never one to skip a shower. Even that night when the power had gone out and the temperatures in the apartment had dropped to near freezing, he'd still jumped into the icy shower.

Invigorating, he had called it. She had her doubts.

"Do you want a light on?" she asked.

"Not especially. It's easier to talk, don't you think?"

"Depends on how much face-reading you want to do."

"And that depends on how much you're comfortable with." He paused, then surprised her by reaching out to take her hand. The meteorologist on the screen still extolled the wonders of the worst ice storm to hit Wyoming since they started keeping records. "I've been thinking of my own mistakes, too. My failings."

"It wasn't you, Luke."

"Oh, yes it was. Quite a bit of it was me. I sensed your unhappiness, but I was awfully quick to let it blow away. If I had the brains of a billy goat, I'd have pressed you a bit, tried to find out what was going on instead of being so self-centered as to think it couldn't have been important. Obviously it was."

"I never thought of you as self-centered. I thought I was."

"Maybe we both were."

A thought flashed across her mind and she decided to share it. Maybe she was evading again, or maybe she just desperately needed some levity. "I know a guy who raises goats as pets. A billy goat is pretty smart, Luke."

A short laugh escaped him. "Okay, if I'd had more brains than lichen. Anyway, you weren't the only one evading. I see that now. I'm willing to take my full share of blame."

She turned that around, thinking about it. Maybe he *had* had a share in the making of the mess, but she still felt she had been the biggest cause. A few good fights, even over silly things, might have made a difference.

Certainly digging a deeper hole through silence had only created a grave.

"My resentments *were* silly," she said finally. "I look back at what I remember now and can only think I was being childish."

"That's one of your parents speaking. Let's leave them out of this. I was gone forty-eight weeks of the year. I missed holidays. I basically left everything on your shoulders. That's okay for a bachelor, but not for a married man."

"But it was your *job*."

"Yeah, but I could have changed jobs. I was all caught up in the travel to exotic places, like some kind of adventurer. I said before and I'll say it again, I could have done something else and been content. I like working outdoors, I like building things, I'm endlessly fascinated by geology. But that doesn't mean I have to live out of a suitcase and never be home. It's different for you. You absolutely love your work, and you couldn't go bouncing around the world with me. Not and do what you love."

"Maybe I could have, if I'd thought about it. There's a call for nurses everywhere."

"In lots of places I wouldn't have taken you. And there was never a guarantee you'd get hired somewhere."

She didn't respond immediately. He had a point. Some of the places he worked weren't friendly to women. She'd have been stuck in a compound, unable to go out and see the world, never mind working. She'd looked into an overseas job, then dropped the idea when she realized she'd have had to sign a contract for a year. That still would have separated them.

But she still felt many of her resentments were childish. "Military wives handle separation all the time."

"Some do. Some don't. No sweeping statements here. You needed more from our marriage than a few weeks a year. I don't think that's childish. It was a legitimate need on your part. But there was more, wasn't there?"

"Yes," she admitted quietly. "The future. Somehow with time that seemed to get bigger."

"We never talked about it," he admitted.

"No. I wanted to have children."

It was his turn to take a deep breath. "Something else we never mentioned."

"I know. My fault. I kept thinking it wouldn't be fair to have a couple of kids who'd never see their father. Damn it, Luke, they'd have practically been raised by strangers. Day care, almost from birth. That seemed wrong to me."

"It would have been. But if you'd gotten pregnant..."

"What?" Her heart had begun to really race now. She wasn't sure she wanted to hear this even after all this time.

"I'd have found a job that would keep me at home. Kids need parents, if they're available."

"Some might be better off without them," she said drily.

He cracked a laugh. "Sadly true."

Her mind was wandering the byways of the past again, trying to remember all the issues she'd had, or thought she'd had. She wondered how trustworthy memory was. The last couple of days, it all seemed to be taking on a different color.

"I'm not even sure," she said slowly, "that I remember all that I was feeling or resenting. Maybe that's a good thing."

"I don't know. Depends on whether it pops up again."

She faced him squarely. "Why would it? I live here

now, and I love it. I grew up in this town, and coming home felt exactly like that."

"Then you'll stay here. And maybe I can stay, too."

"Quit talking like we have a future. You ever break a vase? You can glue it together, but it's never the same."

"I'm not talking about gluing something together. I'm talking about trying out something very different."

His hand tightened around hers, and she wondered if they were both losing their minds. Get past all that ugliness that lay behind them? Not likely. She had wanted to slam the door in his face the instant she clapped eyes on him. Instead she'd been suckered into taking him into her home.

But that had been professional. What they were talking about now was very different, and frankly it terrified her. Sex was one thing. Sorting out some kind of relationship with an eye to a future was a whole different proposition.

She remembered all too well the pain and anguish that had dogged the last months of their marriage, how much the divorce had hurt on so many levels. She couldn't risk that again, and with Luke it would be a distinct risk because they'd mucked it up once before. Could both of them have changed enough to start anew?

People didn't change, she reminded herself. Not really. Look at her: stuck in a rut that had begun in early childhood. Breaking free of it a few times didn't mean she had changed. The old temptations to minimize her feelings remained. Already they were tugging at her, telling her she had been childish before. The only place in life where she had ever felt certain of herself had been in her job.

But for once she decided to face her demons head on. "I'm terrified," she announced.

"Of me?"

"Of us. It hurt so bad before, Luke."

He squeezed her hand. "I remember."

"I don't… I'm not sure I can change enough to make a difference."

"There's only one way to find out. I can guarantee that it won't happen overnight, although I think we both made some great strides tonight."

"Maybe."

He lifted her hand and began to stroke the back of it, lightly. A sizzle of electricity ran through her. He could so easily fill her with desire for him. That ought to terrify her, too, considering it had wound up being the major part of their marriage.

"The question," he said a minute later, "is if you're willing to give it a try, scared or not. I'm not exactly overwhelmed with confidence myself. I was never any good at pushing you to talk. I was too self-centered. And I'd have to start looking for a way to make a living here."

There weren't a whole lot of opportunities for that. Another big question mark. Her world was suddenly full of questions.

"I don't know," she said plaintively. "I just don't know. All these years I've been trying to convince myself that I was glad to be rid of you, but it was never true, Luke. Never."

"Then let's try."

He made it sound so damn easy.

Jack verged on going crazy. The ice storm outside had him locked in his little home at the edge of town.

The roads were being closed by cops, who were telling the occasional car to get off the road.

Walking in this would be insane. He knew that. Freezing rain, sleet, deepening ice, even snow would make any path he chose treacherous. Putting tire chains on his truck wouldn't help, either. The damn things made enough noise to wake the dead. If he went anywhere near Bri's house at this hour of the night, people would know it.

Lights seemed to be on everywhere, too, as if folks had been wakened by the wind and rattling of sleet against their windows and were watching the ice swallow the world.

No one was going anywhere.

Which meant he'd stick out like a sore thumb if he even managed to get to Bri's place. And in an honest moment he had to admit that he'd probably kill himself if he tried to climb the tree to her attic. He'd need to be able to ice skate vertically.

So he sat, filled with anxiety, and it wasn't helping a whole lot to look at the clock and figure that even if he got into that attic it was likely all he would see would be two people watching the storm or sleeping. Man, it was the freaking middle of the night. Bri had worked that day. He'd almost bet she was sound asleep in her own bed, and from what he'd seen, Luke was still pretty much trapped in his hospital bed and wheelchair.

So why was he unable to settle and wait? Because he was growing increasingly terrified the Luke might win Bri back. Oh, he claimed to have come to build the resort, but Jack was more suspicious than that.

He was certain Luke had come for Bri. What man wouldn't want that woman?

Maybe he'd taken things too slow with Bri. Maybe he should have asked her out months ago. But Jack was no fool. He knew he didn't immediately appeal to most women. They had to get to know him first, to recognize his sterling qualities.

He'd been determined to do it all the right way this time, to give her a chance to appreciate him before he even tried to suggest they have lunch together.

But he might have waited too long. He sure couldn't ask her out now, not with Luke there. And while Luke had been nice to him, even kind of offering him a job, he sensed something else in the man. Luke was highly protective of Bri, maybe even a bit jealous of her.

So he stared out at the icy night, stymied in every direction. In theory, Luke should move out of Bri's house soon as soon as he could crutch around safely, which meant the weather had to improve.

Everything seemed to be conspiring against him. Why couldn't the man have died when Jack pushed him? That would have solved everything.

Instead, his competition was firmly embedded with Bri, and Jack was out in the cold.

He couldn't take a second attempt at Luke. That would raise too many questions. But of one thing he remained sure in the depths of his heart: nobody else was going to get Bri. Nobody.

He wasn't quite sure what he was going to do about it, but ideas had begun to grow in the back of his mind. He tried to ignore them, but when he remembered how easy it had been to push Luke over that cliff, he figured it wouldn't be much harder to deal with Bri.

She would be his or she would be no one's. There were only two ways out of this. He hoped Bri had the sense to pick him.

Chapter 12

The weather report continued to worsen. Nothing at all was going to be moving in this part of Wyoming come morning. Roads were being closed. The police were out shepherding stray travelers to safe places to wait. It had now become the storm of the century. Or more, depending on which cautiously intoned forecaster was talking.

"I can't stand this," Bri said finally. "I am not going to sit like a lump all night listening to this."

"What do you suggest?"

"Let me give you a bath. At least I'll feel productive."

"I'd appreciate one," he admitted.

"I can imagine. I remember the two-showers-a-day guy."

He laughed. "Mostly because when I was in the field a shower was a luxury I couldn't often enjoy."

"I'm afraid you won't be enjoying one for about five or six more weeks. But in the meantime, before the ice breaks the power lines, let me heat up some water and some cleanser." She had a natural gas stove, but if the power went out, she wouldn't be able to see anything. Certainly not well enough to bathe Luke.

"Be my guest."

For all she said she needed the activity, however, Bri felt nervous. Somehow she didn't think this was going to be a simple bed bath. No, she feared things were going to get rapidly out of hand.

Or maybe she feared they wouldn't. She was past knowing what she really wanted now. Well, she knew she wanted Luke. But was she honestly ready?

She jumped up and went to get her two biggest pots for heating water. Given the ice buildup, she really did expect power lines to start going down. There was just so much they could handle. Trees, too. She hoped the ones near her house didn't decide to crash onto her roof.

But there was nowhere to go. Not now. If she tried to back out of her driveway, she'd probably slide straight across the street and wind up getting scolded by a local officer.

They were here for the duration. And maybe that wasn't such a bad thing. Ignoring the butterflies in her stomach, she carried the first steaming pot out to the living room.

Luke still sat in his wheelchair.

"Why aren't you in bed?" she asked.

"Because you changed the sheets just last night. It seems a shame to get them all wet. You can reach most of me sitting here, and the rest if I stand and lean over the bed."

"I hear a planner at work," she tried to joke, but it came out sounding weak. She'd bathed him any number of times this week and had managed, mostly, to separate herself from the intimacy of the task. She didn't think that was going to be possible tonight.

"Let's just get you undressed and into bed. Save my back and knee."

"Sorry. Didn't think of that. Self-centered again."

Maybe. Maybe not. She suspected that after what she'd admitted about wanting him, he might be getting some butterflies in his stomach, too. The thought eased her own apprehension a bit. She wasn't used to thinking of Luke as the nervous sort, but why should he be any different from the rest of the world?

A creeping awareness of all that hung on this began to grow in her. One way or another, this wasn't going to end professionally. She knew it as sure as she breathed.

Her heartbeat was already speeding up. She was breathing a little faster. An urge to skip the whole bath and just dive into him was growing, but the idea of having the freedom to explore his whole body again, with the desire no longer a secret, appealed even more.

He would be pretty much at her mercy, given those casts, and that appealed to her, too. A dominant strain she'd never suspected in herself.

Almost before she knew it, a faint smile was growing on her face. The butterflies eased as she anticipated how delightful this was going to be.

Balancing against the side of the bed, he began to pull his clothes off. When it came to his sweatpants and underwear, he perched on the edge of the bed and stripped everything to his ankles.

Bri pulled the rest off. "Now lie on your stomach.

And let me know if you start to get chilled. I can move blankets around."

"Sweetie, I don't think anything could chill me now."

His nakedness was a familiar sight to her, and the years had done nothing to change him. He was still well-muscled, covered with taut, glistening skin. He'd never been a very hairy man, except for a thick beard and great hair. She liked being able to see all his charms with nothing in the way, but she also liked the way the thin dusting of lighter hair on his legs felt so silky.

Laid up though he was, he was still perfect.

As soon as he was facedown on the bed, she drew a blanket up over him.

"Hey," he said playfully.

"I need to change. I'm going to get wet. Be right back."

In her bedroom, she found a set of scrubs and donned them with shaking hands. Was she out of her mind? Probably. But at least starting with a bath would give her plenty of chances to change her mind. She could choose to remain professional and leave it at that. Or not.

She suspected the "or not" was going to be the outcome, but she felt safer knowing she would have a choice at least until she made it, one way or another.

When she returned, he still lay beneath the blanket with his arms over his head. Gathering her courage, she stepped up next to him and reached for the sponge, which she wrung out in the hot water. Then she applied some cleanser to it and tugged the blanket down to his waist.

Any thought of remaining professional fled almost as soon as she began to rub the sponge around his neck. He made a sound almost like a big cat purring, and encouraged her ministrations.

Never before Luke had she thought a bed bath could be sexy. But never before had she bathed a former lover. A perhaps soon-to-be-again lover.

Since he seemed to like it, she leaned into him, massaging as much as washing. Where her fingers touched his skin, she marveled again at how smooth and warm he felt. Memories began to surge, memories of other times when she had caressed him, learned him, loved him.

How had she ever given that up?

With each movement of her hands, the throbbing deep in her center seemed to grow. She fell into a rhythm almost in time with it, wringing, rubbing, leaning into her movements, moving slowly downward, strangely in no rush to finish this task.

By the time she reached his buttocks, he seemed to be moving gently under her hands, as if he felt the same way. As she washed his cheeks, he seemed to buck upward a little, bringing a secret smile to her heart. She loved having him lie beneath her ministrations like this. In the past, any time they had touched, it had been mutual, a joint exploration and expression where both of them had been actively involved. This was a new experience for her and she adored it.

"I'm loving this," he mumbled. "Oh, sweetie, I could stay on this rack forever."

"Rack?"

"If you think I'm not suffering, let me turn over."

A laugh escaped her, one of real happiness. "I'm enjoying your suffering."

"I suspected. Witch."

She laughed again. "Legs first."

"No complaints here. And while you're at it, they're aching from disuse."

"I can only really do one. You'll have to suffer."

"Do you hear me complaining?"

"Cold?"

"Not a chance."

She moved on down his uninjured leg and he groaned as she massaged the muscles deeply. When she reached his feet, she massaged them, as well, washing them first, then rubbing them hard between her hands. He groaned even more deeply, a sound of unadulterated pleasure. Since she loved a good foot massage, too, she could easily imagine how it was affecting him. Something about a foot rub unleashed amazing relaxation. Although relaxation didn't seem to be the direction in which they were headed.

Oh, no. She was about to shatter with the need building in her, but they'd hardly begun. She still didn't know where this would end, but the torment was exquisite.

"Now?" he asked finally.

"Now what?"

"Can I roll over? You're killing me with kindness here."

Again she laughed, loving his honesty. Loving her own honesty, at least with herself. "You're perfect," she said, surprised by the thickness of her own voice.

"You used to say that all the time. I really liked hearing it."

Before she could answer, he rolled over. No blanket covered him, and there could be no mistaking his arousal. He was as ready as she'd ever seen him, and it would have been so easy to toss the sponge aside and simply mount him where he lay.

But there were advantages to drawing this out. The lingering need might be painful, but it was also wonderful. She liked that he had to wait for her to do what she would with him. How seldom had she ever felt that he was at her mercy?

Yet some truthful part of her admitted that at these times he'd always been at her mercy, at least as much as she had been at his.

She drew a deep, steadying breath. She wanted to continue this, continue tormenting him in the most awesome way possible.

"We could skip this," he muttered.

"I'm not going to spare you," she murmured, struggling for breath. "Or myself."

That drew a short, ragged laugh from him. "Have at it, darlin'. I'm all yours."

She took him at his word. She washed his face gently, but as she moved on she became less gentle. His neck, his shoulders, his chest. She had always loved his chest, with smooth muscles developed by hard work. Perfect in every way.

She ran the sponge over him, but now she delayed. Wringing it repeatedly in hot water, she went over his chest again and again. His nipples pebbled until they were hard and she couldn't prevent herself.

Leaning over him, leaving the sponge on his abdomen, she took one hard nipple into her mouth. He gasped, then groaned, as she lashed it with her tongue.

One hand came up to grip the back of her head, holding her close, signaling that he wanted more.

She gave him more. Sucking the nub into her mouth, she drew strongly on it until a guttural groan escaped him. Then she nipped gently with her teeth. His hand tightened on her head and his body arched upward.

She pulled back immediately. "Be careful."

"That's a joke." His voice sounded as if it were coming from under water. She could feel his heart pounding beneath her hand and knew the choice had been made for both of them. All the way.

She leaned farther, taking his other nipple into her mouth and giving it the same treatment. Shudders of pleasure ran through him and caused echoing tremors in her own body. They were becoming one. She could feel it and she was glad. The moment arcing between them was fusing them into a single experience.

"Bite me," he whispered.

So she did, clenching her teeth harder until a deep cry escaped him. The shudder that ran through him this time shook the entire bed. It also shook her to her core.

Had she ever given him this much pleasure before? Had she herself ever felt this gnawing hunger so strongly before?

When she pulled back again he tried to hold her but she slipped away. There was more, a whole lot more, and she wasn't going to miss any of it.

She soaked the sponge again and began to wash him from his pecs and down over his abdomen. His muscles seemed to squirm beneath her touch, and now that she was moving lower there was no mistaking the way his sex jerked at each of her touches.

He was more than ready. So was she, for that matter.

The throbbing between her legs had grown until her entire body joined in, begging for his touches even as she denied herself in favor of teasing him.

During the years of their marriage, they had made love often, sometimes desperately, sometimes playfully. It had always been good, but she couldn't remember ever having drawn it out this way before. Certainly not the first time or even the second on long, lazy days together. There'd been an impatience, even a ferocity at times, but nothing like this. This was amazing.

Several times she danced the sponge away from the thatch of thick hair between his legs. Finally he reached out and grabbed her hand. "Bri, for the love of…"

She turned, smiling at him, not sure he could even see it in the flickering light from the TV. She had him now. He was all hers.

But by the same token, she seemed to be all his. She didn't know how much more she could take, either.

She warmed the sponge again but this time plunged into that thatch, rubbing it over him while another groan escaped him. Only then did she run it up his swollen length.

The shudder than ran through him was epic. For her part, she felt as if sizzling wires were running from her core to her breasts and then throughout her entire body. She would never have dreamed she could get this aroused without being touched herself.

Again and again she ran the sponge over him while his hips rose helplessly.

"Bri…"

She tossed the sponge into the pot and bent again, this time to take him into her mouth. He cried out. His hand clamped the back of her head. He filled her, deeper than she had ever taken him before, and she tasted his saltiness.

"Not this way," he said gutturally. "Please. Not this time."

She was past drawing this out any longer. "Condom," she muttered.

"Like I came prepared?" He swore.

But she was. She always carried condoms to give out when she thought a young patient needed them. In a moment she had pulled one out of her purse, then rolled it on him.

"Now you," he whispered. "Strip?"

She stepped back and pulled the scrub shirt over her head.

"I wouldn't have thought it possible," he murmured.

"What?"

"You're even more beautiful than I remembered. Hurry."

So she dropped her pants, kicked them aside, then climbed carefully onto the bed, straddling him. His hands immediately cupped her breasts and squeezed, then pulled one to his mouth. As soon as he sucked on her nipple, she felt an arc of fire shoot from there to her center. This time it was she who cried out, and her body began to move helplessly in time to rhythms as ancient as life itself.

"Now," he said. "Now."

Reaching down between them, she guided him to her entrance. He found his way home as if he'd been searching for it forever.

When he filled her it was like the answer to everything that had been missing. She felt herself stretch to accommodate him, then every thought fled as she reveled in how good it felt to be joined with him. An emptiness was gone and this was so damn right.

She began to move, sliding along his length, and with the knowledge of familiarity he reached down to touch her sensitive nub, rubbing it just the way she liked, lifting her like a pole-vaulter on the tip of his finger, yet impaling her with his member. She felt strung out on impossible sensations of hunger, need. They drove her higher and higher until she felt dizzy as if she tumbled through the stars.

She felt his final thrust, hard and strong as he shoved deeply into her, and sensitive muscles felt the throb as he jetted his seed. Another movement or two on her part, along with the persistent touch of his fingers, and she followed him, tumbling in free fall to a completion so intense it nearly hurt.

She remained frozen as the sensation went on and on, making time disappear, then slowly collapsed on him.

His arms closed around her.

She had come home. The last place she had ever thought to be again.

She had pulled the blanket up over them when she rolled off him. They lay side by side with her head on his shoulder, waiting for the world to stop spinning, waiting for their breathing and heartbeats to stabilize. Hearing the familiar pounding of his heart beneath her ear felt so good. She never wanted to move again.

The keening wind, the rattle of ice against the windows, only made it feel cozier inside. Cozier in his arms.

"I think I need another bath after that," he mumbled.

She lifted her head a few inches and glimpsed the smile on his face. "Yeah, right."

"Reruns always welcome. Damn, that was fantastic."

It had been. It had also been the only glue for their marriage. As the afterglow began to fade, all the niggling questions tried to rear their heads again. She had loved this man once. Maybe in a small way she still did. But love apparently hadn't been enough.

And this might have been a huge mistake.

But she took out her mental broom and shoved those doubts aside for now. Moments like this deserved to be lived, not worried away.

Nursing had taught her how unexpectedly short life could be. Without warning, all the tomorrows were gone. Maybe that was part of what had troubled her in their marriage. Time was escaping them, lost in long separations.

Slowly she sat up.

"Bri?"

"We've got to talk. Coffee?"

"Always."

She eased across him and pulled on the scrubs she had left on the floor. "Want me to get you some clothes?"

"Do I need to be dressed for this conversation?"

"You can stay right where you are if you want."

"Just hand me the sponge so I can clean up a bit."

She stuck her hand in the water. "It's cold. I still have a pot simmering on the stove. I'll change them out."

She emptied the pot of cold water and returned with

the other. This time she was willing to le himself. She didn't want to get derailed again.

When she got back to the living room with coffee she was surprised to find him sitting up in the wheel-chair, wearing one of the fresh pairs of sweats she had cut to fit over his leg.

"You're doing really well," she remarked.

"Thank goodness for upper body strength."

So once again they sat together, coffee mugs in their hands. The wind howled, flinging so much ice at the windows that it sounds like birdshot.

"So talk," he said.

"I'm trying. I think by now you know it's not easy for me."

He sipped coffee and waited patiently.

"It occurred to me that all those petty reasons I had for being angry? They weren't the real reason. I missed your support at times. I certainly missed you. Sometimes I felt so alone, as if I had to deal with ev-erything by myself."

"I don't think that's petty. In fact, I think you were justified. But you say that's not it?"

"Just now I was thinking about how much I wanted to savor this time with you because I've learned, I've *seen,* just how short life can be. Nobody can be sure there'll be a tomorrow."

He nodded, but she was grateful that he didn't try to answer. Once again she was starting to question her own feelings, and somehow she had to push past that and get it out. Get to the source of all the ugliness and resentment that had started to roil inside her dur-ing their marriage. She owed them both that, however stupid her thinking might be.

...of people die. Too many of
...any of them wound up losing
... hours before they had been
...ut."

...of wisdom. There really is no guar-
... row will come for any of us. I saw a
lot of ... emergency room. It made me aware of
how fast th... was slipping away, and how little guarantee there was that you'd ever be able to make up for
it. Moments are fleeting, then they're gone. What if
there's never another moment?"

He drew a long, slow breath. "My God," he said
quietly.

"Is that stupid?"

"Hell, no." More forcefully.

"So at some level, I think I was feeling that we were
losing our moments. Moments that could never be re-
covered. Time was slipping away while we lived our
separate lives, coming together only for Skype conversations or your breaks. That wasn't a whole lot of moments for us. I was grateful for them, but I also started
resenting the moments we didn't have, and fearing that
the future might never arrive. I couldn't really look at it
that way, though. It was…overwhelming. So I focused
on little moments rather than the big picture."

He didn't say anything immediately, just sat sipping his coffee, appearing lost in thought. The TV,
volume turned down, still babbled on about the sever-
ity of the storm.

Then it winked off. The house was suddenly utterly silent except for the storm outside. The loss of
the forced-air heat was instantly noticeable.

"Better pull out the blankets," Bri said. "It could be a long few days."

"What about the fireplace?" Luke said, pointing to the interior wall of the living room. "Is it safe to use?"

"Jack cleaned the chimney for me in October. It should be okay."

"Wood?"

"Out back, buried in snow and ice. I might need a pickax to get at it, but if necessary, I will."

"I think you can do anything you set your mind to, darlin'. I just wish I could help."

"Not being alone is helping." A painful truth, but still a truth. Alone she'd be wondering how long this would go on, and what she could do about it anyway. Luke's presence made it easier, more pleasant.

She rose. "I'll get more blankets and some flashlights. Be right back."

"I hope so. We still have a conversation to finish."

She doubted it was a conversation that could ever be finished. She'd admitted she wasn't built to be the kind of wife he needed, and she seriously doubted he would give up a career he loved to live in this place. There was no need to even look beyond that. None.

She found two big flashlights in her kitchen pantry. A check of her cell phone showed that she had no signal. The landline didn't even buzz. Right in town, surrounded by neighbors, and they were as cut off as if they lived in an empty field. Nobody was in a position to help anyone else, and certainly nobody would be foolhardy enough to risk their necks out there. Snow was one thing, ice another. As it glazed the world, even walking could be dangerous.

It took her two trips to bring all her blankets. She

used the flashlight to look out of the mudroom at her rarely used woodpile and wondered if the snow beneath the new ice might make it easier to get some of those logs inside. It might, but judging by the way the flashlight reflected off the ice as if it were a mirror, she figured it would be treacherous any way she looked at it. Worse, if something went wrong, there was no way to summon help. Power out, phones out… She hated to imagine the work the utilities crews might even now be trying to do. In this.

God.

She piled the blankets on Luke's bed, then rejoined him. "At least I can still cook and make coffee on the stove, but even the phones are dead."

"I just checked, too. Nothing."

"I meant to check the mudroom door, to see if I could open it." She hopped up.

"Why?"

"If we need wood. Luke, everything is glazed out there. If I have to go out there for wood, I want to take the shortest path possible."

"Maybe we should just hunker down. We can pile on the blankets and share body heat. If you got hurt out there…"

"That did cross my mind. No way to get help."

"So we'll manage. I have winter gear and so do you. We'll burrow in like a couple of polar bears."

She switched off the flashlight to save the batteries, and they sat in a darkness so deep it almost caused vertigo. Not even the familiar streetlights were working, so not a single glimmer of light seeped into the room.

Luke still hadn't responded to what she had said earlier. She wondered if he had forgotten or if he was thinking about it. She had sure made it clear why their marriage had fallen apart: she wasn't the right person for it.

There was certainly no way to change that. She could talk more, she could express her feelings more, but she doubted she could change enough to become the kind of person who would be happy in an absentee relationship.

Luke spoke. "So you needed more?"

His voice startled her out of her thoughts. "More?"

"More of a relationship. A lot more time together."

"A future. Or at least the belief that we'd share more moments together. Otherwise, what was the point?"

"I've been asking myself that."

It was his turn to fall silent. She waited, listening to the storm, feeling the chill in the house grow slowly. Almost as the chill in her heart had grown during their marriage. Just a little at a time, until finally everything was frozen.

So he was asking himself the same question: What was the point? When they'd met at the party of a mutual friend, the attraction had been instantaneous. They'd dated, they'd fallen in love, and even before they married she had begun to live for the times when he would come home. The glow had carried her through. She'd honestly believed it was working, and would work.

Why had she never wondered if his long absences could be a problem? Too blinded by the excitement and love, she supposed. Not thinking rationally at all, but entirely with her heart. And if she were to be honest, with her sexual hunger for him. Everything had seemed perfect and she didn't notice or allow herself to think of the things that might not be.

Even one of her friends, Sharon, had encouraged her. Sharon had been married for eight years, and swore she would trade places with Bri in a heartbeat. "You're so lucky to have a man who isn't underfoot all the time. You get to make your own decisions, do things your own way, without always having to consult. Go for it, girl."

Bri had laughed at the time, enjoying the advice with just a teeny grain of salt. What she hadn't known, couldn't have known, was that having Luke underfoot more of the time was exactly what she wanted and needed.

But how could she even be sure of that? She had seriously missed him the whole time he was gone, but how could she possibly know that she would have been happier if he had been there all the time? She had never experienced it.

Man, she was a mess.

"I wish I could see your face."

She started to reach for the flashlight.

"No, don't," he said. Although it was so dark in there he must have guessed her intention from the sound of her movement. "Some things are easier to talk about in the dark. Besides, I can feel you starting to question yourself."

"How can you possibly tell that?"

"Well, how about we were married and I could sense your moods even if I couldn't read your mind. And now that you've told me how you were taught to question your every feeling, why wouldn't I assume that the nervousness I feel in you has to do with that?"

"Damn, Luke, if I can't figure myself out, how can you?"

"Maybe I'm learning. Anyway, I was trying to say that I've started to question what we were doing, too. I was too busy and self-centered at the time, but I hope I've grown up a bit. You mentioned all the moments we were missing because I was away. I think about that and realize that you're right. The mere fact that we thought we could do that doesn't mean we could, or that it was right for us. I keep coming back to you saying that what we had was an affair, not a marriage. That's really sticking, because it's true."

She felt him reach out and feel for her hand until he grasped it. The warmth of his touch filled her with fire. It always did.

Then she asked the important question. "So where do we go from here?"

Chapter 13

Weak morning light peeked around the edges of the drapes. Bri, securely rolled up in blankets with Luke, felt warm everywhere except her face. Her nose told her that the temperature in the house was falling dangerously toward freezing.

And the howling of the wind outside told her that the storm was far from over. How long could this possibly keep up? The weirdest spring ever, and now an endless ice storm? It just didn't seem possible.

When she moved, Luke groaned a protest.

"Sorry," she murmured. "I need to make some coffee and take care of business. And look outside."

The reluctance with which he let her go actually leavened her heart. Dangerous feelings, feelings that could lead her back to anguish and misery.

She had to stop living in a fantasy world and face

reality. She might care about this man. She certainly had loved him once, but everything about their natures made them wrong for each other.

She slipped out from under the blankets. Before they'd climbed into their cozy little bundle, she'd donned plenty of fleece and heavy wool socks. Even with those, the coldness in the house made her reach for her parka and pull it on.

She'd left the water dripping overnight to ensure that the pipes didn't freeze. It was still dripping, thank goodness. But without power to find out how cold it was outside, she didn't dare turn it off.

Digging around in her cupboard, she found her old percolator and started coffee. The sound of the running water finally caused her to dash for the bathroom, though.

Other things would just have to wait.

If she wanted to wash up, she would have to heat more water. The stuff coming out of her faucet felt barely warmer than an ice cube.

When she returned to the living room with coffee cake and coffee, she found Luke sitting up in his wheelchair, once again dressed in his cut-up sweats. Around his shoulders he'd managed to drape his parka, and a blanket covered his legs.

"It'd be nice if we could get some information," he remarked as she placed cake and coffee in front of him.

"I have a battery-powered radio. I should probably try it, but if the power outage is widespread, they won't be broadcasting much, either. At least not regularly. I don't know if they have a generator powerful enough."

"Well, let's find out."

Which was the simple solution to all her specula-
tions. She paused. "Do I always do that?"

"What?"

"Come up with potential problems before I know
if they exist?"

In the dim light he looked surprised. "I never
thought about it. Train of thought. It doesn't bother
me if you do."

Or maybe, she was yammering to avoid other sub-
jects, she thought as she went to get the radio from the
shelf in her closet. Out in the living room, she turned
the radio on. The crackle of static announced it was
still operational, but no amount of scanning the dial
got them even the faintest sound of a voice.

Luke switched it off. "We'll try again in a little
while."

The cold in the house seemed to increase her hunger,
and Bri ate more than she usually would of the cake,
then went to get more coffee.

"I'm going to have to try to get to the woodpile," she
said finally. She opened the front curtains, revealing a
leaden world coated in ice, and now filled with as much
blowing snow as a snow globe. "This is not promising."

"The company is making it kind of fun."

She glanced over her shoulder at him and drew a
sharp breath as she saw his warm, caressing smile. "We
could freeze to death," she said desperately, trying to
ignore his obvious invitation.

"Or we could warm up another way." But he tilted
his head and shrugged. "I get it. If we don't get power
back soon, we're in trouble. First things first. But
damn, Bri, I'm worried about you going out there to
get wood. You could get hurt."

She frowned faintly. "Yes, I could. Or we could sit here and turn into blue Popsicles that get carried straight to the morgue. I'm worried about the neighbors, too. Nobody's really prepared for a situation like this."

"You can't go up and down the neighborhood on this ice. Won't the police be checking?"

She hesitated. "Probably. Yes, probably. But in the meantime, we need wood. And I know damn well that if you weren't laid up, you'd be headed out there yourself. So don't give me any trouble about it. I'm capable, too."

A shadow passed over his face. "Did I make you feel that you weren't?"

"Sometimes," she admitted. "Anyway, that's not the point. If I can get out either door, I'll be careful, and get back here with some wood."

She pulled on her best boots, warm and fairly slip-proof, and gloves, then zipped up her parka until she was looking through the snorkel. To her vast relief, the mudroom door wasn't frozen closed. It took an extra shove to open it, but it swung open wide enough. Then, not knowing what else to do, she went out front, succeeded in getting onto the porch, and scooped up as much salt as she could into the old milk jug she used for this purpose.

Out back again, she spread it on the porch and steps, hoping it would lend her some traction.

She waited a moment, hoping it wasn't too cold to at least melt into the ice, then stepped out. The salt did its job, making her feel as if she were walking on a stable, gritty surface. She reminded herself not to get carried away. Ice could undo her at any moment. The

woodpile was only twenty-five feet away. If her foot-
ing was good enough, she imagined she could carry
three logs at a time. If not, at least two.

She reached the bottom step when a familiar voice
froze her in her tracks.

"Hi, Bri."

She turned her head and saw Jack, bundled for the
Arctic, walking cautiously toward her. "You shouldn't
be out here," she exclaimed. "My God, it's dangerous.
How did you get here?"

"Walking carefully. Wanted to check on a few people. And hey, you're out here, too."

"Getting some wood to make a fire."

"Why don't you just get back on the porch where
you're safe? I'll get wood for you."

"But…"

He shook his head. "Hey, you're a nurse. If I get
hurt at least someone will know what to do for me."

It was hard to argue with that. Everything Luke
had said about Jack rose up in her mind, though. She
wished she could send him on his way.

Then it struck her as odd that he'd come to her back-
yard. He had no way of knowing she'd be out here.
She remembered, too, that other time she had found
him alongside her house for no apparent reason. Just
checking on the raccoon fencing as he'd claimed? Now,
just here in a storm when the whole world had been
warned to stay home?

Well and truly uneasy with Jack for the very first
time, she climbed slowly onto her porch and waited.
Maybe he was just trying to be nice, but this was really over the top. Risking his neck to check on people?
There were plenty of folks paid to do that who were

probably out there right now. Was he trying to prove himself indispensable?

She bit her lip inside the warmth of her snorkel hood and watched him carefully use his booted feet to hammer holes in the ice to reach her woodpile. She'd planned to go to her garage first and get a pickax. She doubted he was going to find it easy to pull wood out from under all the ice.

But he surprised her. When he reached the wood-pile, much smaller than it had been last fall, he started kicking at it. All of a sudden a bunch of logs rolled free.

For an instant he disappeared as the wind kicked up and the snow became blinding.

"They keep talking about how we're getting warmer," she heard him say as he appeared out of the swirling white fog. "Ask me, climate change is going to be an ice age."

"It feels like it this winter."

"And last, too." He mounted the steps carrying four logs. "Let me bring them in and start the fire going."

Butterflies began to batter her stomach mercilessly. He'd bring in the wood and start the fire? She knew Luke couldn't do it, but she could. She'd done it many times. But refusing his help seemed churlish and she couldn't bring herself to do it.

Nor could she exactly understand why she was get-ting so nervous about Jack. He was just being Jack, helpful as always, except the conditions somehow made it weird. Nor was she especially in a hurry to see how he and Luke would interact.

All of a sudden, she realized what her problem was. It wasn't Jack as much as it was the sense that she now had a guilty secret she didn't want to get out. At least not with Jack. She and Luke had become intimate. What if that raised Luke's jealousy? Or what if… What if what? Jack was just being Jack. If he sensed anything, it was none of his business.

Right.

She stepped aside and let him carry the logs to her living room. He didn't need directions. After all the work he'd done for her, he knew the layout as well as she.

"I'll get more wood once I get the fire going," he said over his shoulder.

"Thank you." To her own ears the expression sounded strained.

Luke must have heard them coming. He'd swung around his wheelchair so he was facing the doorway, and his crutches were near at hand.

"Look," Bri said too brightly. "Jack was out checking up on people and he got wood for us."

"Thanks," Luke said. His voice sounded too level. His expression had grown an edge, even though he managed to smile. So Luke found this odd, too. "Any news on the weather?"

Jack shook his head as he dumped the logs into the box by the fireplace. Bri always kept a healthy basket of tinder next to the fireplace matches. More than once in a winter, the fireplace became a necessity, at least for a few hours.

"Ain't nothing working, not even the radio," Jack said as he squatted and began to lay the fire.

"You shouldn't be out in this," Luke said quietly.

"Maybe not, but I figure the cops are looking in on the old folks. It's the others I got to worrying about. Like Bri here. She's got you to take care of."

That was almost a slap in the face. Bri stared hard at Jack's back, then looked at Luke. He'd apparently reacted the same way, but quickly smoothed his face.

After a moment, Luke spoke. "I'm glad Bri has you to look after her."

"Yeah?"

It almost sounded like a challenge. Instinctively, Bri moved closer to Luke, but he gestured her to step away, as if he didn't want her too close. But why? She could see he was tensing in his chair, and knew he could get up out of it, but what good would that do?

And what was going on with Jack?

He successfully ignited the tinder and applied the bellows. The wood, well-seasoned, quickly caught, sizzling occasionally as some remaining ice melted and water evaporated. Soon a nice blaze was going.

"I'll bring in more wood onto your mud porch," Jack said as he stood, brushing his hands together. "No telling when that power will come back on."

Bri could feel the heat from the fireplace begin to sting her face, but she didn't pull back her hood. Every instinct she had was on high alert, but she really couldn't find a reason for it.

She listened to Jack tromp out through the kitchen and mudroom, heard the door open and close behind him, then his heavy tread on the outside porch and steps.

"What is going on?" Luke asked. "And don't tell me he's just being helpful. There was a reason they were telling everyone to stay indoors, and from what I can tell that reason isn't going away."

"I know."

"This is weird." He reached for his cell phone again

and checked for a signal. "Nothing. It's either a power problem or the tower collapsed under all this ice."

"It wouldn't surprise me." She reached for the cordless set and got the same dead line. "Nothing."

"Maybe you should try the regular line in the kitchen. It only needs the power from the phone line to work, right?"

"I should have thought of that!" Sometimes old-fashioned technology was better than new. It had been precisely for that reason that she'd left a regular phone in the kitchen. No external power needed.

In the kitchen, she caught sight of Jack bringing more wood up to the porch. She also noticed he'd pulled the pickax out of her garage. It wasn't an item she needed most of the time, but the last owner had left it in the garage and she had just kept it. You never knew when you might need to dig a deep hole to plant something...or break your way through ice to get to the woodpile. Apparently Jack had needed to loosen the logs.

The landline in the kitchen was still dead, too. Not knowing what else to do, she started a fresh pot of coffee on the stove. At the very least, even if Jack was making her uneasy, she should offer him a hot drink before sending him back out into this cold.

He might be acting a little oddly, but she was equally certain her judgment of him might be colored by what Luke suspected and what had happened last night. She almost felt like a guilty kid who'd been caught making out in Daddy's car.

Damn, was she ever going to *really* grow up? Her lovemaking with Luke was nobody else's business, and she had had every right to enjoy it. She needed to quit questioning herself about everything and accept that her needs and desires were normal, a part of her. Whether they meshed with someone else's or not didn't really matter.

She and Luke had failed to mesh in important ways. He was hinting that he'd like to change that, and she kept running from the idea. Maybe she should give it a try along with him. After all, giving him up, whatever her reasoning, had been painful beyond belief. She really hadn't wanted to do it until the Barbara thing, and that had apparently been a nasty lie. The real problem had been her inability to fix the problems in their marriage.

But now he was saying he'd been self-centered, and that he had missed her during her absences as much as she had missed him. If they could find a way to be together more, maybe they could fall in love again. And if spending more time together didn't work, either, maybe they could both finish falling out of love. What a thought.

Either way, it could be the cure. They needed to try it, she decided. He hadn't just shown up on her doorstep to defend his honor. Not after all this time. Maybe he'd believed it was his reason, but she didn't because she knew how uninterested she had been in men since her marriage. No one measured up to Luke, for all his failings. Divorce hadn't severed the most important things, apparently.

Jack opened the back door and stepped inside with three more logs and the pickax.

"There's plenty of wood on your porch now, but the snow is turning icy again."

"Thanks a bunch, Jack. But why did you bring the

pickax in?" Just looking at it inside the house creeped her out.

"Because of the ice. I don't want it to rust. I'll put it back when I'm done."

That made sense, so Bri summoned a smile. "Coffee? You must be freezing."

"Coffee would be great. Food, too, if you have it."

The request surprised her because Jack was usually so undemanding, so careful not to put her out in any way. But as he threw back his hood, she thought that not only was he acting differently, he looked different. Something about his dark eyes. A hardness.

She shook herself, sure she was imagining all of this. She poured him a coffee and cut him a thick slice of coffee cake. "Let's go in the living room," she suggested. "There's a table in there you can use and the fire will make it warmer."

"Sure. We wouldn't want Luke to feel ignored."

What the... In all the time she had known him, Jack had never said anything like that, and it didn't sound courteous. It sounded...harsh? She didn't know what exactly possessed her then, but what came out of her mouth surprised her. Him, too, evidently. "You have some objection to Luke? So much that you'd rather sit in the cold kitchen?"

The challenge was unmistakable. Jack's eyes narrowed for just an instant, then his face smoothed over. "He's your ex. He hurt you."

"Maybe I hurt him more." She couldn't believe this conversation.

"You wouldn't hurt a soul." Then he headed for the living room with his plate and cup. She followed quickly.

Things had changed when she got back there. Luke now perched on the edge of his bed, crutches on either side of him, legs to the floor. He appeared relaxed, but she could see tension around his eyes. Only someone who knew him as well as she did would realize that he was ready to spring. On Jack? What was troubling him?

How could she even wonder? This entire situation was troubling, but damned if she could really put her finger on why. Jack out in a storm that was dangerous? Okay, maybe he wasn't so bright about some things. But he also wasn't usually this pushy. He'd started being pushy right about the time he'd offered to build a ramp for Luke, but that could have just been friendliness.

So could this, but it didn't feel like it.

It was almost as if there was a shift in the air in the house, as if a power center had moved. As if it were no longer her house, but Jack's.

What a crazy thought to have.

Jack had taken the office chair and was using the TV tray. Bri, for some reason, didn't want to sit on the couch. Finally she decided to perch on the bed near Luke. Slowly, she unzipped her jacket as she realized the fire was quickly heating the room again.

Jack finished half his chunk of cake before he spoke. "So you two are getting back together."

All of a sudden, no fire in the world would have been able to penetrate the chill that ran through her.

Luke spoke. "Why do you care?"

Bri tensed even more, wondering why Luke was being so challenging. All he had to say was no and it would let the strain out of the room, but instead he had raised it. Was this some kind of machismo thing? Was she missing something important? All she knew was that for some reason she was becoming edgy, so edgy it bordered on fear. Fear of Jack, who had never been anything but kind and helpful? She must be losing her mind. But the anxiety lingered anyway. Something was definitely wrong.

"Just curious." Jack went back to eating his cake. A few mouthfuls later, he said, "Not much of an answer, though."

The words were almost like a thrown gauntlet. She felt a huge relief when Jack stood, picking up his cup and plate. "I'll see myself out, Bri. Keep warm."

"Thanks for all your help, Jack." Basic courtesy dictated she walk him to the door, but she couldn't have moved to save her life. Just as Jack reached the hallway, Luke took her hand to give it a squeeze. Jack glanced back, saw their linked hands, nodded almost as if to himself, then continued on his way.

Bri heard him put his dishes in the sink, heard him open the door to the mudroom. Then it closed.

She had just begun to let out a huge breath of relief when she heard his returning footsteps.

What the...? She looked at Luke, whose face had gone hard as rock. He released her hand. "Maybe you'd better get behind the couch or something."

"What is going on?"

Jack appeared in the doorway, and this time he was carrying the pickax.

Bri gasped. "Jack, what...?"

"I tried to save you from him," Jack said. "I know how much he hurt you. Everyone knows about it. Everyone was talking about what a mess you were when you came back home."

"Jack…"

He shook his head. "Guess I didn't save you. You were always nice to me, Bri."

"I like you," she said with growing desperation. "You're always nice to me."

"Not nice enough, apparently. I was giving you time to realize how good I could be for you. Taking it slow because I knew you had to get over a divorce. Then this. The guy who cut out your heart shows up and just like that you can't see me anymore."

"See you? I never stopped seeing you."

"Yeah, you did when he came back. You looked at me different. Do you know how hard I worked to be the man you'd want? Do you have any idea? Hell, I spent a lot of hours up in your attic listening to you, watching you, figuring you out. I'll bet *he* never spent that much time on you."

The hole Luke had noticed in the ceiling. Not a claw hole at all. Bri's stomach turned over as she realized that Jack had been stalking her for a long time, invading her privacy in the most unthinkable way. She feared she might vomit.

Luke remained silent, but even with a foot between them, Bri could feel him coiling. He couldn't do anything. He had a broken leg and arm. What could he possibly be thinking? But she wondered what he had sensed that had made him suggest she get behind the couch.

Think! There had to be a way out of this, a way to talk Jack down. She was a nurse, damn it. She'd talked a lot of people down over the years. Of course, none of them had been holding pickaxes, either.

She scrambled for soothing words. Useful words.

She tried to stand because it helped her to make a calm approach, but the instant she moved, Luke's hand yanked her back. "No," he said.

"So he's ordering you around again?" Jack said. He shook his head. "You're a strong woman, Bri. You shouldn't take orders from him."

"I'm not taking orders. I'm wondering what's going on here." She tried to keep her voice as soothing as possible, but no amount of effort could entirely prevent a tremor from becoming audible. "Jack, you know I like you."

"Sure you do. And I thought it would become something more once I knew exactly how to care for you. That's why I tried to get him out of the way. I don't know what excuse he used, but the minute he came to see you I knew he was up to no good."

"Get him out of the way?" At last it penetrated and Bri understood exactly what she was dealing with here. "Did you push Luke off the cliff?"

"Of course I did. If he'd died, there wouldn't be a problem, would there?"

She felt Luke moving, almost infinitesimally, beside her. What did he think he was going to do?

"Jack," she said, "we can talk about this. Luke is only here until his job is over. And didn't he offer you work?"

"Just to keep an eye on me. He figured it out, Bri. He knew I wanted you. I could tell. Guys know those things."

"But he'll be moving out as soon as he can take care of himself!"

"Too late. You think I can't smell what you two were doing in here? Sex. The place reeks of it."

Bri sucked air, her mind scrambling for some way to defuse the situation. If Jack hadn't been holding that pickax, she'd have known they could work it out. The fact that he'd brought it in here meant his idea of working it out meant someone was going to get hurt. Maybe killed.

Being a nurse had made her physically strong, but she doubted she was strong enough to take out a stronger man wielding that kind of weapon.

Luke spoke. "So what you want to hear is that I'm leaving and I don't want Bri back?"

"That's a start."

Luke edged forward on the bed, his hands closing on his crutches, not as if he were about to stand, but as if planned on swinging them.

"There's just one problem, Jack," Luke said.

"What's that?"

"What makes you sure Bri will want you after you've threatened her with a pickax?"

"I didn't threaten her!"

"No? Then why are you standing there holding it?"

Silence filled the room. The keening banshee of the wind was the only sound, filled with foreboding.

Jack looked down at the pickax he held, and for just an instant Bri thought he was going to drop it. Hope died swiftly when he looked up again.

Never had she seen such hardness in Jack's face. His eyes looked almost blank, as if he had gone somewhere else. As if his body were inhabited by something besides the Jack she had always known.

"Too late now," Jack said, his voice curiously flat.

"It's not too late," Bri said quietly. "You can walk

out of this house right now and nothing will change." Desperation and nausea warred within her.

"No, it's too late," Jack said. "I tried to kill him. Now you both know that and you'll tell on me. He should've just died and things could have been okay then, but not now."

"Jack…"

"Shut up," he snarled. "I should have guessed you weren't good enough for me. Cheap, like every other woman. But I thought you were special, Bri. You're not special at all."

This time she didn't even try to speak. She was watching Jack intently, every muscle in her body tensed to respond if he moved. She could shove the hospital table at him. The TV trays were useless. There was the office chair. But overall, the room was devoid of weapons and protections.

Luke let go of his left crutch. She hardly noticed that it flipped over and landed right beside her.

"Why make things worse for yourself, Jack?" Luke asked, sounding amazingly reasonable. "There's a world of difference between getting in trouble for assaulting someone and actually murdering them."

"I don't care anymore. Bri was everything to me. If I can't have her, no one can."

The room filled with ice in an instant, seeming to Bri to become so cold that the fire might never have been lit.

Jack hefted the pickax, gripping it with both hands. The time for talk had apparently passed. Bri looked quickly around, desperate to find a way to stave off a blow from that ugly tool. She had to protect Luke, as well, because he was still in casts, and they had no idea whom Jack was going to come for first.

Then she glanced down. For the first time she noticed that Luke had removed the rubber feet from the crutches. All of a sudden she got why one of them had rolled to her side. Moving slowly, she closed her hand around it.

Jack's eyes darted from Luke to her and back, as if he were making a decision. "The cripple or you?" he mused aloud. "Probably you. The cripple can't move that much."

Now he was turning them into objects. Distancing himself from their common humanity. Bri recognized it and a shudder ran down her spine.

She eased forward so that her weight rested on her feet more than the bed. She had to get between Jack and Luke. She had to protect Luke at any cost. Not that she'd be able to withstand more than a single blow from that ax. Somehow she had to get it out of his hands. She'd only have one chance to do it.

"Jack, you're a good man. Do you think I never noticed? I *relied* on you. I counted on you. Don't disappoint me."

Wrong thing to say. She saw it instantly.

"Disappoint *you?* What do I care about your disappointment? You disappointed me. I thought you were better than this."

"Better than what?" She was gauging distance now, trying to decide how best to move. It was then she noticed that Luke was nearly standing, as well. On his broken leg? My God...

A switch flipped in her. All the fear vanished as

fury rose blindingly in her. This idiot was going to hurt Luke. Not without killing her first.

She tightened her grip on the crutch. If she could tangle it with the pickax before he hit either of them… Thought gave way to action before the idea even finished forming.

Jack lifted the ax and started to move in. He was eyeing Luke, as if planning to strike him first, then Bri. Not while she had a breath in her body. She straightened, raising the crutch, and started to move toward Jack.

Surprise flickered over his face, then it twisted into fury. He charged.

Luke moved, striking as fast as a snake. He shot his crutch forward, catching Jack in the knees. At a near run, Jack fell forward onto the floor. Bri jumped aside just quickly enough to miss the falling pickax that might have hit her leg.

Then Luke rose from the bed, astonishing her, and fell on Jack's back, pinning him.

"Get the ax," he demanded. "Get the damn ax away from him."

Jack struggled and managed to grab the ax again, trying to roll over beneath Luke.

Bri forgot every vow she'd ever made never to hurt another person. Lifting the crutch, she jabbed the pointed end down on Jack's upper arm with every ounce of strength she had.

He howled and his hand flopped open. Oh, God, the nurse in her said, she'd hit his brachial artery. There was no mistaking the arterial spray. He could be dead in minutes.

"The ax," Luke said breathlessly. "I'll hold him."

For good measure, he fisted his good arm and punched Jack in the side of the head.

"The artery." But he was right. Bending, she grabbed the pickax, ran to the front door and threw it out into the storm.

Still running, she came back to the living room and found Luke still holding a struggling Jack.

"You're going to get hurt," she warned Luke.

"I don't care. Hey, Jack! You hear me? Did you hear what Bri said? You're bleeding from an artery. You stop fighting this instant so she can do something about it or you're going to bleed out before I let you go."

Adrenaline still ruled her. Bri looked down at her handiwork and only automatic responses kept her from doing more damage. He'd wanted to kill her and Luke. That still seethed in her, a temporarily caged beast.

Jack went still.

She studied the side of his face she could see. "He's weakening." If she hadn't seen it before, she would have been astonished by the amount of blood spurting nearly three feet into the air and pooling around him.

"Not enough," Luke said. "I can feel it. What's it going to be, Jack? Death or help?"

Bri didn't wait for a response. She went for the emergency kit she kept in the bathroom. When she returned, blood was everywhere, even on Luke's back, but Jack was looking pale. Very pale.

Without a word, she knelt beside him and pried open the kit, pulling out a tourniquet.

"Thank God I didn't hit him any higher," she muttered. "He needs the E.R., stat."

"I hope we can get some help."

She tightened the tourniquet until the spurting

stopped. "Ten minutes, then release the pressure. I gotta try the phone again."

Luke gave a nod of his head. She noticed he was sweating, which meant he must be in pain. What kind of damage might he have done to himself?

God, at that moment she could have cheerfully pulled off that tourniquet and let Jack go for good.

But whatever her rage, her instincts remained. Save the patient.

She raced to the kitchen and lifted the phone, hopelessness seeping through the adrenaline, fear and rage. It hadn't worked all night. Why would it work now?

She almost sagged to the floor when she got the dial tone.

"Nine-one-one, what is the emergency?"

"Hi, Stacy. It's Bri. Arterial bleed at my place. I have a tourniquet on, but it's bad. And you might need to send two ambulances. I think I have two patients."

"The roads are treacherous, but I have at least one unit within five minutes."

"We'll start with the worst first."

"Hang in there. You want to stay on the phone with me?"

"I have a patient to take care of. And I need the cops, too."

Then she hung up the phone and returned to the scene from hell.

Bri helped Luke back onto his bed when the EMTs arrived. She warned Tim and Ted that Jack was irrational and dangerous, so they strapped him safely to the gurney as soon as they established an IV and started him on a bag of lactated Ringer's solution.

"Back for you shortly, big guy," Tim said to Luke.

"Take your time. Those roads are bad."

"Tell me about it," Ted said.

"Remember," Bri said before they got out the door. "He's dangerous. He tried to pickax us."

They paused, exchanging looks of concern. "Got it," Tim said. "I'll warn them at the E.R."

"Thanks."

As soon as they were gone, Bri turned her attention to Luke. She still seemed to be running on automatic, which was probably a good thing. She'd have time for a nervous breakdown later.

"Now we need to get the blood off you," she announced. "I'm getting the bleach."

"Bleach?"

"Routine. If Jack hadn't been in such bad condition, Tim and Ted would have doused you. HIV."

"Oh."

She doubted Jack had any such thing, but until a blood test proved it, she was taking no chances. She poured some bleach in a bowl. "Sorry I can't mix it with water," she said as she returned, "but I might as well bathe you in ice. I don't know how much shock you can take."

"I'm fine."

"You don't look fine. What were you thinking?"

"The same thing you were. And what about the blood on you?"

She ignored the question. His blood exposure seemed to be limited to his back, neck and good arm, so she stripped his shirt and set about working him over with a sponge. "They'll do more at the hospital."

"I don't need the hospital."

"You need it until I'm sure you didn't dislodge that pin in your leg. My God, the way you fell on him…"

After that he said no more, enduring her ministrations. Little by little reality began to sink in, and her hands started to tremble.

"Luke?" she said quietly.

"Yeah." He sounded gruff.

"You were…magnificent."

"I kinda thought you were."

Battering at the door told her round two had arrived. She let in Sheriff Gage Dalton and Police Chief Jake Madison. One look around the room froze them both.

Gage spoke first. "Does this have anything to do with the pickax sticking up out of the snow?"

The adrenaline that had kept Bri going deserted her then. She sank onto the office chair, ignoring the fact that she was covered in blood, too, and tears began to roll down her face.

"Jack," she said. It was all she could say.

So Luke told the story. She hardly heard him. All the emotions she had put in cold storage suddenly thawed out, leaving her an absolute mess.

If there had been a dark, quiet corner, she probably would have curled up into a tight ball and hidden in it.

Jack could have killed them both. Worst of all, he could have killed Luke. He had tried to kill Luke.

She would have died if he had succeeded. Her heart would have shriveled into a lump of coal.

The horror of it all came home.

Hours later, Dr. Trent finally let her get out of the hospital bed, don some scrubs and head for the bay where they had Luke. She'd heard them take him for

X-rays. Heard that they needed to replace at least one cast, but that was it. She needed to know more.

She had successfully fended off offers of sedation. She endured being bathed in bleach. She'd put up with being watched for delayed shock, but she had had enough of being a patient. She hated herself for collapsing, but she'd been through a nightmare, she had survived it, and at least she'd kept her head until she had done all she could.

She found Luke in bay three. He didn't exactly look like a happy camper, but at least he didn't appear to be in pain.

"Bri." He held out his hand and she went to his side to take it.

"What's the skinny?" she asked him.

"I'm fine. Just needed a new cast because I cracked the other one. How do I get out of here?"

"You'll have to ask the doc. What's the rush?"

"I want to go home with you and take care of you." He peered at her with intensity, his gray eyes sharp. "How are you?"

"I'll survive. No damage, except I have a new nightmare to live with."

"God, it was awful. I was so frightened for you." He squeezed her hand. "Let's get home. You know those moments you talked about the other day?"

"What about them?"

"I watched them vanishing a few hours ago. You were so right about them. No guarantees."

"None."

"So let's go home, Bri. We've got a lot of things to figure out."

"I don't think my living room is going to be habitable for a while. Regardless, the roads are still a mess. They told me we shouldn't leave yet."

"Hell." He sighed and tightened his hold on her hand. "Then let me take you away."

"To where?"

"Who cares? Just let me take you."

Chapter 14

Luke had taken over, and for once Bri didn't mind not being consulted. After all, he'd managed to get a small plane to get them out of Conard County, he'd arranged for a crew to restore her living room, and he'd swept her away for a vacation on a beach in the Florida Keys.

She wasn't sure where this was going. They hadn't discussed much of a personal nature at all. They'd talked about Jack, though, and were still talking about him.

She watched him crutch his way through the hotel dining room and thought that he looked more magnificent than ever. He accepted help from the waiter, who pulled out a chair across the table from her, and ordered a bottle of wine for them.

"Did you learn anything?" she asked him.

"Gage was very forthcoming. Your ex-handyman

is under psychiatric observation to determine if he's fit to stand trial."

"He needs help, Luke. Did you see the change in him? Something went very wrong in his head."

"I agree." He sighed, then shook his head. His face hardened briefly. "But remember, this is a guy who poked holes in your ceiling so he could watch you whenever he felt like it."

That still creeped her out. She suppressed a shudder, and felt once again the sickness in her stomach. "None of that was normal."

"No, but as I understand, the question is not whether he's normal, but whether he could understand right from wrong."

"True."

"He's going away for a long time, darlin'."

"I hope so."

"And what I'd dearly love to see again is a smile on your face." He extended his hand across the table, and she barely hesitated before giving him hers.

"I'll get there. I'm still shocked. Still baffled. I'm just so glad he didn't hurt you."

"I'm glad he didn't hurt *you*. That guy was awfully close to death from the moment he threatened you. Messed up or not, I'd have found a way to…" He stopped. "Enough. We've seen enough violence. I don't want you to see me that way. Ever."

"I've never even thought of you that way. Not once."

"Good." He sat back to taste the wine and waited until it had been poured and the sommelier had departed. "Are you ready to order?"

"Not yet." She looked out the window beside the

table and watched aquamarine waves wash up on a white beach. "It's beautiful here."

"I'm enjoying it. I wish you were, too."

Her gaze tracked back to his face. "What makes you think I'm not?"

"Because I can feel it. You've gone away somewhere inside. You're distant. You're building walls. Do you want to be rid of me?"

"Luke, I'm still trying to deal with all of this. A man I thought was a friend tried to kill us both." But deep inside she knew he was right. She'd had enough, and she had hidden away. If nothing could touch her, there'd be no more pain, right?

"Moments," he said significantly.

She got it. She just didn't know how to get back. At least not yet. "Give me some time," she asked.

"All you want."

After a lunch involving a conch dish that was out of this world, they sat outside on the terrace, listening to the waves, but talking very little.

The endless waves had a strong effect on her, soothing her with their constant susurration, while making her feel extremely small. The sea was eternal. Those waves would wash ashore forever. But she was insignificant, a mere blip on the time line. Her footprints in this world would wash away as quickly as they did when the waves rolled over them.

She closed her eyes, feeling the sun and breeze on her face, hearing the lullaby of the sea, feeling the large hand that held hers so gently.

And little by little she focused on that hand. It held her, it was real, and it was asking her to come back.

To leave some more footprints. Footprints that would matter.

All of a sudden, her heart seemed to crack open. The shell that had been protecting her was gone. She felt pain again, but she also felt something more.

Opening her eyes, she looked at Luke. He was watching her with concern. "You really want to try again?"

"Our marriage?"

"Maybe. Let's start with relationship."

"Fair enough. What brought this on?"

"Footprints," she said enigmatically. "Let's go upstairs."

They took the elevator to their room with its balcony view of the beach and water. Beyond the glass doors, a cruise ship was sailing out toward the sea. Tonight there'd be the sunset celebration at the dock. They hadn't gone yet because she hadn't really wanted to, but again it struck her that she was wasting precious moments.

Moments that she ought to be turning into memories.

Luke stretched out on the bed with a pillow under his broken leg. She joined him, sitting cross-legged beside him, studying him.

"I don't want another broken heart," she said.

"Me, neither."

"But I don't know how much I can change myself." She thought back to all the times she'd dismissed her own feelings. It was still her inclination as she knew all too well.

"How about we do this, then?" he said. "I won't ask you to change. I'll just drive you crazy with questions instead of ignoring it when you seem bothered. Can you live with that?"

"We could try it."

"Just promise me you won't get mad every time I prod you."

The faintest of smiles curved her mouth. "I can promise to try. But I'm still not a very good judge of my own feelings."

"They don't need to be judged. They just are, and are an integral part of all of us. Spew away so we can talk about it. Then you'll have a basis for judgment."

She thought about that and realized she could probably manage it. But her awareness had begun to focus on him and him alone, driving everything else away.

"Luke?"

"Hmm?" He squeezed her hand as if to offer reassurance.

"I would rather have died than see you hurt."

His grip tightened so much that it became nearly painful. "I felt the same way."

"That means something, doesn't it?"

"It probably does." He sounded cautious.

She couldn't blame him for that after all she'd put him through in the past. What a vague way to describe what she had felt: that means something. Something? God, she needed to be clearer.

The tear in her heart was opening wider with each passing minute, bringing back pain, but bringing back a much more important feeling. "It means," she said, "that I never stopped loving you."

Then before she could start thinking she was foolish, she broke into the tears she had been withholding since the incident with Jack. Luke might have died.

The words seemed to be stamped in fire across the universe. She might have lost him for good, and while a few weeks ago she had been telling herself she was glad they had divorced, now she faced the fact that she had never been glad, and had never stopped missing him. All she had done was compound the things that had bothered her into a full-blown case of loneliness. Because life would always be lonely without him.

He tugged her down until she lay curled on her side, her head pillowed on his shoulder. One arm held her near while his other hand stroked her arm and back.

"It's been hard," he murmured. "So hard."

She managed a nod, but she was sobbing so strongly that she couldn't speak. She had always hated crying, had considered it weak, and then she understood where that feeling had come from. Her mother had never let her cry, at least not where anyone else could see. She'd had to hide it away or get yelled at, until she stopped crying altogether.

"Oh, God," she choked out. "Oh, God."

"What?"

"I wasn't allowed to cry, either."

He swore then, succinctly and with a great deal of variety. Oddly, the words and his evident anger began to soothe her. Her sobs eased into hiccups, and finally stopped.

"I'm messed up," she said brokenly.

"No, you're not. Well, everyone's messed up, so why should you be any different? This is hard on you. It's wrong. You can always cry with me. Whenever, however."

She lifted her hand and laid it on his chest. "I'm so glad I didn't lose you."

He shifted onto his side and pulled her close. She knew what was coming, what had always come for them when they were together. Instead of fighting it, instead of thinking it was a distraction, she welcomed his kiss, drawing his tongue deeply into her mouth. The fire and passion began to build. Familiar, yet fresh, she began to ache for him. She needed him. This way and every way. How could she have ever thought otherwise?

He was doing a lot better, but she still needed to help him get out of his clothes. Her own she tossed aside carelessly, desperate for the feel of his skin against hers.

He still couldn't mount her, but that was okay, too. She rolled on top of him, and looked down into the gray eyes that had lingered in her memory all these years like a promise not kept. She could have been patient, but he was impatient and made no secret of it. Seizing her hips, he lifted her onto his rigid manhood and brought her down swiftly, filling her, piercing her, reaching her heart.

Then he lifted his hands to cup her breasts. Rubbing his thumbs over her nipples, sending wildfire along her every nerve ending, he demanded in a thickened voice, "Hard. Fast. Let's soar."

Soar they did. Propping herself on her hands, knowing he could see her and titillated by it, she rode him, rocking her hips against his, taking him deep again and again.

How had she ever thought this was a diversion? This was an essential expression beyond words. Need, hunger, passion, all fueled everything else in life.

She felt herself cresting the wave, riding it like a surfer who wanted to stay at the highest point forever.

"Now," he mumbled.

She barely heard him, but it didn't matter. She crested that wave and slid almost painfully down it until it crashed over her, blinding her, deafening her, sweeping her beyond any control.

She felt him rise up one last time and knew he had crested with her. Perfect. Just perfect.

When she collapsed on him at last, dewy and slick and welcomed by his arms, she knew she belonged nowhere else.

They dined on their little balcony, the soft tropical breeze stirring the palms, making their fronds clatter quietly. The blue of the sky was changing as the sun sank toward the sea. The sounds of music reached them from the streets and shops below, a cacophony of Jimmy Buffett mostly, but occasionally mixed in with the distant sound of a bagpiper. They saw the nightly schooner trip heading out to watch the sunset, accompanied by scores of small boats.

"Where else," Luke asked, "does sunset bring such celebration?"

"I bet there are other places, but who cares? This is unique for me."

"We'll get down there tomorrow, I promise. I'll take the wheelchair and you can shop for silly T-shirts and we'll see the sword swallower, and the acrobats, and the musicians…"

"I'd love that."

"What else would you love?"

"A couple of children. With you." Taking her courage in her hands, she looked at him and waited. For all she knew, she'd just expressed a foolish wish.

But a slow smile curved his mouth. "I'd like that, too. What else?"

She hesitated, biting her lip, suspecting that he was going to make her say what she was really thinking, not slip away from it as she had so often in the past. This was the first day of the rest of her life. A trite but true reality.

"I want you to be home more. I need that, Luke."

He nodded. "Already working on it."

Her heart nearly stopped. Finally she drew a breath. "Really? But will that make *you* happy?"

His gaze never wavered. "*You* make me happy. Let me tell you a story." He reached out and took her hand, bringing it to his lips for a kiss before he continued.

"Once there was a young guy who thought he had the best job in the world. He loved traveling all over, dealing with all the difficulties of different climates, different cultures, different ideas. But then he got married to this wonderful woman, and little by little he realized that he was missing her all the time. The travel was necessary, but it was no longer good."

Her heart began to lift. "Really?"

"Really. He started thinking about what else he might be able to do, but the more he felt this beautiful woman was dissatisfied with him, the more reluctant he was to part with his job. It was almost as if he felt he was going to lose her, so he might as well keep the one thing he used to enjoy: his job. Little did he guess that he was doing exactly the wrong thing. But...she never told him what was wrong."

"Oh!" A pang squeezed her heart.

"He thought maybe she was getting tired of him. But he never screwed up the basic courage to ask. And then the trouble would blow away and he wondered if he was imagining it."

"I'm so sorry," she whispered.

"Anyway, this young buck was a little too self-centered for his own good. Instead of trying to find ways to please his lady, he just let it lie. Never should have done that."

He paused, and for a few moments looked out over a sea that was turning a darker blue as the sun settled toward it. When his gaze tracked back to her, she could see pain.

"The fool lost the one thing that mattered to him most, and he didn't even realize that it was the most important thing until it was gone. He threw himself into his work, never really understanding all that had happened, except the woman he loved believed he had cheated on her."

"Which he never did," she said quietly.

"I'm so glad you know that now. Nothing could have made me cheat on you. Anyway, a few years later, a little older and wiser, this guy decided to look up that very important woman. He thought it was because he wanted to clear his name. He was quite convinced of it. But what he wanted more than anything else in the world was to see her again, because she still owned his heart."

"Oh, Luke!"

"That hasn't changed, Bri. I still love you. I still need you in my life. Take as much time as you need. Let me prove that I mean what I say about changing jobs. I'm already working out something. My current employer may let me finish this job then stay on permanently as the facility manager."

"Oh, wow." She wanted to fling herself at him, but he didn't seem done yet.

"I want everything we didn't have before, Bri. A full-time marriage and a family. I want roots, and I want to plant them where you are. But only if you want me. And like I said, you can take all the time you need. I'll be on your doorstep every night when I get off of work. I won't give you much room to change your mind because I can't. I love you too much. But I'll give you the time to agree with me." He said the last with an almost impish smile.

It was her turn, and she knew there had never been a more important time in her life to be honest. "I never stopped missing you. Even when I was furious with you, a part of me still loved you. I resisted the feelings because, well, it was over, wasn't it? Only it wasn't over, and I knew it for certain when I could have lost you. Strange, that I needed to face that to face myself."

"Facing death can be clarifying," he agreed.

"I love you. I want to be with you always. I want that family." She waited, wondering if she was being too precipitous. Why should he believe her after everything?

But apparently he did. He reached out, tugged her out of her chair and onto his lap. Brushing her hair back and bringing his lips close to hers, he said, "We'll make it this time, Bri. I swear we will. I can't lose you again."

Then he kissed her just as the sun sank into the western sea in a crimson blaze of glory.

"Forever," he murmured against her lips.

Forever, her heart agreed.

* * * * *

MILLS & BOON®

Power, passion and irresistible temptation!

The Modern™ series lets you step into a world of sophistication and glamour, where sinfully seductive heroes await you in luxurious international locations. Visit the Mills & Boon website today and type **Mod15** in at the checkout to receive

15% OFF

your next Modern purchase.

Visit **www.millsandboon.co.uk/mod15**

1014_PROMO

MILLS & BOON®

Why not subscribe?
Never miss a title and save money too!

Here's what's available to you if you join the
exclusive **Mills & Boon Book Club** today:

✦ *Titles up to a month ahead of the shops*
✦ *Amazing discounts*
✦ *Free P&P*
✦ *Earn Bonus Book points that can be redeemed*
  against other titles and gifts
✦ *Choose from monthly or pre-paid plans*

Still want more?
Well, if you join today we'll even give you
50% OFF your first parcel!

So visit **www.millsandboon.co.uk/subs**
or call Customer Relations on **020 8288 2888**
to be a part of this exclusive Book Club!

JBS_2014

Snow, sleigh bells and a hint of seduction

Find your perfect Christmas reads at
millsandboon.co.uk/Christmas

1014/MB506

MILLS & BOON®

Why shop at millsandboon.co.uk?

Each year, thousands of romance readers find their perfect read at millsandboon.co.uk. That's because we're passionate about bringing you the very best romantic fiction. Here are some of the advantages of shopping at www.millsandboon.co.uk:

* **Get new books first**—you'll be able to buy your favourite books one month before they hit the shops

* **Get exclusive discounts**—you'll also be able to buy our specially created monthly collections, with up to 50% off the RRP

* **Find your favourite authors**—latest news, interviews and new releases for all your favourite authors and series on our website, plus ideas for what to try next

* **Join in**—once you've bought your favourite books, don't forget to register with us to rate, review and join in the discussions

Visit **www.millsandboon.co.uk**
for all this and more today!